SONGBIRD

SONGBIRD

Sydney Logan

For Mackensey,
because this is her favorite.

Chapter 1

Callie

The neon numbers on the hotel alarm clock shine like a beacon in the night.

1:15 AM

Why did I ever agree to this?

Tossing off the satin cover, I climb out of bed and walk toward the French doors that lead out onto the terrace. I don't bother opening them, knowing the chilly Nashville air will rattle my bones. Instead, I gaze at the city through the glass, my eyes gravitating toward the Batman Building. That's what we Nashvillians call the thirty-three story skyscraper, the top of which resembles the superhero's mask. It's visually stunning, especially at one in the morning.

You won't be stunning tomorrow, Callie.

It's true. A maid of honor is supposed to be bright-eyed and bushy-tailed, but that won't be happening. It'll be a miracle if I sleep at all. I'm typically calm under pressure, but dealing with my best friend, Megan, and her Bridezilla tendencies, has had me on edge for weeks. Months. Years.

Twenty years to be exact.

That's when Megan and I promised to be in each other's weddings. We were ten years old at the time. I think we even pinky swore.

Are pinky swears admissible in court?

Tonight's train wreck of a rehearsal only added to my restlessness. Simon, the groom, had shrugged off the fact that one of his groomsmen failed to show. He then spent the rest of the evening promising his bride-to-be that his cousin's behavior isn't unusual and that he *will* be at the wedding. It was impressive, watching Simon tame Megan's raging temper, but as the maid of honor, I can't deny that I'm still worried about the jerk not showing up at all.

Maybe a drink will calm my nerves.

Unimpressed with my room's mini-bar selections, I suddenly recall the piano bar downstairs in the lobby. Maybe a little relaxing music is just what I need to chill out and finally get some rest.

I change into a hoodie and jeans and run a brush through my hair before heading out into the deserted hallway. Ignoring the elevator, I walk toward the spiraling staircase that leads to the lobby. The hotel, classy and elegant, is utterly extravagant and totally Megan. Chandeliers hang from the ceiling and the walls and furniture are adorned with rich shades of red and gold.

When I pinky swore all those years ago, I'm pretty sure

I imagined myself as the maid of honor in a much smaller affair. Maybe in a small country church. Or, better yet, in someone's backyard. Had I known my best friend would someday plan such a huge ceremony—with a guest list of more than two hundred—I might have kept my pinky to myself.

But tomorrow is not about me.

When I reach the piano bar, I'm not surprised to find the lights low and the place nearly empty. Sadly, the pianist has called it a night. I choose a stool and order a drink while gazing wistfully at the grand piano in the corner.

The bartender brings me my drink. "You play?"

I shrug. "A little."

The guy looks exhausted. Despite that, he still manages to flirt with me. I flirt back, but only because I want to play the piano. It takes two cocktails and giving him a fake phone number, but he finally gives me permission to play a few songs.

Playing piano never fails to relax me. Performing live isn't my favorite thing to do, but the bar is practically empty, and my anxiety, my exhaustion, and the alcohol make me brave.

Sitting down on the bench, I let my fingers drift aimlessly along the keys. I switch on the microphone and start to play the opening bars of my favorite Fleetwood Mac song.

Closing my eyes, I play and sing, allowing the music to soothe my troubled mind. I'm at the final chorus when I feel someone's eyes on me. It's the most incredible sensation—instinct alerting me to the penetrating stare of some stranger in the dimly lit bar.

I slowly open my eyes, and my fingers slip off the keys when I see him.

He's seated at a table just a few feet away. His tie is undone, as are the first couple buttons of his shirt. He gazes at me, and I watch as his finger lazily trails along the rim of his glass while I struggle to remember the words to a song I've loved all my life.

The man rises from the seat, his eyes never leaving mine as he picks up his glass and walks over to the piano. I break the spell, forcing myself to look down and focus on the keys. Without asking permission, he sits down on the bench next to me. I take a deep breath and pray for instinct to take over as I finish the song.

After I play the last note, silence hangs in the air between us until he lifts his hand and brushes my hair away from my shoulders.

"Play something else," he says, his voice deep and smooth against my ear.

So I sing, paying no real attention to the words as we stare at each other throughout the song. I have no idea how long we sit there, but it's apparently too long for the bartender because he announces last call.

The handsome stranger stands up and reaches for me.

"Come with me, Songbird."

The look in his eye is unmistakable, filling me with a sense of longing and excitement that I haven't felt in so very long. I know I'm too tired, too lonely, and probably a little too tipsy to accept this man's outstretched hand.

I do it anyway.

The alarm clock blares in my ear, and I slap blindly at the offensive clock. With a groan, I stretch my arms above my head and immediately regret it. My entire body aches.

What did I do?

My eyes flash open as images from the previous night flood my mind.

The piano bar.

Three cocktails.

Deep brown eyes.

Oh no.

I slowly turn my head, expecting to see him staring back at me. Or at least snoring next to me.

He's gone.

Of course he is.

With a disgusted sigh, I climb out of bed and head to the shower. I don't have time to feel ashamed. I'm already late for breakfast with the wedding party, and the last thing I need is a pissed off bride to go along with my throbbing headache.

Stepping inside the shower, I pray the sting of the water washes away my humiliation.

I don't do one-night stands.

Ever.

As the scalding water flows down my skin, my guilt

deepens as I recall little details about last night. Our desperate kisses in the elevator. Me pulling him by his tie and leading him to my room. The name he called me as we . . .

Name. I don't even know his name. Or if we used protection.

My shame now at a fever pitch, I climb out of the shower and quickly get dressed. Thankfully, breakfast is casual, so there's no need for me to try to make myself look presentable. After glancing at my cell to confirm that I am indeed late, I grab my room key and head out the door. It's when I'm in the elevator that my shame turns to rage.

He just left in the middle of the night? What kind of cold, heartless jerk does something like that?

I'm still wallowing in my stupidity as I make my way down the hallway and toward the bridal suite.

Megan and Simon have ignored all traditional beliefs, opting to spend the night together and treat everyone to something called a Bridal Breakfast. It's sort of like the rehearsal dinner, except this party is at the break of dawn and includes scrambled eggs and bacon.

My stomach twists at the thought of food.

Get it together, Callie. Today is Megan's day, and you are the maid of honor. You can wallow later. You can vomit later. For now, you have to put on a brave face and concentrate on helping your best friend through the most important day of her life.

It's not much of a pep talk, but it's the best I can do. Taking a deep breath, I plaster a smile on my face and knock on the door. It swings open, and I'm greeted by the absolutely glowing bride.

"Happy wedding day!"

Megan immediately tilts her head and purses her lips. "What's wrong?"

Crap.

"What makes you think something's wrong?"

"Gee, I don't know," she says, waving me inside. "You're late, which never happens. And you look like you pulled an all-nighter."

"I just need coffee. Very strong coffee."

Megan narrows her eyes. This is what happens when you're best friends with someone for twenty years. Keeping a secret is impossible. Thankfully, she lets me off the hook.

"You'll tell me eventually. In the meantime, coffee's on the terrace."

I follow her through the French doors and out into the way-too-bright Nashville morning. The sunshine makes my head throb even more. The groom leaps to his feet as soon as he sees me.

"You look like you could use this," Simon says, handing me a steaming cup.

"Bless you."

He kisses my cheek and offers me the first empty chair, which is unfortunately right next to his best man.

"How's it going?" Owen asks with a wide grin.

His plate is overflowing with eggs, bacon, and gravy . . . and it's all mixed with some kind of disgusting jelly that makes me want to barf. Desperate to calm my queasy stomach, I reach for a piece of toast and take a small bite.

"You have a rough night, too?" Owen asks.

Too?

I don't ask him to elaborate. I just nod.

Owen's laughter booms, causing my head to pulsate. I've met him on more than one occasion, and normally, he's a lot of fun to be around. This morning, however, I might just kill him.

I pick up the butter knife and eye it longingly before using it for its intended purpose. I take a bite, and the buttered toast settles my stomach immediately.

Megan, clearly not amused, stabs at a piece of fruit and glares in my direction.

"I can't believe my maid of honor thought it was okay to get completely smashed the night before my wedding. I expect that kind of crap from Simon's cousin who can't manage to get to a rehearsal dinner—not to mention this breakfast—on time, but my best friend should know better."

With the patience of a saint, Simon reaches for her fork and gently pries it out of her hand. He then spears a slice of melon and lifts it to her lips. Megan takes a bite, and the two of them whisper to each other in between kisses.

Simon really is The Bride Whisperer.

"In my defense, I didn't get completely smashed," I mumble in between bites of toast. "I remember most of it. Almost all of it."

Owen laughs and pours himself another glass of juice. "What is it about this hotel? My brother, Devin—that's the groomsman you've yet to meet—found himself in a similar predicament last night."

"And where is the rogue groomsman this morning?"

"Apparently he's having trouble recovering from his *epic hookup*. His words, not mine."

"According to Devin, his hookups are always epic," Megan mutters before turning toward me, suddenly all smiles. "But I don't want to talk about Devin McAllister. I want to talk about you."

"What about me?"

"I have a small favor."

My radar instantly registers the soft and coaxing tone of her voice. She uses it whenever she wants me to do something that I probably won't want to do.

"Would you try on your dress . . . just one more time?"

Owen chuckles. I shoot a glare in his direction.

"Megan, today is your wedding day. If the dress doesn't fit by now, it's not going to. Besides, I tried it on yesterday, and it was fine. You said so yourself."

"But I didn't see it with the shoes."

I cannot wait until this wedding is over.

I throw my napkin onto the table. "Fine. Where is it? And where is Lorie?"

Megan rises from her chair and takes me by the arm. "Lorie's dealing with the wedding planner. Apparently, there's some problem with the band."

"And Lorie offered to go kick someone's ass so Megan didn't have to," Owen says with a wide grin. "Hey, is Lorie single?"

I roll my eyes as Megan leads me toward a bedroom in her suite. The place looks like a wedding superstore, filled with dresses and tuxedos and shoes.

"There's your dress," Megan says, pointing to one of the dresses hanging on the rack. "And here are the shoes. Just come out when you're ready!"

She flashes me a pearly-white grin before closing the door behind her.

I reach for the peach halter dress. This will be the tenth time I've tried it on.

At least it's pretty.

The heels, however, are not.

I strap on the stilettos and pray I don't fall.

As I look in the mirror, I pull my hair into a twist, just to get an idea of how I'll actually look once we're walking down the aisle. I tilt my head, and that's when I see a small mark on the side of my neck.

What is that? Is that a . . . hickey?

With a groan, I let my hair fall back down to my shoulders.

"Megan," I yell as I walk out onto the terrace. "I'm going to need some concealer to hide this—"

The sound of a fork crashing against a plate makes me stop in my tracks. Every head in the room turns toward the noise, and I stop breathing when I find myself staring into the very familiar eyes of the rogue groomsman.

Chapter 2

DEVIN

I'm suffering from the mother of all hangovers. That's the only explanation for the beautiful hallucination that's standing right in front of me.

I try to act nonchalant, as if I'm not at all affected by the sight of the woman on the terrace. She was gorgeous last night, in just her hoodie and jeans. This morning, in her peach bridesmaid's dress and strappy killer heels, she's breathtaking.

And she's pissed. I can tell by the fire flashing in her eyes.

Owen, my little brother, fakes a cough.

"You two know each other?"

I just grin and drink my juice.

"Why do you need concealer?" Megan asks, scrutinizing the girl's face. "I don't see anything."

She turns toward the crazy bride. "Do you want me to

wear my hair up?"

"Yes . . ."

"Then I'm going to need some concealer. It seems that I have a . . . blemish on my neck."

I laugh, and the girl's head whips around like something out of *The Exorcist*.

I smirk and pick up my fork, never breaking eye contact with her as I stab at my scrambled eggs.

Yes, I marked her.

No, I'm not sorry.

She all but drags the bride toward the bedroom. I chuckle and pour myself another glass of juice. Simon sits down beside me, effectively sandwiching me between my friend and my brother.

"You didn't," Simon says quietly. "Please tell me you didn't."

Owen grins. "You did. *Please* tell me you did."

"Did what?"

"You and Callie."

Callie.

I lazily pop a strawberry into my mouth. "Is that her name?"

My brother offers me a congratulatory fist bump. Simon curses and buries his head in his hands. This wedding has turned him into such a girl. Megan's cute, but I'm not sure any woman is worth this much aggravation.

Simon groans. "Megan will kill you. Why, Dev? Why *her*? Why today?"

"Well, technically, it was last night."

Owen cackles. "You're a hotshot attorney, and that's all you've got? Dude, you slept with the maid of honor. Surely you have something eloquent and poetic to say."

"You know me, little brother. I never kiss and tell."

"Since when?"

Simon continues rubbing his temples.

I roll my eyes. "Would you relax? The fact that I slept with the maid of honor—and quite thoroughly enjoyed it, I might add—has nothing to do with your precious wedding. I didn't even know she was *in* the wedding."

"You would've known if you'd bothered to show up to the rehearsal dinner," Simon mutters.

I ignore that. "Besides, I'm a groomsman. Aren't hook-ups within the wedding party fairly customary?"

"It's tradition," my brother agrees.

Just then, a door slams. Owen's eyes glaze over when a busty redhead suddenly appears on the terrace.

"Who's that?" I whisper.

"Lorie. Yet another hot bridesmaid," Owen says, his eyes never leaving her face.

And the tradition continues.

"Where are the girls?" Lorie asks.

Simon sighs and points toward the bedroom. "Looking for concealer."

Lorie narrows her eyes in confusion before stomping back inside.

"She seems fun."

"Doesn't she? I'm making it my mission to find out," Owen says with a firm nod.

The groom groans in frustration.

I grin. "So, what's on the agenda? Do I have time to get a massage before we do this thing?"

Simon's eyes grow wide. "Please, for the love of God, don't be late. I'm begging you, Dev."

"Dude, I'm just going to get a massage. I won't even leave the hotel. What time do you want me here?"

"Pictures are at four," Megan says as she breezes back onto the terrace. To my great disappointment, she's alone. "You need to be here at three to get dressed. If you are late, Devin McAllister, I will hunt you down and kill you. Are we clear?"

"Crystal." With a grin, I stand up and walk over to the bride, giving her a quick kiss on the cheek. Megan smiles. Either I'm forgiven for the hickey or Callie kept her mouth shut. I suspect the latter.

"I'm coming with you," Owen says. "How about it, Simon? You look like you could use a massage. Maybe relieve some pre-wedding tension."

Seeking permission, Simon looks to his bride.

"*Fine*, just don't be late." Megan sighs heavily and heads inside. We follow her into the suite. "Besides, I don't have time to babysit you guys. I have to find some concealer because my maid of honor allowed some asshole to put a massive hickey on her neck last night."

Owen laughs and nudges my shoulder. "So, who is he? Did Callie say anything about the guy?"

Megan unzips a makeup bag and pulls out a lipstick tube. "Not really. She said it was *pretty good* . . . whatever that means."

My head shoots up in disbelief.

Pretty good? She said it was pretty good?

"It was freaking epic," I mutter under my breath.

Owen laughs loudly as he and Simon grab me by the arms and shove me out the door.

Chapter 3

Callie

"I want a name."

I ignore Lorie and drink my water through a straw. I'd love something stronger, but I've vowed never to drink another drop of alcohol for as long as I live. Booze is evil. Anything that can make you completely lose your mind like I did last night really should be illegal.

"You have beautiful hair," my stylist says.

"Thanks."

Fascinated, I watch as the hairdresser works his magic with the curling iron. The concealer had done a decent job of hiding the gross purple bruise on my neck, but I still wasn't comfortable with the up-do Megan wanted. It only took thirty minutes of begging to convince her. In a show of bridesmaid solidarity, Lorie decided to wear her hair down, too.

"Why can't I make my hair do that?" I ask as one of my blonde curls bounces into place.

"I'm waiting, Callie Franklin."

I sigh and glance across the room. Megan's in a pedicure chair and well out of listening range.

"Trust me, Lorie. You don't want a name."

"So, I know him."

I nod.

"That's some hickey on your neck. Is he a teenager?"

"No, he's not a teenager!"

Every head in the salon turns our way. I flush with embarrassment and drop my voice to a whisper.

"Is it really noticeable?" I reach up and gently touch the mark. "You'd think I'd remember that happening, wouldn't you?"

"Not necessarily, and stop touching it! We nearly used the entire tube of concealer to cover it up the first time."

I quickly drop my hand back down into my lap.

"Look on the bright side, Callie. At least you have a date for the wedding. I'll be stuck dancing with one of the McAllisters."

At least I know his name.

Devin McAllister.

The rogue groomsman.

"I don't have a date." I shake my head, earning me a glare from my hairdresser.

"You didn't invite him to the wedding?"

"Oh, he'll be there."

It's not enough that I have to endure—not to mention

wear—the shame of my one-night stand. Do I really have to look at him all night, too?

I can tell Lorie's curious, but she doesn't push for details.

Three hours later, we're all perfectly primped and ready for pictures. True to their word, the guys make it back in time. I can feel Devin's gaze on me, but I avoid looking at him, even when we all gather in the elevator. When we finally make it down to the Spanish Ballroom, I'm a bundle of nerves and trembling in my five-inch heels.

"What's wrong?" Lorie whispers.

I just shake my head and follow the directions of the photographer as she places us in some of the most ridiculous poses. When pictures are finally over, Betsy, the wedding planner, herds us into an adjacent room to wait. Megan's mom adjusts the bride's veil, and Lorie hands me a glass.

"Drink this. You seriously look like you're about to puke."

Despite my booze boycott, I allow myself one long sip, hoping it'll calm my nerves.

It doesn't.

"Are we ready?" Betsy asks.

The three of us nod, and her face is beaming as she barks instructions into her headset. We line up in the hallway, and I chance a glance at the guests in the crowded ballroom. Suddenly, I feel a hand on the small of my back.

"Aren't you going to say hello?"

His warm breath tickles my ear, making me tremble. I ignore him and stare straight ahead.

"It's show time!" Owen shouts, clapping his hands. "All boys to the front!"

I exhale a shaky breath as his hand quickly disappears. Betsy murmurs something into her headset, and the music starts to play. It seems like forever before Lorie finally makes her way inside the ballroom. She glides down the aisle like a runway model, which does nothing to calm my racing heart.

"Callie!"

Megan's frantic whisper interrupts my inner turmoil. I look behind me, and the bride's frazzled face quickly reminds me of my duties.

"What's wrong? And where's your father?"

"In the bathroom. The man's bladder is the size of a toddler's." Megan looks toward the ballroom. "Cal, I'm doing the right thing, right?"

"What?" I look toward the altar. Lorie's nearly there.

"I mean, I love Simon, and I know he loves me. But is this *right*?"

Not once has Megan ever questioned her relationship with Simon. They've been together so long it's hard to remember a time when they weren't Megan and Simon.

"Callie, you're up," the wedding planner says.

"Back off!" Megan suddenly yells, grabbing my hand. "I'm having a moment here and I need my best friend."

"I'll . . . just go find your dad," Betsy says. She rushes away while muttering frantically into her mic.

Do your job, Callie.

Pulling the bride by the hand, I lead us out of view of the wedding guests.

"Megan Young, look at me."

Her eyes dart around the room. *Is she looking for an exit?*

"Breathe, Meg. You're just nervous."

"I'm not nervous. I'm petrified. Tell me this is right. Please, Callie. You'll tell me the truth. Tell me I'm not making a huge mistake."

I sigh softly. I'm no expert on relationships. My parents divorced when I was a kid, so that's pretty much skewed my views on love and marriage. My own relationships—what few I've had—have been purely physical with absolutely no emotion involved. What do I know about happily ever after?

Nothing at all.

But I know my best friend, and I know how much she loves the man standing at the altar. So, I do what any good reporter would do.

I plaster on a smile and make it up as I go along.

"Simon loves you. He worships the ground you walk on, and I know you feel the same about him. I can't think of any other couple who are more right for each other than the two of you. You are going to make gorgeous babies and live happily ever after."

"Really?" Her voice shakes with relief.

"Really. And he's waiting for you. He's ready to make you his forever. Isn't that the most amazing feeling in the world? This man is going to love you until the day you die."

Megan sniffles softly. "It is. It's incredible."

I smile. "So, let's do this."

Her face splits into the most beautiful smile I've ever seen before she kisses me on the cheek.

"Thank you, Callie."

Betsy arrives with Mr. Young, and I give her a nod.

She sighs with relief before ushering me through the door. Ignoring the confused but smiling faces of the guests, I make my way down the aisle. I'm so overjoyed not to be falling on my face that I make the mistake of looking toward the altar. When I do, I find myself staring into the eyes of Devin McAllister.

I should look away. I should focus on anything but him. But the intensity of his gaze actually grounds me, and for the first time today, I'm blissfully calm.

The wedding march begins, and I force myself to look at my best friend as she makes her way down the aisle with her father by her side. When Megan places her hand in Simon's and the preacher starts the ceremony, I'm once again swept into the web that is Devin's steely gaze.

Vows are spoken.

Rings are exchanged.

Simon kisses the bride.

I'm sure it's beautiful, but as the newlyweds make their way back down the aisle, I realize I can't remember any of it.

Part of my duty as maid of honor is, of course, a speech at the reception. I'm a journalist, so naturally, I'd written my speech well in advance and practiced it in the car to and from work every day for the past week. It's a little humorous and somewhat sappy—and I rarely do sappy—but I can appreciate that this day warrants it, and I love them both, so I wrote it.

The DJ hands me the microphone, and I nervously rise from my seat at the head table. I force my gaze to remain on Megan's face as I start to speak.

"When Megan and I were ten years old, she and I made a pinky promise that, someday, she would be my maid of honor and I would be hers. If I'd known she planned to strap me in five-inch stilettos when the day finally arrived, I might have kept my pinky to myself."

The crowd laughs. The groomsmen whistle. I ignore them. When I'm not looking at Devin McAllister, it's so much easier to pretend he isn't here.

"They aren't five inches," Megan mutters, but her face beams with happiness as she smiles at me.

"Despite that *torture*," I continue with a smirk, "I want you both to know how much I love you. I've seen very few instances of true love in my life, but trust me when I say that Simon and Megan have found it in each other. We should all be so lucky. I wish you nothing but joy and happiness. Congratulations."

The guests raise their glasses to toast the happy couple. Relieved, I sit back down while Simon and Megan share their first dance. Forgetting my no-alcohol stance, I take a sip of champagne and glance at Lorie. Her head is close to Owen's. His arm is around the back of her chair, and she giggles when he whispers into her ear.

Lorie never giggles.

I sigh dejectedly. I'd been counting on Owen for a dance

partner. I watch in despair as the two of them make their way onto the dance floor, leaving me and Devin alone at the table.

Thankfully, he's *way* down there.

"Darlin', please explain to me why you're sitting here looking all pitiful when there's a beautiful man at the far end of the table who can't keep his eyes off you."

Leo!

Leo's our entertainment reporter at the *Journal*. He's cute and funny and one of the few male reporters who doesn't hit on me. All pluses, so I'm happy to call him my friend.

"Leo, dance with me. I'm begging you."

He chuckles and downs his glass of champagne.

"Can't. I'm afraid I'm spoken for tonight."

He points across the room to Oliver—his boyfriend and my favorite photographer at the paper.

"You're spoken for every night," I grumble.

"Is that jealousy I hear?"

"It's just not fair. Why are all the good guys taken or gay?"

Leo laughs. "I know. It's such a curse."

I sigh loudly and reach for my glass. "Fine, go dance with your beautiful boyfriend and desert me in my hour of need."

He grins mischievously as someone sits down beside me. I don't even have to turn around. I call tell by the glazed expression on Leo's face that it's Devin McAllister sitting by my side.

"Oh, look. Desertion avoided. Have fun!"

With a wink, he's gone.

Traitor.

Devin places his arm along the back of my chair and

leans close to my ear. "You know, you can't ignore me all night. It's actually quite rude."

My temper flares, but I refuse to turn my head in his direction. I'm obviously unable to look at him without losing my mind.

"You'd know all about rude behavior."

"What's that supposed to mean?"

With a resigned sigh, I tilt my head in his direction. He's right *there*, with his piercing brown eyes.

I take a deep breath and steel my resolve.

"Marking me and leaving me without even the courtesy of a goodbye qualifies as rudeness, don't you think?"

A slow smile creeps across his face. "I wanted you to have something to remember me by."

"You're a pig."

"And you're gorgeous. Come dance with me."

I grab a nearby glass—probably Lorie's—and down it quickly before placing it back on the table.

"No."

"We shared a bed, but you won't share a dance with me?"

"I was drunk."

"You weren't *that* drunk."

I wave my hand toward the guests. "There are literally hundreds of women in this room. Take your pick."

"I just did."

I snort. *Smooth.*

"I think that's a very bad idea."

Devin slides his hand along the back of my neck. My skin tingles beneath his touch.

"Just one dance, Songbird," he says softly, letting his nose trail against my cheek.

Songbird. It's the name he used to charm me in the bar last night. The same name that charms me *now*—right out of my chair and onto the dance floor, where I find myself in his arms.

Devin pulls my hand to his chest while he rests his palm on the small of my back. He holds me close, and our bodies sway to the slow rhythm of the music.

"I know it's a little late now, but my name's Devin McAllister."

I glance anxiously around the room. "Callie Franklin."

"So, Callie Franklin, I guess you're pissed about last night?"

At least he has the common decency to keep his voice low.

"Yes, I am."

"May I ask why?"

"Because I don't do one-night stands. Ever."

He smirks. "Well, if that's what's bothering you, I'm sure I can be persuaded into a repeat performance. I wouldn't want you to feel unnecessarily guilty when it's so easy for me to make it right."

"You're a pig."

"You said that already."

"Still true."

He shrugs. "Maybe. Doesn't change the fact that your dress and those heels are killing me."

"You don't want me. You want to sleep with me. Big

difference."

"Not to me there isn't."

"You really are a p—"

"A pig. I know. So what? We both get what we want."

"And what makes you think I want you?"

"Because last night was epic and you know it."

"It was so epic you couldn't be bothered to say goodbye?"

He tilts his head. "That really bothers you, doesn't it?"

"It really does. But the hickey bothers me more. What are you, sixteen?"

"A hickey which made it possible for you to wear your hair down tonight, which I love, so I'm not apologizing for that, either."

"I get the feeling you don't apologize for much."

Devin weaves his hand in my hair and pulls me closer. Nervously, I glance across the room. My eyes lock with the bride's. Megan's expression is livid.

"We can't, Devin."

His mouth hovers close to mine. "We can. And if it's really that important to you, I promise to say goodbye this time."

I shake my head, but it's half-hearted, and he knows it.

"Say yes, Songbird."

Can I do this? For one weekend out of my lonely life, can I allow myself this? Devin McAllister is a gorgeous man, and for some reason, he wants me. It'll be meaningless and amazing, and then he'll walk out of my life for good. And when it's all said and done, the only reminder I'll have of this weekend will be the hickey on my neck.

"One condition."

His eyes glow with triumph. "Anything."

"This time, leave your mark where only I can see it."

Luckily, the elevator doors open right in front of his suite.

Devin pushes me against the door and presses his forehead to mine as he fumbles for his room key. I stumble back when it finally opens, but his strong arms catch me and lift me off the ground. With a surprising sweetness, he lets me slide slowly down his body before he touches his lips to mine.

Tonight's different. *He's* different.

Gone are the frantic kisses and wild groping from last night. Tonight, Devin's kissing me and touching me with a gentleness that confuses me and thrills me at the same time.

He leads me to his room and sits me on the edge of the bed. Without breaking my gaze, he drops to his knees in front of me and lets his hand creep down my leg before unstrapping one heel, and then the other.

Leaning forward, I loosen his tie and let it fall onto the floor before reaching for the buttons of his vest and shirt. He finds the straps of my halter, giving them a tug and letting the fabric fall.

"You really are beautiful, Callie."

I lay back. Within seconds, I hear his zipper, and then he's hovering above me. I run my hands along his chest, making him shudder beneath my touch. Devin lowers his head, letting his lips slide gently across my collarbone. His kisses drift lower, and I moan softly when he sucks forcefully on my heated skin.

"There, baby," he whispers. "My mark . . . where only you can see it."

The tenderness in his voice breaks me.

"Don't do that."

Devin raises his head. I can see the confusion etched on his handsome face.

"Don't do what?"

Don't make love to me.

Getting attached to this man is the last thing I need to do. I can deal with the scorching kisses from the night before. What I can't handle is tonight's slow caresses and soft kisses when I know I'll never see him again.

"Don't be sweet, Devin."

Something flashes in his eyes.

"Whatever you say, Callie," he says, covering his body with mine. "But for tonight, you're mine."

"I'm yours," I whisper softly, because it's true.

For tonight. I'm his.

When I wake up the next morning, I feel well-rested and wonderful. A quick glance at the alarm clock explains why.

It's noon?

"Devin, wake up. We've probably already missed checkout."

I reach behind me, only to find cold sheets.

My eyes snap open.

"Devin?"

I turn over, but all I find is his pillow and a long white rose.

And a card.

I sit up in bed and bring the flower to my nose, inhaling deeply.

I guess it's too much to hope that he's in the shower.

With a resigned sigh, I wrap the blanket around me, letting his smell completely surround me as I open the note with fumbling fingers.

Goodbye, Songbird is all it says.

Chapter 4

Callie

It's Monday, and as usual, the newsroom is buzzing with excitement. An overnight fire at a restaurant in Brentwood had our news crews out early. This afternoon, there's an impromptu visit from the governor at the zoo, and an upcoming charity benefit has just been announced for the Children's Hospital. I watch in jealous dismay while my colleagues scurry around the room—synchronizing itineraries and negotiating for the best cameramen.

With a weary sigh, I drop back down into my chair in my cubicle. I reach for my coffee and stare at my computer screen, begging the words on the screen to sound as if I really enjoyed the community theater production of *The Sound of Music* I'd been forced to watch last week.

The play was good.

No wonder I'm stuck in a cubicle.

I angrily press the delete key while glancing around my tiny workspace. Hanging on the wall is my journalism degree—taunting me in its frame.

I'm not naïve. I know I have to pay my dues in the news world. But I've been working for the paper for over a year, and not once have I been given something substantial to cover.

Frustrated, I close the document and open my email instead. Our mail is heavily monitored, so I'm surprised to find a message from my honeymooning best friend. I open the message and regret it immediately.

> *Hey Callie!*
>
> *I'm currently lying on Lanikai Beach watching as my husband (my husband!) windsurfs. I've decided there's nothing sexier than my handsome husband (I love saying that) riding a wave. I'm taking lots of pictures. I'll text you a few.*
>
> *Speaking of pictures, I'm attaching a few shots from the wedding that the photographer sent to us. I think one photo will be of particular interest to you. Don't think I've forgotten how you deserted me during the reception! I expect a heartfelt apology and all the juicy details when I get home!*
>
> *Love,*
>
> *Mrs. Megan Anderson*

I take a deep breath and click on the attachments.

There I am, dancing in the arms of Devin McAllister.

Since checking out of the hotel yesterday, I've tried to block the entire weekend out of my mind. I'm not used to feeling ashamed and stupid. Not that I'm innocent. I've had boyfriends since moving to Nashville, but few that I'd consider serious and none that I could imagine spending the rest of my life with. Work, as frustrating as it can be, is my first priority, and I want nothing, and no one, to get in the way of my becoming a serious journalist. Because of that determination, I'm typically far more levelheaded when it comes to men, which is why my attraction to Devin McAllister is so unnerving.

And *stupid* . . . if the tabloids are to be believed.

Last night, in a moment of weakness, I checked him out on the Internet. Devin's really quite accomplished, with his Harvard law degree and his private practice. I'd searched through the news articles and learned that, along with his devotion to charities, he also has quite the reputation as a womanizer. This didn't surprise me, considering he'd managed to charm me.

Twice.

Our second night together is proving the hardest to forget, and I know it's because he had the decency to keep his promises. The new hickey was visible only to me, and he said goodbye this time.

On a note.

I have to admit the rose was a nice touch.

The mark on my skin and the pretty rose would naturally

fade with time, and the note can be ripped to shreds. Those mementos will disappear, so I'm thankful I won't be subjected to any lasting reminders of my wild weekend.

"Please say you did."

Leo's voice makes me jump in my seat. I quickly close the email and pretend to work on my article.

"Did what?"

"Don't play innocent with me. I saw you drooling over that picture of Devin McAllister."

"I have no idea what you're talking about." I can't face him. I know my face is beet red. "Megan just sent me some pictures from the wedding."

"Right."

"And how do you know his name?"

Leo laughs. "Are you kidding? Everybody knows Devin McAllister."

"I didn't. Not until this weekend. And I'm not giving you any details."

"Just a few? *Please* let me live vicariously through you."

"You'd have to, because I promise you're not his type."

Leo's eyes light up. "Callie Franklin, I am *so* proud of you."

"Really? Because I am *so* ashamed of myself."

"Oh, stop that," he says, sitting down on the edge of my desk. "You had fun, right?"

"Fun. Yes, it was fun."

My head screams at me, obviously offended that I'd chosen such a lackluster adjective to describe it.

Leo sighs wistfully. "Ah, to be single again. I miss it

sometimes. And you were careful, of course."

"Of . . . course. Yeah."

He narrows his eyes. "Callie?"

"Hmm?"

"You *were* careful, right?"

I suddenly become very interested in my shoes.

"Are you insane? That man has slept with half of Nashville."

"Says who?"

"Says *who*? Do you even read our newspaper?"

"Umm . . ."

"Good lord. Get on our website and search for his name. Immediately."

The muffin I inhaled at breakfast starts to churn in my stomach.

"Devin McAllister is pictured with a different woman at every event he attends," he says, reaching for my mouse and clicking through the photos. Sure enough, there's Devin. And on his arm in every single picture is a new woman. Redheads. Blondes. Brunettes.

Good to know he's an equal opportunity womanizer.

"That doesn't mean he sleeps with all of them, Leo."

"But what if he does?"

"I'm on the pill."

"A baby would be the least of your worries!"

I sigh tiredly. "Look. I haven't slept. I'm emotional. I'm ashamed. I know I was stupid. I'll get tested as soon as I can get to a doctor."

Leo's face softens. "Promise me."

He really is such a good friend.

"I promise."

Five o'clock arrives, and I gratefully take my tired ass home. I pick up some take-out along the way, and after dinner is devoured, I snuggle into my favorite pajamas and curl up on the couch with a banana freezer pop. I became addicted to them during my summer vacations with my dad. After my folks got divorced, my summers were spent with Dad in Brandywine, our little hometown in the hills of East Tennessee. Mom never allowed sugary snacks in the house, but Dad insisted that kids should be kids, and his fridge was always stocked with my favorite banana freezer pops whenever I'd come to visit.

I'm dreaming about freezer pops and summer when I'm jostled awake by my cell. Afraid it's work, I jump off the couch and grab it out of my bag.

"Callie Franklin."

"Oh, good, you're alive," Lorie says. "I was beginning to wonder if Owen's brother kidnapped you. I haven't seen or heard from you since the reception."

"No, I'm fine. Sorry to make you worry."

"It's okay, although I'm not thrilled that you ditched me."

"Whatever," I mumble sleepily. I can still recall the way she giggled with Owen. "I'm sure you were well taken care of in my absence."

"I *was*." I can practically hear her smile. "We had a good time. We're still having it actually. We kept the room for a few days. He's in the shower."

"Oh, so you called to brag."

"Not at all. I called to check on you." Her voice grows low. "I know it was Devin who put that ugly hickey on your neck, and I saw you leave with him. You know I'm not one to fish, but I'm fishing."

"And I'm not taking the bait. Besides, there's nothing to tell."

"Nothing at all?"

"Nothing beyond what happened this weekend."

"You just don't usually do that sort of thing, so I just wanted to make sure you were okay. And I know you were careful."

She says it so matter-of-factly, because I'm always the responsible one.

Almost always.

"I promise I'm fine. Just sleepy. I'll call you tomorrow. Tell Owen I said hi."

We hang up, and I head to my bedroom. I haven't unpacked, so I take the time to toss my dirty clothes into the hamper and empty my suitcase. I place my medications— my morning vitamin and my birth control pills—in their usual spot on my nightstand. Next to them, for no reason whatsoever, I lay the white rose and Devin's goodbye note.

"I'm such an idiot."

I climb into my bed for the first time since Thursday.

I'd been so exhausted last night I hadn't even made it to my bedroom before falling asleep on the sofa. Sleeping in my own bed and getting back in my regular routine is exactly what I need in order to put this weekend behind me, once and for all.

After setting the alarm on my phone, I reach for my bottle of water and my birth control pills.

My hands freeze as I glance down at the pack.

With trembling fingers, I gingerly touch the pills labeled Thursday, Friday, Saturday, and Sunday. The little white pills are there—staring right back at me and reminding me that, not only had I been reckless this weekend, but I'd also been forgetful.

Very, very forgetful.

Chapter 5

DEVIN

I straighten my tie and take one last look in the mirror. There's enough morning sunlight shining through the window for me to get dressed without having to turn on the light. And I'm grateful, because the last thing I want to do is wake her up.

Before I leave, I glance back at Nina, who's undeniably gorgeous with her long black hair and creamy skin. Last night's benefit had been particularly dull, and when it was appropriate to do so, my date and I ditched the party and escaped to her hotel room. Unfortunately for Nina, my heart just wasn't in it, and I'd fallen asleep as soon as I climbed into her bed.

She'll probably never forgive me.

Once I'm outside, I hail a cab and give the driver my address so that I can shower and change. Thirty minutes later, I'm driving toward my law office. As I head downtown, I think about law and sex. One's logical. The other's physical. These are things I understand. What I don't understand is why the sexual part of my life has suddenly become nonexistent. I noticed a difference right after Simon's wedding. He said his vows a month ago, and since then, I couldn't be less interested in the opposite sex.

While it's true I enjoy spending time with gorgeous women, I'm not quite the playboy they portray in the tabloids. Sure, I'll have my picture taken at a benefit with some beautiful woman on my arm, but more times than not, I come home alone. And that's exactly how I want it.

When I finally reach my office, my secretary greets me with a smile.

"Good morning, Mr. McAllister."

"Good morning, Alicia."

Alicia is yet another beautiful, desirable woman in my life, except this woman is my employee, and I never mix business with pleasure. She's hard-as-nails and keeps me in line, which is exactly what I need. During her initial interview last year, I accidentally called her "sweetheart." She immediately threatened to file a sexual harassment suit against me.

Impressed, I hired her on the spot.

"Here are your messages, Mr. McAllister. You have a breakfast meeting with Gavin Hammond in the conference room at nine. Pastries are on the way, and the rest of your schedule is on your phone."

"Thanks, Alicia."

I head into my office, closing the door behind me. I'm grateful to have an hour before my meeting with Hammond. It'll give me the chance to catch up on some paperwork that's been piling up for the past few weeks thanks to my shitty attention span.

Flipping open the first manila folder on the pile, I give it a quick glance before cursing and tossing it back into the pile.

I'm completely useless.

I check my phone, answering a few texts and ignoring others. That's when I spot a text from Owen.

**Check out these pictures from the wedding.
What a crazy weekend! --BigO**

The first picture is of Simon with Megan's garter between his teeth. The bastard looks so happy, and who can blame him? The bride has killer legs.

The second picture is of Lorie, the new object of my brother's affection. Owen seems to really like her, which is unusual for him. He doesn't like to get tied down, either.

I click on the final picture, and I gasp when bright blue eyes suddenly appear on my screen. Callie's walking down the aisle, her long blonde hair flowing down her shoulders. Without thinking, I let my finger trail along her face.

My memory doesn't do her justice.

For a brief moment that weekend, I thought I might actually feel something for this girl—something that went a little deeper than just sexual attraction. Luckily, she'd snapped me out of my madness when she begged me not to be sweet. Her words had been just the reality check I needed in the heat of the moment.

When I awoke in the middle of the night—with Callie wrapped in my arms—I'd felt an inexplicable urge to watch her sleep. So that's what I did. I held her and watched her sleep until the sun rose in the Nashville sky.

She'd asked for only two things from me. Having already fulfilled one of her requests—thanks to the perfect placement of my latest hickey—I carefully climbed out of bed and scribbled a goodbye note. Sensing it needed something more, I quietly called guest services and asked for a single white rose. I placed it, along with the note, on my pillow where she'd be sure to find it.

A few days after the wedding, I met Owen for breakfast. He begged for details about the weekend. I shared just enough to shut him up. When I told him I wouldn't be seeing her again, he seemed almost relieved, muttering something about Callie being a sweet girl and far too good for me.

After a day filled with boring-ass meetings and more paperwork, I drive home, change clothes, and immediately go for a run, hoping the exercise will help clear my head. It works, until I see another runner in the distance with a blonde ponytail. Like an idiot, I chase the woman until she stops to stretch.

I feel like a complete dumbass when I realize it's not her.

For punishment, I make myself run another five miles. When I finally make it back to my apartment, I collapse on the couch without even taking a shower.

That night, for the first time in weeks, I don't have one dream about blue eyes or white roses.

Chapter 6

Callie

"Callie? I came as fast as I could." Lorie's voice is unnaturally soft from behind the bathroom door. "I ran three red lights and had to flirt my way out of a ticket, but I'm here. Can I come in?"

"Yes," I reply shakily.

The door opens, and Lorie's wide eyes immediately find me, sitting on the edge of the tub and surrounded by open boxes and various brands of pregnancy tests.

"How can they all be positive? How can ten different tests from ten different companies say the same thing?"

Lorie sighs heavily before making her way over to me. Kneeling on the ground, she lifts my chin and smooths my hair out of my tear-stained face.

"Did you seriously pee on all of these?"

I sniffle quietly. "I thought if I kept trying, I'd eventually get a different result."

Lorie sits down on the tile floor. Despite my embarrassment and fear, I can appreciate the fact that my normally outspoken friend is resisting the urge to tell me how irresponsible and stupid I am.

"How, Callie? I mean . . . *how*? Aren't you on the pill?"

"I got busy. And stupid. And I forgot to take them for a few nights."

She frowns. "I didn't realize you were even seeing anybody."

"I'm not. I haven't. Not since . . ."

I can't finish the sentence, because no matter how terrified I am that I'm pregnant, nothing can compare to the sheer terror in confessing the father's name.

After what feels like forever, Lorie finally gasps.

"Devin? Devin McAllister's the father?"

All it takes is the sound of his name to make me dissolve into tears.

Deciding she can't handle my breakdown without assistance, Lorie calls Megan, who shows up an hour later with a pint of ice cream and three spoons. They manage to coax me out of the bathroom and lead me to the living room.

The three of us snuggle on the couch and wrap ourselves in my favorite blanket while we take turns eating triple chocolate chip right out of the carton. In between mouthfuls, I tearfully confess every detail of my weekend with Devin. They gasp and giggle appropriately. Megan even sighs wistfully when I tell them about the white rose. Lorie's not so easy to impress.

"Forgive me if I'm not bowing at his feet for giving her a flower," she says. "He left her. Twice."

"But he said goodbye the second time," Megan says with a nod.

"No, he left a *note* that said goodbye. You don't think two nights with our beautiful best friend warrants more than a card and a rose? The man couldn't be bothered to spend the night?"

"Devin didn't owe me anything. I knew exactly what I was doing and now I'm paying for it." I angrily jab my spoon into the ice cream. "I mean, just because I thought the weekend was amazing doesn't mean he felt the same way."

"I happen to know for a fact that's not true," Lorie says, then immediately covers her mouth with her hand. "Shit."

"What do you mean?"

"Nothing. Ignore me."

"You're lying!" Megan shouts. "Take her spoon!"

I quickly snatch the spoon out of Lorie's hand.

"What the crap?"

With a smirk, I wave it in front of her face. Lorie narrows her eyes before exhaling a deep breath.

"Fine! Owen and Devin had breakfast a few days after the wedding. He said Devin wouldn't shut up about you. However, he wouldn't give any steamy details, which, according to Owen, is pretty unusual. Devin's typically a big bragger when it comes to women."

This information shouldn't make me happy, but it does.

"Anything else?" Megan asks.

Lorie grins at me. "Devin said the weekend was *epic.*"

Megan squeals.

I roll my eyes. *I bet he changes his tune when he finds out I'm pregnant.*

"What are you thinking?" Megan asks me. "How are you feeling?"

"I'm pretty freaked out, to be honest."

"Totally understandable," Lorie says.

"Sure, but aren't you excited? I mean, it's a baby."

"It sure is." My sarcastic tone sounds harsh even to my ears. "That's bad, isn't it? I'm going to be a terrible mother."

Lorie shakes her head. "I think it's completely normal to feel freaked out. You should take a few days off, see a doctor, and consider your options."

"And you should tell Devin," Megan says quietly.

Fear clenches my stomach. I can't even imagine making that phone call. What would I say? What would *he* say? Would he even care?

"She should get confirmation from a doctor first. Then she can tell Devin."

Megan shakes her head. "Maybe she wants Devin to go with her to the doctor."

"And maybe she's independent and doesn't need him to hold her hand."

"Maybe she *wants* him to hold her hand!"

"*She* is right here!" I toss my spoon in the carton and throw the blanket aside. "Thank you for coming. I'll call the doctor first thing in the morning."

"I think she's kicking us out," Lorie mutters.

I nod. "Megan, I don't like asking you to keep this from

your husband, but I would appreciate it if both of you would stay quiet until I figure out what I'm going to do."

"Absolutely," she says.

"Of course," Lorie says, nodding.

"Thank you. Now, I'm tired, emotional, and cranky, and I want to go to bed."

My best friends envelop me in their arms and promise me everything's going to be okay. I walk them out and lock the door behind them.

All I want to do is sleep.

As I lay down in my bed, I let my hand drift along my stomach. Could ten pregnancy tests be wrong? I haven't had any weird cravings or nausea—unless you count those brief moments of vomit-inducing fear when I was checking the test results on those stupid sticks. My only real clue is the fact that my period is nine days late.

Could I be worrying for nothing?

I allow myself a tiny glimmer of hope before falling into a deep sleep.

I don't even bother opening my umbrella as I make my way out of the doctor's office. I'm thankful for the rain falling on my face, because it'll mingle with my tears, and no one will be able to tell my entire world has just fallen apart.

My gynecologist confirmed what I already knew. My

sobs alerted him to the fact that this isn't exactly happy news, and he spent the next hour discussing my options. He sent me home with pamphlets, vitamins, and a reminder of my next appointment.

For the next two hours, I drive around the city and pray for divine intervention to help me make the right decision. This isn't in my plan. I want to write. I want to win a Pulitzer. I want to have a real career, and *then* I'll settle down and have a family. Not *now*.

That stupid wedding is going to haunt me for the rest of my life.

I can't help but laugh when I remember how much I wanted no reminders of that weekend. The hickey has long since faded and the flower's dead. All that remains is the handwritten note.

And a baby.

It's times like these when a girl needs her mother. That's a phone call I dread, because my mom will be horrified that I'm following in her footsteps. Thanks to my unexpected arrival, she and Dad had married young. Since I was old enough to date, Mom had instilled in me her belief that *smart girls* always waited. Smart girls never allowed hormones to override common sense. Smart girls don't get knocked up by guys they'd just met in a piano bar.

So, no, I won't be calling her anytime soon.

I've just pulled into my apartment's parking garage when my cell vibrates in the passenger seat. A quick glance at the screen makes me curse under my breath.

Frank.

I really don't want to talk to my editor today.

Guilt wins out, and I turn off the ignition before answering.

"Callie Franklin."

"You're covering tonight's hospital benefit."

This is Frank's typical greeting. No hello. No how are ya. He just barks out orders.

"Hospital benefit?"

"Children's Hospital? Ring a bell?"

Snap out of it, Callie.

"Of course, yes! Umm . . . I thought Kayla was covering that."

"Kayla has the flu. You keep saying you want a shot, so here's your shot. It's formal, so dress . . . formally. Interview some members of the hospital administration, maybe a few benefactors, and even a parent or two if they're willing. I need copy on my desk by midnight in time for the morning edition. Stop by the office and pick up your press pass."

I can't help but smile. This day just became infinitely better.

"Who's my photographer?"

"Oliver. Meet him at the hotel entrance at six. He'll text you the address."

Even better. I love Oliver.

Grateful to have a break from my personal drama, I thank him for the opportunity and then immediately call Megan.

"So?" she answers breathlessly.

"So . . . yeah. Positive."

She squeals as if this is wonderful news.

"What are you going to do, Callie?"

"Nothing right now. I have a more pressing issue, believe it or not."

I tell her about the last-minute assignment to the charity event. I have nothing formal in my closet, and Megan owns a downtown boutique. I give her a budget, and she promises to have a dress and shoes delivered to my house within an hour.

With that out of the way, I head inside. I've barely made it into my apartment when my cell rings again.

"I heard," Lorie says with a sigh.

"About the baby or the event?"

"Both."

Good news travels fast.

Knowing I won't have time to eat later, I make myself a sandwich while we talk.

"I'm so glad you'll be there tonight, too," she says.

"Too?"

"Owen invited me. It's a total meet-the-parents moment. Apparently, the McAllisters are big-time benefactors of the hospital."

I nearly choke on my turkey sub. "Will they *all* be there?"

"Relax. Devin's out of town."

Thank God.

"You'll have to face him eventually, Cal."

"I know, but *eventually* doesn't have to be tonight."

"Agreed. It's a pretty special night to them, according to Owen. His parents have donated millions to the hospital, particularly to childhood leukemia research."

"That's pretty specific. Wonder why?"

"I don't know, Lois Lane. That'd be a great question for the benefactor."

I grin. "You're right, it would. Thanks, Lorie."

After we hang up, a pretty black dress arrives, and I get ready in record time. By five o'clock, I'm headed to the paper to grab my press pass. Frank barks last minute instructions as I race out the door, and forty minutes later, I'm walking into the hotel.

"Wow!" Oliver whistles as I make my way to him. He's standing at the entrance, leaning casually against the wall with his camera around his neck. "Definitely hot. Too bad you're not my type."

"Yeah, that's a real shame." I grin and adjust his gold bowtie. "You look great, too. Maybe we should have color coordinated."

Oliver rolls his eyes. "It's not the prom, Callie. Come on, let's get a drink."

We flash our press passes and step inside the ballroom.

"We're not here to socialize, remember?"

He ignores me and steers me toward a waiter. Oliver winks at him before taking two glasses of champagne from the guy's tray.

"You're shameless," I mutter as the server walks away. "Now, where's the press room in this place?"

"I'm gonna look around," Oliver says. "I'll text you when I find it."

"Thanks."

I hold on tight to my glass and navigate my way through

the crowd, hoping to find Lorie and Owen's table. I spot them at the same time they find me, and the two of them wave me over. As soon as I approach the table, I don't even get the chance to say hi before Lorie's smile turns to a pissed-off frown.

"What is *that*?"

Suddenly nervous, I glance down at my dress.

Did something pop out? Did the seam split?

"I'm serious, Callie. What is that in your hand?"

My hand?

I lift my glass. "Umm . . . champagne?"

"I know what it is. Why are you holding it?"

I narrow my eyes in confusion before I realize what she means.

"Oh!" I quickly hand her the glass. For an entire half hour, I totally forgot I was an unwed mother. "I didn't take a drink, I swear."

Owen glances curiously between the two of us before saying hello.

"You scared the hell out of me," Lorie murmurs before lifting the glass and downing my drink.

How unfair.

"Well, I can't believe the two hottest girls in the room will be sitting at our table tonight," Owen says with a lazy grin. "And I know someone who's going to be *very* happy to see you, Callie."

I glance anxiously at Lorie.

"Yeah, about that . . . Callie, would you come with me to the ladies' room?"

It's more of a demand than an actual question, because Lorie grabs me by the arm and all but drags me down a long hallway leading to the restrooms. The sinks are lined with women checking their hair and make-up.

Lorie pulls me into a corner. "Devin's coming."

No. No. No.

"I thought you said he was out of town!"

"He was. But this is a huge deal to his family. Owen says he never misses it. I'm so sorry, Callie."

I take a deep breath. "It's okay. This is work, and that ballroom is a big place. Maybe he won't notice me."

She eyes me from head to toe. "In that dress? Good luck with that."

Doesn't she realize I'm desperate here?

"Besides, it's been six weeks. Maybe he doesn't even remember me. Everybody says he's a total playboy, right? I'm probably just one more notch on his bedpost."

Lorie doesn't look convinced as we head back. When we reach the table, we find Owen sitting next to a handsome, tuxedoed man with salt-and-pepper hair. By his side is a beautiful woman with hauntingly familiar eyes.

"Ready to meet the parents?" Lorie whispers.

My stomach flips as Owen makes the introductions.

"How nice to meet you both." Valerie McAllister smiles at us. "And don't you look beautiful tonight."

"Thank you," we reply in unison.

William McAllister grins. "You both look like you could use a drink."

You have no idea.

"Callie works for the *Journal*," Owen says as he leads Lorie to her seat. My friend's barely in her chair before she's nervously downing her glass of champagne.

I hate her.

Mrs. McAllister motions toward the table. "You should join us, Callie."

"Oh, thank you, but I'm actually working tonight. I need to interview a few donors and then head back to the newsroom."

"You should interview Dad," Owen says. "He worked at the hospital for years. He's retired now, but he and Mom are still major benefactors."

Valerie places her hand on her husband's shoulder. "The hospital is very near and dear to our hearts. You'd be happy to be interviewed, wouldn't you, William?"

"Of course. Please, Callie, have a seat."

I *do* need this interview, and it'd look suspicious if I turned it down. Besides, I'm a professional. I can forget that I'm interviewing my unborn child's grandfather. Once it's over, I'll get Oliver to snap a few pictures, and then I'll make my escape before Devin even knows I'm in the building.

Reaching into my bag, I fish for my phone and send a quick text to Oliver before opening the recorder app on my cell. I place it on the table between us.

"Are you ready, Mr. McAllister?"

He smiles. "Please call me William. And yes, I'm ready when you are."

For the next fifteen minutes, William McAllister gives me a brief account of his work at the hospital. For years, he studied Hodgkin's disease before shifting gears to childhood leukemia research.

"Why leukemia?" I ask.

With that question, I feel a distinct change in the mood of everyone at the table. I glance around. An unusually subdued Owen bows his head, while his mom dabs at her eyes with a tissue. Lorie—stone-faced and confused—stares wide-eyed at me. She's probably thinking what I'm thinking. *There's definitely a story here.*

"Leukemia is the most common form of cancer diagnosed in children and teens," he explains softly. "If my past research or our donations can keep one family from feeling the pain we've felt . . . well, that's time and money well spent."

The pain we've felt. A good reporter would ask what he means by that, but something stops me. Maybe it's the emotion in his voice. Maybe it's the tears in his wife's eyes. I'm glad I don't, because when he starts telling me about the recent developments in leukemia treatments and research, everyone's mood brightens.

"Thank you so much for your time, Mr. McAll—"

"William."

I smile. "William. Would you mind if my photographer snaps a few pictures?"

"Not at all. Although, we should probably wait for Devin. Heaven knows his face isn't in the news enough."

Everyone laughs, but I can tell their amusement isn't mean-spirited. The McAllisters seem like a tight-knit family, and they've been so nice to me.

Will they still be nice when they find out I'm carrying their grandchild?

Anxious to get out of here, I rise from my chair and quickly send another text to Oliver.

Where are you?

"Now that work is out of the way, you really should join us for dinner," Mrs. McAllister says. "We'd love for you to meet Devin."

"We've met," a smooth, familiar voice echoes from behind me.

Great. I close my eyes in defeat when Devin appears at my side.

"Oh?" Mrs. McAllister's eyes twinkle as she looks between the two of us. "Son, you didn't tell us that you'd met such a lovely young woman."

"Lovely is the perfect word to describe her."

His burning brown gaze sweeps over me, causing butterflies to erupt in my already queasy stomach.

"It's nice to see you again, Devin."

Thankfully, Oliver finally arrives and I introduce him to everyone. Lorie joins me while Devin takes a seat next to his father. The McAllisters lean close together as Oliver snaps a hundred photos.

"He can't keep his eyes off you," Lorie murmurs.

"I think I'm gonna puke on my four hundred dollar shoes."

She glances down at my silver Manolos. "Oooh, pretty. Do you get to keep them?"

I roll my eyes.

"I think we're good," Oliver says.

Breathing a sigh of relief, I thank them once again before dragging my photographer away from their table.

"What's going on between you and Devin McAllister?"

My eyes dart around, looking for the nearest exit. "There's nothing going on."

"Please . . ." Oliver smirked. "That man's eyes didn't leave your body for a second, and you're all fidgety and nervous."

"Shut up and please tell me you found me someone else to interview."

He steers me toward the press room. "The hospital's CEO is taking questions for the next twenty minutes. You'll probably find some benefactors in there, too. But this discussion isn't over, Callie Franklin."

We spend the next hour talking to the hospital administrators and a few more supporters. When I'm sure I have enough information, Oliver takes some pictures of the partygoers before the two of us head to the exit. I've nearly made it out the door when I feel someone wrap their arms around my waist.

"Don't leave," Devin murmurs against my ear.

I stop abruptly.

"What—?" Oliver looks behind me and smirks. "Oh, I see."

"I'll meet you back at the office."

Oliver looks between the two of us. "You sure?"

I nod.

He says goodnight, and I take a deep breath before

turning around to face the music. I'd have to deal with Devin eventually. I know this. I was just hoping it wouldn't have to be tonight.

But we don't always get what we want.

"Devin, I—"

"You're stunning."

"Thanks. Listen, I really have to get back to the office. I have a deadline."

"Just one dance, Songbird."

He looks so hopeful it makes me laugh despite my anxiety.

"Right. Just one dance. I've heard that before."

Devin chuckles and runs his fingers down my bare arm. "That was some dance. Some night, too."

I ghost my hand along my stomach.

"Devin, about that night . . ."

He looks around, and suddenly, I'm being pulled toward a darkened hallway just outside the ballroom.

"That weekend was amazing," he whispers, his face just inches from mine.

"Yeah. We really need to talk about that."

"I'd love to talk about it. I'd love to recreate it."

"Don't you have a date?" I glance over his shoulder. All I need is some crazy supermodel bimbo trying to kick my pregnant ass.

His lips softly brush my cheek. "No. I haven't really dated much lately."

I tremble when his hands wrap around my waist.

"Why not?"

"I don't know, Songbird. Maybe you've ruined me for other women. Is that possible?"

"I . . . don't know."

"Come dance with me."

"I have a midnight deadline. If I miss it, I'm fired. Please, Devin . . ."

With a sigh, he closes his eyes and presses his forehead against mine.

"What about later? Can I see you?"

"I have no idea how long I'll be at the paper."

"Doesn't matter. Text me when you get home and I'll come right over. Where's your phone?"

Like an idiot, I offer him my cell. Devin enters his number, and I promise to call as soon as I get home. The poor guy smiles as if he's won the lottery. I almost feel guilty, because I know what he's expecting when he gets to my apartment.

I don't have the heart to tell him he's going to be deeply disappointed.

Chapter 7

DEVIN

It's suddenly so clear.

The sleepless nights. The zero interest in the opposite sex. The agitation and restlessness. All the frustration that's consumed me for weeks suddenly makes perfect sense.

I've been missing her.

I make this startling discovery as I head back to our table. When I sit down, the whole family's saying *what a lovely girl Callie is*, while my brother grins like an idiot. Lorie glares at me over her champagne glass like she's going to kick my ass.

What's her problem?

I can't worry about her right now. The only thing keeping me in this seat is the fact that tonight's important to our family. My mind needs to be on the benefit and not on the beautiful girl I just let walk out the door.

I've never missed a woman. Ever.

"How did you meet Callie?" Mom asks.

I recognize the sparkle in her eye, and I hate like hell to disappoint her. She's always on my ass about meeting a nice girl and settling down, but nice girls are few and far between. Besides, who wants a nice girl? Certainly not me. Nice girls want the picket fence. Nice girls want a commitment.

The last thing I need is anything that remotely resembles a commitment.

"I met Callie at Simon's wedding. She was the maid of honor."

My voice is nonchalant, as if I don't know every curve of the woman's body or the sound of her quiet sighs as she sleeps.

"It's too bad she couldn't have joined us for dinner," Dad says.

I agree, because these benefits are full of gold-digging tramps. That's why I always try to bring a date—to at least give the impression I'm involved with someone. News that I'm here alone is sure to spread like wildfire.

I spend the next two hours listening to speeches and watching my brother and his girlfriend whisper into each other's ears. After a few raffles and one last video presentation that brings tears to everyone's eyes, the benefit finally starts to wind down. I begin to write my customary check when my phone vibrates in my pocket.

I'm home. 453 Tangerine Lane. #3A.

"Look at that smile," Mom says.

Owen smirks knowingly. "Must've been some text."

I grin and slip my phone back into my jacket. After writing my check, I pass it to Dad. Mom eyes me curiously when I stand up and kiss her on the cheek.

"Headed home already?"

"Early meeting tomorrow."

I promise to call her later in the week and tell everyone goodnight. I've almost made it to the exit when someone grabs my arm.

"Dev, wait."

I turn and find myself face-to-face with my brother and his girlfriend. Owen looks serious. He's rarely serious.

"We need to talk."

"Can't, little brother. I'll call you tomorrow." I then smile at his girlfriend. "It was nice seeing you again, Lorie."

She grabs my arm. "Listen to me, Devin McAllister. I know where you're going, and I know what you think's gonna happen when you get there. If you hurt my friend, or make her cry, or do anything to upset her, I swear they'll never find your body."

"And I'll help her dig," Owen says firmly.

I narrow my eyes. "What are you guys talking about?"

"You're going to see Callie, aren't you?"

"It's none of your business, but yes."

Lorie's eyes flash with anger. "Oh, it's my business now. Maybe it wasn't my business when you put that disgusting hickey on her neck. And it probably wasn't my business when you left a card on her pillow to serve as some bullshit goodbye. But make no mistake, *this* is my business now, and if you do anything to hurt—"

"Why are you assuming I'm going to hurt her?"

My brother shakes his head. "Dude, just . . . don't be an asshole tonight, okay? And call me in the morning, because I'm pretty sure you're going to need to."

What the hell?

"I don't have time for this," I mutter. "I promise I won't upset her, and I'll call you in the morning. Is everyone satisfied?"

"For now," Lorie says.

"Awesome. Goodnight."

Traffic's insane, but I finally make it to Callie's apartment just after two. I anxiously knock on the door, ridiculously eager to get my hands on her. Maybe she'll be wearing some flimsy lingerie. Maybe she'll be naked. My mind's busy conjuring all the possibilities when she opens the door . . . wearing a sweatshirt and jeans.

"Hey," she says softly, stepping aside to let me in.

"Hey. You okay?"

She looks pale as a ghost. Is she sick? She looks sick. Maybe I should call an ambulance. Or my dad.

"I'm okay." Callie leads me over to the sofa. "Look, Devin, I know you probably have some plans for us for tonight, but *that* won't be happening."

"Oh." Disappointment floods me, but if the nauseated look on her face is any indication, it's probably best. Besides, there's the next night. And the next.

"But we need to talk, so I'm glad you're here. I have something I need to tell you." She abruptly jumps to her feet and walks toward her kitchen. "Would you like something to drink?"

I can't tell if she's being a good hostess or simply stalling, but I ask for a beer. It looks like I'm gonna need it. I hadn't pegged her for the kind of woman who needs to *talk about her feelings*.

When she returns to the living room, Callie hands me a bottle and sits down next to me. I notice she only brought one.

"You're not drinking?"

She curls her feet beneath her. "Unfortunately, no. I won't be drinking for a long time."

I've had it with the riddles.

"All right, what's going on? My brother and his girlfriend threatened to murder me if I make you cry. Something's obviously up with you because you just want to talk."

Her forehead creases. "Don't you ever just *talk* to a woman?"

"Not if I can help it."

"Why not? The girls you usually date don't have enough sense to carry on an intelligent conversation?"

"I don't date, Callie."

"I see. You just sleep with them."

"Sometimes. Is there something wrong with that?"

"And are you careful?"

"Careful?"

"Safe," she says softly. "We didn't use protection. I just wondered if that's typical for you."

Oh. It'd be easy to blame the alcohol, but honestly, using protection was the very last thing on my mind that night.

"No, that's not typical. I'm sorry about that."

"So am I."

Callie seems far more relaxed after my apology. *Maybe this night won't be an epic failure after all.* I slide closer to her, but she raises her hand in warning.

"We're not finished."

I groan and lean back against the couch.

"Devin, I need you to listen. Something happened that weekend. I'm almost positive you won't want to sleep with me after you hear what I'm about to say."

"I seriously doubt that."

"I don't." Callie sits up a little straighter and squares her shoulders. "I want you to know I expect nothing from you. Our weekend together was a mistake, and I'll deal with the consequences of it. I don't know exactly what I'm going to do at this point, but I thought you should at least know what's going on."

"What's going on?"

Her eyes flood with tears.

"Devin, I'm pregnant."

Pregnant.

Pregnant?

I stare at her. She stares at me. I watch her closely, hoping that at any moment she's going to burst out laughing.

But she's not laughing. She's crying.

I hear Lorie's voice in my suddenly throbbing head.

Don't make her cry.

"Why . . . why are you telling me?"

She wipes her eyes. "What do you mean?"

"You're assuming it's mine?"

"Of course it's yours!"

I snort. "Really? How can you be so sure? Maybe it was that bartender in the hotel's piano bar. Or maybe it was the guy who sat with you at the reception. Or maybe—just maybe—it was the photographer you were with tonight. You two seem pretty close."

Even as the bitter words drip off my tongue, I know better. Her face is just too furious . . . her eyes too heartbroken.

Suddenly, Callie stops crying. Her eyes flash with fury just seconds before she slaps me across the face.

Despite the ringing in my ears, I can hear my brother's warning.

Don't be an asshole tonight.

Too late.

I groan as bright sunlight floods the room. Muttering a curse, I cover my face with one arm and tighten my grip on the bottle of whiskey in my hand.

"Oh, good. You're already dead. Saves me the trouble."

I feel like death. *How much did I drink?*

"What time is it?"

I struggle to sit up. When I open my eyes against the harshness of the sun's rays, the room immediately begins to spin. Groaning, I lay back down.

"Don't you mean what *day* is it?" Owen snaps. "Your secretary called. She was concerned. Why are you on the floor?"

I'm on the floor?

"Hell if I know."

"Get your sorry ass up. You've had two days to wallow in your self-inflicted misery. Now stand up, take a shower, and be a man for once in your life."

"What is your problem? And why are you screaming?"

"Because you lied."

"I did?"

I groan as he helps me to my feet. When I'm halfway steady, I glance down to find myself wearing a tux—a very wrinkled and whiskey-stained tux.

The room starts spinning again, so I stagger to the couch.

Owen sighs loudly and sits down next to me. "Yes, you did. You promised me you wouldn't be an asshole. You lied."

I squint against the blinding sunshine and try to focus on his face. It's too much effort, and my head starts to pound as memories flash through my mind. Some moments are a little fuzzy—and some don't make sense at all—but there's one memory that's clear as crystal.

Callie's pregnant.

"You're right. I'm an asshole."

My brother listens as I try to piece together the past two days. After Callie slapped the shit out of me and told me to get the hell out of her life, I found myself at a seedy bar on the outskirts of town. I remember a redhead, and I recall really wanting to sleep with her in hopes it'd purge my head of any and all thoughts of the girl I'd been missing for the past six weeks. But this girl was all wrong. She didn't have long blonde hair and bright blue eyes.

Bright blue eyes that I brought to tears.

So, I took a cab home, where I apparently drank myself into a stupor and passed out for two days.

My brother, always finding humor in the worst situations, begins to chuckle.

"Nothing about this is funny, Owen."

"Oh, I beg to differ. I find it hilarious. Callie has ruined you for other women."

"It's not that I *can't*. I just don't . . . want to. It's complicated."

"It sure is."

I bury my head in my hands. "Callie's pregnant."

"Yep."

"I'm the father."

"It would seem so, yes."

I rub my face. "Look, I know I handled this badly. But what did she expect? I don't know this girl at all. I'm just supposed to assume this kid is mine because she says so? It was a gut reaction."

"I know, but you also shouldn't have accused her of being a tramp, which is basically what you did. It's no wonder she slapped the shit out of you."

"And how do you know about that?"

"Girls talk."

Lorie.

"That's your problem, Dev. You're a brilliant attorney who can convince a jury to acquit a stone-cold killer if you turn on the charm, but outside the courtroom, you don't think before you speak. Did you shut up long enough to even consider the possibility that this woman could be the mother of your child?"

No, I hadn't considered it. Not for a second. Because that would mean I'd be forced to accept it.

"I can't be a father, Owen."

"Yeah, well, it's not like you get a choice. Besides, Lorie says that Callie's not one to sleep around. If she says you're the father, then it's probably the truth. Especially since she hasn't dated anyone since the wedding."

"But what about before the wedding?" I ask, hanging on to my last thread of hope. Not that I really want to imagine another man's hands on her, but at this point, I'm desperate.

Owen shakes his head. "I don't think so. The doctor says she's about six weeks along."

With a groan, I cover my face with my arm. "What the hell am I gonna do?"

"You're going to be a man. You're going to get out of that nasty-ass tuxedo, take a shower, get dressed, and go over to Callie's and knock on her door."

I chuckle darkly. "Not happening."

"Oh, yes. And if she doesn't shoot you on sight—which

I admit is definitely possible—then you're going to get down on your hands and knees and beg for forgiveness. You're going to tell her that she can count on you for whatever she needs. Callie's scared to death, man."

Of course she's scared. It's not like either of us planned this. She'd been so brave in telling me, and what had I done? Insulted her and left her in tears. I'd hurt this beautiful girl who'd occupied my every waking moment for the past six weeks . . . this amazing woman who'd made it impossible for me to be even remotely attracted to anybody else. Because they weren't her.

Can I fix the mess I've made?

Will she let me?

Do I even know how?

My stomach clenches with terror when I think about it. What do I know about raising a kid? I don't even like kids. They're loud and messy and annoying. I'm selfish and arrogant, and there's no doubt I'll completely screw it up. What do I know about being a father?

"What if I don't want to?"

Owen frowns. "Don't want to what?"

"Be a dad."

"Dude, didn't you hear me? You don't get a choice. It's not like you can say *not my problem* and walk away."

"Really? Guys do it all the time."

"You'd know, since you prosecute deadbeat dads all the time."

Shit.

"Besides, Dev, you have other things to worry about."

"Such as?"

"Our mother. Please make sure I'm around when you tell Valerie McAllister that she has a grandchild on the way and you want nothing to do with it."

Mom has been begging us for grandkids for years. We'd all placed bets, and I'd been happy to participate, because I was certain Owen would find himself in this predicament long before me.

"But most importantly," he says quietly, "there's Callie."

The mere sound of her name fills me with shame.

"What about her?"

"You've broken the heart of the only girl you've ever really wanted."

I snort. "I've wanted lots of women, Owen."

"But Callie's different, isn't she?"

I shrug and avoid his gaze.

"Pregnant or not, Callie's gotten under your skin. I saw it at the wedding. And then I watched your eyes glaze over when you saw her at the benefit."

I can try to deny it all I want, but Owen's right. There's something about Callie that's unforgettable. She's beautiful and smart. And the sex . . .

Then I remember sex is the reason I'm in this mess.

My stomach lurches.

"Dev?"

I quickly stand up and immediately vomit on my hardwood floor.

Chapter 8

Callie

Whoever came up with the phrase *morning sickness* is a complete liar. Mine is the twenty-four hour a day kind. Thankfully, my child shares my love for banana freezer pops, because, according to my baby bible, I'm probably going to be enjoying my morning sickness throughout my entire first trimester.

That's what it says—*enjoying*.

Pretty sure the baby bible was written by a man.

I glance wearily at the book in my lap. The chick at the bookstore said it was the most popular book for expecting mothers, so of course that's the one I bought. Lord knows I'm in desperate need of a baby survival guide.

After my post-Devin breakdown—which consisted of three days of tears and numerous ice cream interventions with Lorie and Megan—I decided it was time to get a grip.

I'm a thirty-year-old, professional woman. There's absolutely no reason that I can't raise this baby by myself and be a good mother. I certainly don't need an asshole like Devin McAllister in the picture. All I need is . . . me. Am I scared? Of course. Do I have a clue? Not at all. But I'll figure it out because single women raise babies every day, and they do it well.

And now . . . I'm joining the club.

With that in mind, I decided to attack this whole pregnancy thing with the same determination I used when studying for final exams in college.

I crammed.

When I'm not working—or throwing up—I'm reading baby books. If I'm not reading, I'm surfing pregnancy websites on my laptop. I'm like a woman possessed, eager for any and all information that can get me through the next eight months without any further emotional breakdowns.

I've shed my last tear for Devin McAllister.

A knock on the door makes me jump, sending my precious baby book onto the floor. I quickly pick it up and place it on the table before heading to the door.

"Who's there?"

"It's Uncle Owen!"

I roll my eyes before glancing through the peephole. Sure enough, Owen's there, smiling like an idiot and carrying a variety of colorful bags.

"What do you want?"

"I come bearing gifts! Come on, Callie. It's just me."

With a sigh, I open the door. Owen barrels through,

hitting me with one of the gigantic bags on his way to the sofa. When he's finally settled, he grins at me and nods at my freezer pop.

"Banana, huh?"

"They help with the nausea."

"I prefer grape."

"What are you doing here, Owen?"

"Just checking on ya."

I look at the bags. "And what's all this?"

"*This* is for my nephew."

I fight back a grin. "It's a boy?"

"Yep."

I sit down beside him and gaze at the overwhelming amount of gift bags. "You know, your nephew or *niece* is the size of a raspberry right now."

"Doesn't matter. Babies need toys." He grins and hands me a small blue bag. "Open this one first."

His enthusiasm's infectious, and I find myself excitedly digging into the bag. Thanks to my baby book, I'm able to correctly identify the little blue onesie.

"Tennessee Titans," Owen says. "There's a matching bib, too."

I smile. "I see that. Those are cute, Owen. Thanks."

"Oh, but there's more!" He chuckles and tosses me another gift. After four more bags, I can't help but notice a pattern.

"Don't think I'm not appreciative, because I totally am . . ."

Owen frowns. "But?"

"Everything's blue. You know, there's a distinct possibility this baby's a girl."

"Not gonna happen. There hasn't been a McAllister girl born in more than thirty years."

"Hmm." I don't have the heart to tell him this baby's a Franklin. He's brought gifts, after all, and I really don't want to rain on his parade. "I really appreciate all this, Owen."

"You're welcome," he replies quietly before taking a deep breath. "Listen, I want to talk to you about Devin."

My entire body bristles at the sound of his name.

"I know he was a complete ass and totally deserved that slap across the face. But he's had some time to reflect, and he's going to try to make it right."

"How?"

"Umm . . . I sorta convinced him to come over and beg for your forgiveness."

I laugh. "Seriously?"

He nods.

"Well, you can tell him not to waste a trip because I'm not in a very forgiving mood where your brother is concerned. Is that what this impromptu baby shower was all about? Because if so, you can take your gifts and shove them—"

He shakes his head. "No, that's not why I brought them. I really just wanted to bring my nephew some toys and clothes. No strings attached."

I bow my head, ashamed to have jumped to conclusions so easily.

"I'm sorry, Owen. I'm just . . . I really don't want to talk about your brother. Or *to* him, for that matter. He made it very clear he wants nothing to do with this baby. I don't want or need his money. I don't want or need his help."

"I know you don't, but—"

"No buts. I told him the truth. The baby's his. I tried to do the right thing, which is more than I can say for him, so tell your brother he can save his apologies because I don't need them . . . or him."

Owen sighs sadly. "I wish you'd hear him out. He really likes you, Callie. And I know that sounds juvenile or whatever, but he really does. I've never seen him look at another woman the way he looks at you, and trust me, I've seen Devin with plenty of women through the years."

"I'm sure you have," I mutter, rubbing my stomach. "I think I need another banana pop."

"I'm on it."

Owen leaps off the couch and makes his way to the fridge. When he returns, he actually takes the time to unwrap it for me. I thank him and lean back against the couch, nibbling slowly.

"Callie, the last thing I want to do is upset you, but I'm begging you. Please let him try to fix this. I really want to know my nephew, and my parents will be ecstatic when they find out they have a grandkid coming. We're good people, honestly. Devin's good, too, beneath that mask of immaturity and arrogance."

"Just because Devin's chosen not to be part of the baby's life doesn't mean I'm going to the shut out the rest of you. I'm not selfish."

"I don't really think Devin made that choice. He just

freaked out. A baby just wasn't part of his plan, you know?"

"You think it was part of mine? I don't know what I'm doing! I'm throwing up all the time. I cry for the stupidest reasons. And I'm scared out of my mind. Unlike Devin, I don't have a choice." I point to my stomach. "There's a baby in there. I can't just throw a temper tantrum and ignore it."

"I don't think he's going to ignore it for much longer." Owen reaches into his pocket and pulls out a business card. "I gotta go. Here are all my numbers. I want you to call me, day or night, if you ever need anything. More banana pops. More blue toys. A shoulder to cry on. Whatever. Okay?"

"Thanks, Owen. And thanks again for all the gifts." I lean over and kiss him on the cheek before taking another look at all the presents. "I really, really hope for your sake it's a boy."

We both laugh as I walk him to the door.

"Will you do me a favor?" he asks.

"Maybe."

"Will you at least think about what I said about my brother?"

I sigh. "I just need some time. I want to concentrate on my baby and avoid drama. I won't beg him to be part of his child's life, and we'll be just fine without him."

After he leaves, I take all the toys and clothes and place them in the guest room. Or rather, the *nursery*. I've never decorated in here because I've never had guests. Right now, the walls are stark white with a full-sized bed in the corner. Obviously, that'll have to go. I've yet to reach the furniture part of my baby research, but I'm assuming he or she'll need a crib, changing table, a dresser . . . maybe a rocking chair.

And, of course, a wall for books, because my kid is going to be a reader.

Suddenly starving, I grab my bag and baby book and head to the coffee house just down the block. It's my favorite place to eat in Nashville because it's close to my apartment and has the best veggie burgers in town. After placing my order, I find a corner booth and open my book. I'm deeply involved with the chapter "How to Break the Happy News to the Family" when I feel someone's eyes on me. I look up to find myself staring into the beautiful face of Valerie McAllister.

She smiles brightly. "Callie! I thought that was you. How are you?"

Swallowing nervously, I quickly close my book. "Mrs. McAllister, it's nice to see you again."

"You, too. And please, call me Valerie," she says, waving toward the empty seat across from me. "May I?"

I nod. *First the uncle and now the grandma?* All I need is Devin to show up and we can have our first official family reunion.

"William loves this place, so I thought I'd grab him some lunch."

"I love it, too. I'm just waiting for my veggie burger."

"You look a little pale, sweetheart," she murmurs softly, patting my hand. "Are you feeling okay?"

I smile gratefully. Valerie's so sweet and motherly, which is something I desperately need right now.

"Umm . . . no, actually. I've been pretty nauseous lately."

"A stomach bug?"

Obviously, the McAllister men have kept their mouth shut. *Figures.*

The waitress interrupts our awkward conversation. She places my burger in front of me and tells Valerie her order will be up in just a few minutes. We both thank her, and I immediately take a bite.

Valerie grins at my enthusiasm. "Nausea gone?"

I wipe my mouth with a napkin. "It's so weird. I'm starving one minute. Vomiting the next. There's no rhyme or reason to it."

"Hmm."

She grows quiet, and that's when I see her gazing at my book.

Crap. Crap. Crap.

"Well, that certainly explains the nausea and cravings. Congratulations, Callie."

"Thanks," I mutter.

Her face softens. "I take it by the sound of your voice this isn't great news."

"It's . . . complicated. I'm trying to be happy. I really am."

She nods. "How far along are you?"

"About six weeks."

"And how are you? Do you have a good doctor?"

"I do, and I'm okay, honestly. I'm going to figure it out. My baby and I will be fine."

The waitress brings a take-out carton. Valerie thanks her without taking her eyes off me.

"Callie, I know this is none of my business, but the father . . . is he being supportive?"

It's actually very much your business. I take a deep breath and gaze into her eyes . . . the same deep brown eyes of her son. I can't lie to her, but maybe I can be vague.

"Not exactly, but we'll be okay."

"What do you mean, *not exactly*?"

Something about the tone of her voice makes my stomach lurch.

"He . . . just made it very clear he's not interested in being part of this baby's life."

Anger flashes in her eyes.

Mine fill with tears.

Does she know? Could she possibly?

"Callie?"

"Valerie, I can't. You need to talk to your son."

"My s—"

"Enjoy your lunch."

"Callie, wait!"

But I don't wait. I grab my book and bag and run toward the restroom. Slamming the stall door behind me, I drop everything and hover over the toilet. This isn't morning sickness. This is anxiety, because I'm pretty sure I just outted Daddy Devin to his mother.

After washing out my mouth, I make my way back into the restaurant. I breathe a sigh of relief when I see that Valerie's gone. I sit back down in the booth and push my cold burger to the side before burying my head in my hands.

What should I do?

Deciding I better warn at least one brother, I dig in my bag until I find Owen's card. I add him to my contacts and send him a text. It's just two words, but I know he'll understand my cryptic message.

Grandma knows.

Chapter 9

DEVIN

I wonder how many thirty-year-old men need to give themselves a pep talk just to walk out their door.

For the past two hours, I've been unable to convince my feet to do just that.

My brother really put into perspective what an asshole I've been. Typically, that doesn't bother me, but when it comes to Callie Franklin, it bothers me a lot. I can't imagine how hard it must have been for her to confess to me that she's pregnant, and what did I do? Treat her like crap.

I deserved to be slapped.

I deserve worse.

After Owen left, I really did some soul-searching. I can try to ignore it all I want, but the fact is I'm going to be a father. The mere thought scares the hell out of me.

You should probably tell her that.

Will she even let me?

Determined to try, I've actually placed both feet on the floor and stood up when my cell vibrates in my hand. I take one look at the message from Owen before falling back onto the couch.

Grandma knows. You're a dead man.

Before I can reply, I hear a fist pound on my door, immediately followed by the furious voice of my mother.

"Devin Wayne McAllister, open this door right this minute!"

Shit.

Sighing tiredly, I walk over to the door. I've barely opened it before I'm knocked down by the force of my tiny mother barging into the room. She looks livid, and suddenly, I'm a kid cringing under the weight of his mother's pissed-off glare.

"Why are you on the floor?"

"Because you knocked me on my ass."

"You deserve it," she says, huffing with annoyance before stepping over me on her way to the couch.

I climb to my feet. "Actually, I was just on my way ou—"

"I don't care. Would you mind explaining to me why I just saw a visibly upset and very nauseated Callie Franklin at the coffee shop?"

"You saw her?"

"Yes, I saw her—looking positively pale and reading a baby book. It was easy to connect the dots. When I asked if she had plenty of support, she told me a particularly horrifying story about a man who told her he doesn't want to be part of her child's life. Then, she told me she couldn't talk to me anymore and that I needed to speak to my son."

I swallow nervously but keep my mouth shut.

"I'm assuming by the way you couldn't keep your eyes off her at the benefit that Owen isn't the one I should be talking to."

Embarrassed and ashamed, I bow my head and stare at my feet.

"Callie's pregnant."

"I know *that*!"

"The baby's mine."

A deathly silence hangs in the air. Finally, Mom reaches out her hand. Out of complete desperation, I take it and let her pull me to the couch.

"Devin, did you really tell her you wanted nothing to do with your child?"

"Not in those exact words, no, but . . ."

My mother holds my hand while I spill my guts. I leave out the more graphic details of the wedding weekend, but when I'm finished, my mom knows everything I know about Callie Franklin. She listens intently and doesn't interrupt . . . that is, until I tell her I haven't been able to get Callie out of my mind.

"You have feelings for her," she says softly. I detect a hint of amazement in her voice. "I could tell at the benefit that you were completely smitten."

"It doesn't matter if I do. I've completely screwed it up."

"Then you're just going to have to fix it."

"I don't know how."

"You apologize, for starters," she says. "You tell her you're an idiot—"

"Wow, don't hold anything back there, Mom."

"Well, you acted like an idiot."

I nod. "I did. You're right."

"Tell her you *are* going to be a father to this child and that she can rely on you for anything for the rest of your lives."

I chuckle nervously. "The rest of our lives?"

Mom searches my face. "You don't understand, do you? You may not end up romantically committed to this woman, but you have created a child with her. Like it or not, the two of you are now connected forever. She's scared, Devin. She needs to know she can depend on you."

I anxiously rub the back of my neck. "I *so* didn't sign up for this."

"And she did?"

"That's not what I meant."

Mom sighs. "I know you're scared, and I don't mean to dismiss that, but think about how frightened you are and then multiply it by a thousand. *That's* how scared Callie is right now. All this anxiety isn't good for her or the baby."

"She hates me."

"That's why you're going to do whatever it takes to fix this. Right now."

Without letting go of my hand, my mom leads me out the door.

"Oh, and Devin?"

I lock the door behind us. "Yeah?"

"She'll probably tell you to go away."

"Oh, I'm prepared for that."

"What will you do?"

I look down into my mother's proud, trusting eyes. My mom knows me better than anyone, and she knows that, despite my faults, I'll do whatever it takes to make things right.

"I'll beg to stay."

I check my watch. *How can she not be home?*

I keep knocking and pray her neighbors won't call the cops on me. I've been standing at her door for thirty minutes. *Maybe she's home and just doesn't want to talk to you. Maybe she's at work. Maybe she's sick and can't answer the door. Maybe . . .*

With a groan, I slide down her door and sit on my ass. *Where is she?*

The elevator dings, and Callie walks out into the hallway. In her arm is a bag of groceries. When she sees me standing by the door, she stops in her tracks and drops the bag.

"Sorry." I rush toward her and kneel to the ground. "I didn't mean to scare you."

She remains silent as I pick up her ice cream, crackers, and something that looks suspiciously like spinach. After putting everything back in the bag, I offer to carry it inside for her.

"What are you doing here?"

"We need to talk, Callie."

"You've said enough."

"No. I—"

But she doesn't give me the chance to finish. She reaches for her bag and snatches it out my hand. Without another word, she pulls her keys out of her pocket and unlocks the door.

"Callie, please talk to me."

She steps inside her apartment and promptly kicks the door closed right in front of my face.

Chapter 10

Callie

"Callie! Open the door!"

I ignore his relentless knocking and put away my groceries. *How long has he been here? Have my neighbors seen him? Maybe I'll get lucky and they'll call the police.*

After half an hour, I grab my phone and put my earbuds in. Singing along, I start opening ingredients to make my grandma's chicken noodle soup, hoping it'll settle my queasy stomach. While it simmers, I throw in a load of laundry. I've just closed the door on the washing machine when I get the first text.

I'm not leaving.

Great. Totally forgot that I gave him my number.

I pull out my earbuds and toss my phone onto the sofa.

Thankfully, he finally stops knocking, but I hear a distinct thump, which leads me to believe his legs have finally given out and he's now propped against my door.

I ignore the sound and grab a banana freezer pop before collapsing on the couch.

My phone chimes again. I wait a whole ten minutes before glancing at it.

I know I'm an ass. I'm sorry.

I gaze at the screen. Sorry for what? For being an arrogant jerk? For knocking me up? For accusing me of being a tramp? For dismissing me—and our baby—so easily? For pounding on my door for God only knows how long?

My fingers ghost along the screen, eager to ask what he's apologizing for.

You aren't talking to him. Remember?

I wish I could just turn it off, but I'm too afraid I'll miss a call from work.

Almost instantly, there's another text.

Please talk to me.

I smirk. Now he's begging.

Good.

By ten o'clock the text messages stop, and I breathe a sigh of relief. Grateful that he's given up and gone home, I quickly clean up the kitchen and load the dishwasher before grabbing my baby book and going to bed. I climb under the blanket, looking forward to the chapter on relaxation techniques for a stress-free pregnancy.

Before I can even open the book, I'm fast asleep.

I wake up the next day feeling relaxed, well rested, and starved.

Excited that I'm not hugging my toilet this morning, I rush to the kitchen in hopes of having a real breakfast for a change. I glance in the fridge, and my stomach growls when I spy a fresh package of turkey bacon.

Yes!

Usually, I prefer my eggs sunny-side up, but the baby book warned about eating raw yolk, so I scramble them instead. I add a couple slices of toast and then sit down to enjoy my first decent breakfast in weeks. A moan actually escapes my lips when I take the first bite.

Note to self: Baby likes scrambled eggs.

After breakfast, I get ready for work. I'm feeling so good I actually dress up a little today, choosing a knee-length skirt to wear with my flats. As I check my reflection in the mirror, I'm amazed how *happy* I look . . . all because I didn't throw up this morning.

It's the little things in life.

Confident that it's going to be a great day, I grab my bag and phone and head out. When I open the door, a man's body—and his head—fall at my feet. I find myself staring down into Devin McAllister's brown eyes.

So much for my great day.

"Good morning, Songbird."

"What the hell are you doing here so early?"

He smirks and climbs to his feet. "You're actually acknowledging my presence this morning?"

Shit. I snap my mouth shut.

"And, for your information," he continues, leaning close as I lock my door. "I never left. I told you I wasn't leaving."

He slept out here?

"You're a jerk."

"No argument here. Please just talk to me."

I sigh deeply and turn to face him. He's right *there*, staring at me with those brown eyes that make me lose my mind.

"I'm gonna be late for work."

"Meet me for lunch. Dinner. Whatever you want."

Devin McAllister is the most infuriating man I've ever met. How dare he camp out at my front door all night long and make me feel sorry for his arrogant ass.

"Why are you here, Devin? You made it very clear how you feel."

He leans closer. "That's not how I feel. I'm here because this is where I should be. You have to let me apologize."

"I don't have to do anything."

He sighs. "Of course you don't *have* to. But would you at least let me try to make it up to you?"

"I don't need your apology. Now get out of my way and

leave me alone."

I hold his gaze, and he holds mine, neither of us willing to let the other one get the upper hand. Devin's used to getting his way. A cocky, high-priced attorney who pours on the charm to get whatever he wants. Six weeks ago, I would have fallen for it. I did fall for it. Twice.

Never again.

"I'm going to work. If you're here when I get back, I'm calling the cops."

His eyes flash with fury. I take pride in the fact that I'm pissing him off.

"You can call the National Guard for all I care. I'm not giving up, Callie."

"You don't have a choice, Devin."

He opens his mouth, but I don't give him the chance to argue. I just step around him and head to the elevator.

DEVIN

Pissed and exhausted, I haul my ass to my apartment to shower and change before driving to the office. When I walk in, my secretary regards me with a smirk before handing me a pile of messages.

"Good morning, Mr. McAllister."

"Hello, Alicia. What's all this? My punishment?"

"*This* is what happens when you disappear for two days. I can weed through them if you like? Trash the unimportant ones?"

I hand them back to her. "Yes, please."

"Oh, and your dad called. He'd appreciate it if you'd stop by the house sometime today. They'll be home all afternoon."

Great.

"And I'll bring you some coffee. You look like you need it."

"Thanks, Alicia."

I head into my office and fire up my laptop. I regret it immediately because I find over two hundred emails.

Heaven forbid if I ever take a vacation. My inbox would explode.

I delete what I can before losing all patience and calling Alicia, begging her to work her weeding magic on my email, as well. By the time she brings me my coffee, I only have twenty phone calls to return and about fifty emails requiring my attention.

The rest of the morning is spent replying to clients. To be honest, I'm glad to have something to concentrate on besides Callie and the baby. Then my brother calls and asks about the two things I've been trying hard not to think about.

"Has she let you in yet?"

"Shut up, Owen."

"You know, if you keep stalking her, eventually she's gonna call the cops."

"Good. Maybe they'll lock me up and put me out of my misery."

His laughter grates on my nerves. "That girl hates you, man."

"I'm aware."

"I mean, she even let *me* in the house."

"What do you mean?"

"Uncle Owen arrived with gifts. Brought my nephew some kickass toys."

"Neph—what? How do you know it's a boy? Did she tell you that?"

"Wow, you really don't know anything about pregnancy, do you? It's not like they can tell the gender yet. But I know, man. Uncle Owen knows."

I roll my eyes and resist the urge to throw my phone against the wall.

"You know, Dev, *that's* what you need to do. Gifts, man. Not for the baby, but for Callie. Something to soften her up."

"Right. So, how is she?"

"Callie? She's okay, I think. Mad at *you*."

"So you said."

I glance at my watch. *Wonder what time she goes to lunch? What does she like to eat? Is she having any of those weird pregnancy cravings?*

These are things I need to know.

Camping outside a woman's apartment puts things into perspective. Last night, while I struggled to sleep against her door, I admitted to myself that I obviously have feelings for this woman. It's impossible to deny it when I seem to get excited about the most inconsequential things. Like the way her eyes sparkled this morning when she opened the door to find me there.

She'd deny it, of course, but I know what I saw.

After hanging up with Owen, I finish responding to the last of my emails before closing my computer and heading out the door. I can't concentrate, anyway.

"I'm headed out for a while, Alicia."

She looks up from her computer screen. "Do you promise to come back this time?"

I grin. "I promise."

"Don't forget to stop by your parents' house. Your dad seems anxious to see you."

I bet. "I won't forget."

"Is there anything I can do for you while you're out?"

Owen's advice rattles around in my brain. *Gifts, man. Not for the baby, but for Callie.*

"Actually, there is something you could help me with. You're a girl—"

"Last time I checked, yes."

"What kinds of gifts do women prefer?"

She smirks. "You've never bought a gift for a woman?"

"Does my mother count?"

"No."

Shit.

"What's the occasion?"

How much should I tell her? I decide to be honest. Everybody's going to know soon enough, anyway.

"I need a gift that says *I'm sorry for being a heartless bastard when you told me you were having my baby.* Any suggestions?"

My usually stoic secretary's eyes grow wide.

"I don't think Hallmark makes a card for that, Mr. McAllister."

She's trying hard not to laugh, which is good, because I really don't want to have to fire her.

"I really could use some advice here, Alicia."

"Of course, sir. May I ask a question?"

"Sure."

"Just how big of a heartless bastard were you?"

"Fairly epic."

She nods. "Then I'd probably start with flowers. I can call the florist if you'd like."

That's a great idea. Girls like flowers, right?

"Roses. White roses."

Will Callie remember? Will she even care?

"White?"

"Yes. A dozen?"

Alicia taps her pen against her chin. "Better make it two. And I suggest you stop by and take care of the message on the card. It'll mean more to her if it's in your handwriting."

I smile. "Perfect. Thank you, Alicia. Remind me to give you a raise."

She's already dialing the number.

"Oh, don't worry. I will."

Before dealing with the florist, I decide to make the drive to my parents' house. I don't normally dread spending time with them, but I am so not in the mood for a lecture, and I know one's coming from my father. After all, he's the one family member who hasn't offered his opinion about the baby situation.

I don't bother knocking. I just walk in and head straight to the study. That's where I always find him. Sure enough, he's sitting behind his desk, gazing out the window.

"Hey, Dad."

He turns his head and smiles.

"Good morning, son. You look like shit."

"Thanks a lot."

Dad chuckles and offers me a seat on the leather couch.

"I'd ask if you'd like a drink, but it's not even noon. Besides, you've probably had enough for a while."

"I see you've talked to Owen."

"And to your mother. They're both very fond of Callie."

"I know. My whole family's in love with her."

"What about you?"

"What about me?"

"Are you in love with her?"

I glance at the mini bar. Maybe I *could* use a drink.

"Is that even possible?"

Dad stands up from his desk chair and joins me on the couch. "Oh, I think anything is possible, son. You're going to be a father. I'd be willing to bet that Satan himself is wearing a parka because hell has officially frozen over."

I grin. "True. At least Mom will get the grandbaby she's always wanted."

"That will be fun," Dad says, his eyes twinkling with happiness. "It's about time something wonderful happened to this family, don't you think? We've been sad for too long."

"So you think this is a good thing."

"I think it's wonderful. It'll be even more wonderful when Callie finds it in her heart to forgive you."

When. My father, the eternal optimist.

"Callie seems like a very intelligent, compassionate

woman. Pregnancy can be a frightening thing, especially for a first-time mother. Make her feel special. Make her feel safe. That's what she needs right now."

"I'm trying, Dad."

"By camping outside her apartment?"

I shrug.

"She's scared, Devin. Even more so than you."

"I can't imagine how that's possible."

"Think about it," he says softly. "*You* can walk away. You can choose to wash your hands of the entire situation and pretend it never happened. Callie doesn't have that luxury."

"I won't walk away."

"I'm very glad to hear that. Callie needs to hear it, too. "

I glance at my watch. *I could invite her to lunch and tell her then.*

"Give her some time."

"I'm not a patient man."

"I'm well aware," Dad says with a laugh. "Think of it as practice for the future. You're going to need tons of patience to be a father. It's really quite exhausting."

"I'm sorry that I'm always testing your patience."

He shakes his head. "Devin, you've never been a bad son. You've handled your heartache the best you could, just like the rest of us. I think this baby will be the best thing that's ever happened to you. You'll finally have the chance to look forward to the future instead of always focusing on the past. Shyann would want you to be happy."

I close my eyes. The sound of her name never fails to rip my heart out.

"I don't want to forget," I whisper.

Dad sighs sadly and places his hand on my shoulder.

"And you never will."

Chapter 12

Callie

My amazing breakfast and my heated clash with Devin keeps a smug smile on my face all morning long. I'm proud of myself for not falling for his crap. Did he really think he could bully me into talking to him? Just because he camped out by my door doesn't mean I'm going to forget the horrible way he acted.

While my personal life's a mess, my career is finally showing signs of life. Frank called me into his office to say how impressed he was that I'd scored an interview with William McAllister. Apparently, the McAllisters are notoriously private when it comes to talking to reporters about their personal involvement with the benefit. Like a good newsman, Frank was curious about the family's passion for childhood leukemia research, and more than once hinted that I should dig deeper. As I left his office, he reminded me to check the assignment board. I'm never excited to check it because I'm always given some trivial fluff piece, but today, I've been assigned to interview one of the city's mayoral candidates for next week's special election edition.

I practically skip all the way back to my cubicle.

"She's alive!" Leo shouts from across the room.

I smile and wave, grateful to see he's on the phone. I really don't want to talk to him. Not yet. I'd called in sick the past two days. I'm not quite ready to admit the truth and Leo has an uncanny ability to drag it out of me.

I spend the morning doing research on my mayoral candidate and confirming the interview date and time with his office. I'm just about to head to lunch when I hear someone clear his throat.

"You're far too pretty to be hiding in a cubicle."

With a sigh, I look up to find Devin peeking over my wall.

"Are you deaf? I told you to leave me alone."

"And I told you I'm not giving up."

"And I told you that you don't have a choice!"

A hush falls over the newsroom. *Great.*

"You know, I think you're the most frustrating woman I've ever met."

"Yeah, well, you can blame it on the mommy hormones surging through me," I whisper. "Now leave me alone. I'm going to lunch. My child's hungry."

Devin's eyes dance with something that vaguely resembles . . . *joy?*

"*Our* child," he says softly. "Let me take you and our

child out to lunch."

"*My* child. And no."

Suddenly, Leo's standing beside me. I'd like to think he's coming to my rescue, but I know better. He's just nosy.

"Hey, Callie. Everything okay here?"

Devin's eyes narrow when Leo wraps his arm around my shoulder.

Is he seriously jealous? Ha!

I smile at my friend. "Everything's fine. Would you please take me to lunch?"

"*I'm* taking you to lunch," Devin says, his gaze fixed on Leo's arm on my shoulder. I almost giggle at the absurdity of the situation. He obviously has no idea that Leo's gay, so I use this to my advantage and snuggle into my friend's embrace.

Thankfully, Leo gets the hint. "Sure, Callie. Let's go to lunch."

I shoot Devin a glare. If I had any compassion for him at all, I might be concerned for his health. With his fire engine-red face, could he possibly be having a stroke? Should I maybe call 911?

Yeah, it's a good thing you don't have feelings for the man.

"Good, because I'm starving."

"Callie . . ."

I don't give him the chance to say anything else. Looping my arm through Leo's, the two of us walk up the stairs and out into the sunshine.

"I can't believe we're having a baby! And with Devin McAllister!"

After my shameful display in the newsroom, Leo managed to get a confession out of me over lunch. I wish I could say his enthusiasm's infectious, but all it's doing is making me queasy.

I nibble on my chicken salad sandwich and watch the birds flutter around the park fountain. "*We're* not having a baby. I am. *Me*."

"With that gorgeous, gorgeous man."

"That gorgeous man's a jerk, Leo."

"Granted, he handled this totally wrong, but it seems as if he's trying to make it right. You should let him."

"Why? Why should I?"

"Because he *wants* you, Callie. I'm surprised I made it out of there with my arm intact. You know I'm a lover, not a fighter. What would Oliver say if I came home all mangled and broken because I helped make your baby daddy jealous?"

"Stop calling him that. And he's not jealous. He just thinks he can bully me into getting what he wants."

"Not true. I saw it at Megan's wedding reception. The man's into you. Why are you fighting it?"

I roll my eyes and toss my unfinished sandwich into the nearest trashcan. "I told you what he said to me. Am I supposed to just forgive and forget?"

"No, but you can at least let him apologize. Don't you owe that to your kid?"

"He made it very clear he wants nothing to do with the baby. He even accused *you* of being the father! Well, one of the fathers."

Leo shudders. "No wonder he's ready to murder me. But none of that matters."

"Why not?"

"Don't you think he's being pretty persistent for someone who doesn't want to be in your life? Besides, you're not without fault here, Callie Franklin. *Two* people were irresponsible that weekend. Two ambitious, power-driven people who had an amazing weekend together, which has led to *this*. You know nothing about each other. If the situation were reversed, wouldn't you have questioned him?"

"Of course, because you said he's one of the biggest manwhores in town."

"Allegedly. Allegedly one of the biggest manwhores."

"You never said *allegedly*."

Leo rolls his eyes. "Anyway . . . the point is you would have questioned him, too. He knows nothing about you. Why should he assume you're telling him the truth?"

"That's . . . valid, I guess."

"He absolutely handled it badly, but it seems he's realized that, and he wants to fix it. Shouldn't you let him try?"

Back at the office, I'm still thinking about what Leo said when I hear my name being called from the stairs.

Good grief. What now?

I slowly peek over my cubicle. A delivery guy's standing there with a gigantic bouquet of roses.

White roses.

"I'll take those," Leo says, smiling at the delivery boy. He glances at the card and grins. "Oh, Callie! That horrible, terrible manwhore has sent you these beautiful flowers!"

I mutter a curse and drop back down in my chair. Leo walks over and places the vase on my desk.

"Wow, a whole dozen this time."

I try to ignore how beautiful they smell and how pretty they look.

Leo snorts. "No, honey, that's *two* dozen."

"You counted?"

"Of course! And here's the card."

I snatch it out of his hands. *As if you don't know who sent them?*

With a laugh, Leo heads back to his desk. I slink down into my chair and slowly open the tiny card.

You look beautiful today.

I bow my head as tears fill my eyes. *Stupid hormones!*

But one thing's for sure.

Either Devin McAllister's full of shit, or I'm in serious trouble.

Please don't be here. Please don't be here.

I continue mumbling that prayer as I step out of the elevator. Taking a deep breath, I peek over the top of the flowers in my hand. Of course he's there, standing against my door.

"Oh, you got the flowers. Here, let me help you with them."

I let him, because nobody tells you how heavy two dozen roses can be.

"I didn't think about how you'd get them home. I guess I assumed you'd leave them on your desk."

"My desk's too small." I reach into my bag and find my keys.

"Do you like them?"

"Yes, Devin. They're really beautiful."

"Like you."

His voice rings with sincerity, so I resist the urge to roll my eyes. Instead, I open the door and step inside the sanctuary of my apartment.

"Thank you for the flowers."

"You're welcome, Callie."

I close the door.

The next four days are exactly the same.

Each morning, Devin's waiting for me outside my apartment. At noon, he's in the newsroom begging to take me to lunch, despite the fact I always say no. The poor delivery boy shows up around three o'clock with a fresh bouquet of white roses. And every afternoon, I find him waiting at my door. I always thank him for the flowers and then close the door in his handsome face.

Every day is the same. Only the cards are different.

Always handwritten, the messages have become more heartfelt each day. Instead of saying something flattering about me, he's started telling me things about him. Things that are completely unexpected.

You look beautiful.

I want to take care of you and our baby.

I can't stop thinking about you.

I dream about you every night.

After reading today's message, I take the collection of tiny cards out of my drawer and line them up on my desk. I obsess over them, trying desperately to read between the lines.

Today's embarrassment of flowers and sweet card hit me the hardest. In his perfect handwriting, Devin wrote four little words.

Please forgive me, Songbird.

Maybe it's the pregnancy hormones, or maybe he's just wearing me down with all the sappy love notes, but it's getting harder and harder to close that door in his face every night.

As we walk to my apartment later that evening, I beg Lorie to tell me what to do. She'd remained uncharacteristically quiet throughout this entire ordeal. Lorie's so good at separating emotion from logic. I rely on her to be my voice of reason.

"What do you want to do?" Lorie asks.

"I have no idea."

"What does Megan say?"

"You know Meg. She's a romantic at heart."

"She thinks you should forgive him?"

I shrug. "She thinks I should at least have a conversation with him."

Lorie loops her arm through mine as we head toward the elevator. "You know, I'll hate him forever for treating you the way he did, but I think Megan's right. I believe he's sincere when he says he's sorry."

We step into the elevator and press the button for my floor. "Owen's turned you into such a softie."

"Maybe, but he knows his brother better than anyone, and apparently, Devin's a mess. And Valerie's worried about both of you because all this drama isn't good for the baby. This kid's going to have the best grandparents, Callie. The McAllisters are amazing people."

At least my child will be loved by one side of the family.

"Fifty bucks says he's at my door right now."

She smirks. "I'm not taking that bet. He's been camped out there all week."

We laugh as we step out of the elevator and make our way to the door. As predicted, Devin's there, sitting outside my door. He quickly stands up when he sees the two of us.

"Hello, Devin," Lorie says sweetly.

"Hello, Lorie."

"Don't you have a home?"

I bite my cheek to keep from laughing.

Devin clears his throat. "Yes, I do. My home's wherever Callie is."

Lorie's face softens, and she shoots me a glance. I shrug helplessly. He's been saying sweet shit like that all week.

"You're either the smoothest bastard I've ever met or you're absolutely crazy about her."

I take advantage of his stunned silence by unlocking my door. Once it's open, I turn around and stand in the doorway, watching as my best friend and the father of my child stare each other down.

"Which do you think it is?" he asks.

"I'm going to let Callie decide. Try not to screw it up this time, McAllister." She grins and walks back toward the elevator. "Goodnight, you two."

Devin turns to me, excitement etched across his handsome face. His brown eyes sparkle with anticipation as he leans against the doorway.

"I can't help but notice your arms are empty. Do I need to fire my delivery guy?"

"Oh, no, he delivered them. I just couldn't carry *four dozen* roses home. I hope you don't mind, but I gave them away. The girls—and some of the guys—loved them. Nearly every desk in the newsroom has flowers. One of our advertisers stopped by and thought he'd walked into a florist."

He laughs. "Did you at least read the card before you gave them away?"

"I've read every card. We should probably talk about those."

"Okay."

I take a deep breath and step aside.

"Are you coming in or what?"

Happy but hesitant, Devin slowly follows me into my apartment.

"Have a seat. Would you like something to drink? I have

water, juice . . ."

"Juice is great."

I can feel his eyes on me as I head to the fridge. The open floor plan of the apartment was the first thing that attracted me to it, but right now, I could've used a wall to give me a few minutes to gather my nerve. Instead, I ignore his penetrating stare and grab two juices.

"I'm going to make a sandwich. Would you like one?"

"No, thanks."

I grab the mayonnaise, turkey, and cheese out of the fridge. As soon as I flip the top on the mayo, my stomach does a somersault. *Weird.* I've craved mayo every night this week.

I shrug it off and finish making my sandwich. After putting everything on a tray, I carry it to the living room and sit down next to him on the couch.

"Thanks," he says.

I nod and curl my feet under me. He watches me while I eat, which normally would have made me self-conscious, but I'm too starved to care.

"I can't believe you let me in."

"That makes two of us. I guess you wore me down with all the flowers and sappy cards. You can stop sending them now, by the way, although I'm sure your florist will miss you terribly. He . . . or she . . . can probably retire now."

He grins. "It was worth every penny if it means you'll talk to me."

"I'm not talking to you because of the roses. I'm talking to you because a very good friend reminded me that, if our situations had been reversed, I might have had the same reaction you did."

"What's your friend's name? I'd like to send her a dozen roses for helping me out."

"*His* name's Leo. You met him, remember?"

Devin's eyes darken. I stifle a giggle.

"I think he likes tulips, though. Oh, and don't put your name on the card. Oliver—his boyfriend—might get jealous if you do."

He blinks rapidly. "Wait, Oliver? The photographer?"

I nod and sip my juice.

"Leo and Oliver are a couple?"

"That's right."

"And I accused you—"

"You sure did."

Devin bows his head. "So I'm an even bigger asshole than I thought."

I don't agree or disagree, because neither is productive to the conservation we need to have.

"So, yeah, Leo reminded me that you don't know me at all, so your reaction—while insanely rude—was understandable."

"I just panicked," he says quietly, his voice breaking. "But that doesn't excuse what I said to you. I'm so sorry, Callie."

"It's okay—"

"No, you have to let me do this," he says urgently, climbing off the couch and falling to his knees before me. "You have to let me say these things because you might never give me another chance."

Please don't let me cry in front of this man.

"I'm sorry I hurt you. I'm sorry I made you cry. I'm sorry I made you feel like you were all alone. I was scared, and I'm still scared, but I know you're scared, too, and I just want the chance to make this up to you. I have never begged for anything in my life, but I will beg for this."

My breath hitches when he takes my hands and slowly laces his fingers with mine. I've been so strong these past few days, but being this close to him when he's on his knees and pouring his heart out is going to break me.

I blink back tears. "Why, Devin? Why are you doing this?"

"Because this is my baby, too, and I want to be part of its life. I have absolutely no idea what to do, but I really want to try." He lets go of one of my hands and brushes a strand of hair out of my face. "I want you to trust me, but I know that'll take time. Please let me try."

He isn't asking me to forgive him. Somehow, he knows I'm not ready for that. He's just asking to try, and he's begging me to give him a chance to do so.

Can I do that?

Maybe.

"Will you get my bag? It's on the kitchen table."

Confusion flashes across his face, but he doesn't question it. When he returns, he hands it to me and falls back down to the floor.

"You don't have to beg on your knees, you know."

"Yes, I do, Songbird."

Sighing softly, I slide down to the carpet next to him and

reach into my bag to pull out five tiny envelopes.

"Tell me about the cards, Devin."

"Which ones?"

In all honesty, the more flattering cards are pretty self-explanatory. I'm more interested in what he has to say about the more heartfelt notes he sent later in the week. I hand him those, and he reads them before gazing at me with a look that melts my heart.

"I think about you all the time. I've done nothing but think about you since Simon's wedding. I can't even look at another woman without thinking about you, so I finally stopped trying."

"You don't seem like the kind of guy who likes to be alone."

"The only woman I want hasn't been answering my calls. Or my texts. Or my—"

"Okay, okay."

We smile at each other.

"And that last card? Is it true?"

"It's true. I dream about you every night."

"Every single night?"

"Every night since the wedding," he says, then he grins. "Well, there was that one night I didn't dream at all, but I'd run ten miles that afternoon. I was too exhausted to do anything except collapse on my couch. But otherwise, yes, I dream about you every night."

He gazes at me, and I have to look away just so I can process everything he's said. Suddenly, his finger is on my chin, tilting it so that I'm forced to look at him. During our conversation, our bodies have somehow drifted closer, and his face is just inches from mine.

"Good dreams?" I whisper.

"The best."

He trails his finger across my bottom lip. My entire body shudders.

"I shouldn't kiss you," he murmurs roughly.

"You shouldn't kiss me."

There isn't an ounce of conviction in either of our voices

"Callie," he whispers, and like a moth to a flame, I close my eyes.

Chapter 13

DEVIN

My mind screams at me, telling me it's stupid to let ourselves get carried away. But that doesn't stop me from sliding my hand along the nape of her neck and pulling her face to mine.

Just as our lips touch, her eyes suddenly fly open.

"Callie?"

In an instant, she's out of my arms and rushing toward the back of her apartment. I jump up and follow her down the hallway and into the bathroom where she's kneeling over the toilet.

"Go away," she says with a groan.

"Not a chance."

I hold back her hair while she loses her dinner. After a few minutes, her body finally stills, and she sags against me.

"I thought it was over," she whispers, reaching for a

nearby towel. "I guess the baby doesn't like mayo anymore."

"I thought morning sickness was just . . . in the mornings?"

Callie walks over to the sink and quickly washes out her mouth. "Not mine. But I'm okay. Please go back to the living room."

"Are you sure you're okay?"

"Yeah. I just need a minute."

I nod and slowly head back to the living room. *Does that happen a lot? Has she been sick this entire time?*

A few minutes later, Callie returns to the living room. She's pulled her hair into a ponytail and changed into a T-shirt and sweats. I watch closely as she walks straight to the fridge and pulls out a banana freezer pop.

"Do those help?" I ask as she makes her way to the couch. I'd love to hold her, but I don't know how she'd react to that after vomiting in front of me.

She nods. "They do. Sorry about that. I haven't thrown up in days, so I was really hoping that fantastic phase of pregnancy was over. The baby bible says it can last up to three months. Some lucky women are sick the entire time they're pregnant. I will *die* if I'm one of them."

"The baby bible?"

"In my bag."

"May I?"

She shrugs, which I assume is permission. I sprint off the couch.

"It's supposed to be the best book for expectant parents."

I sit back down and immediately start flipping through

the pages. Food. Furniture. Childbirth. *So not ready for this.*

"How are you feeling now?" I ask, handing the book to her.

"I'm okay." She smiles softly—an honest to God smile that thrills me. She's beautiful, even after vomiting. "Thanks for holding my hair."

"Thanks for letting me."

"You didn't really give me a choice."

I take her hand in mine. "I told you I'm not going anywhere. Vomiting. Cravings. Mood swings. Nothing's keeping me away from you."

Her eyes shimmer with tears. *Hormones?*

"You really want this?" she whispers.

"I really do. And I want to be at your next appointment."

"Okay." Callie stifles a yawn and giggles. "Sorry, this is my life most days. Eat. Puke. Sleep. Work. Rinse. Repeat."

I grin.

"Come on." I pull her by the hand and lead her down the hallway. Her bedroom is easy enough to find, and I pull the blanket back as she crawls under it. She pulls down her hair before lying down against the pillow.

"Don't send anymore flowers," she says softly.

Unable to resist, I reach over and play with a strand of her hair.

"Okay, I won't."

"And don't sleep outside tonight. You can stay here."

"Really?"

She shrugs. "What's the worst that can happen? It's not like you can get me pregnant."

I chuckle. "That's true. Are you sure?"

"Come to bed, Devin."

Her words are music to my ears.

We've made so much progress tonight, so the last thing I want to do is give her the impression there's an ulterior motive in my accepting her invitation to spend the night. For the first time in my life, I'm climbing into bed with a beautiful woman for completely innocent reasons.

I'm exhausted.

Her bed looks awesome.

And I really, really don't want to leave her.

I slip off my shoes and climb into bed, resisting the urge to pull her against me. I can remember with startling clarity how she felt in my arms while she slept that last night at the hotel, and I find myself absolutely aching to touch her.

But I have to be patient.

With a heavy sigh, I lie on my back, close my eyes, and beg my body to ignore the beautiful woman lying next to me.

"Devin?"

"Yeah?"

"I'm sorry I interrupted our kiss."

"That's okay. Maybe you'll give me another chance someday."

She giggles. "Maybe."

"A man can dream."

"Speaking of . . . do you think you'll still dream of me, even though you're sleeping right next to me?"

I can't help but smile.

"I don't know, Songbird. I'll tell you in the morning."

Suddenly, I feel her soft hand gently brush against mine. We lace our fingers together, and I listen to the steady rhythm of her breathing until we both fall into a peaceful sleep.

Chapter 14

Callie

The next morning, I wake up with a pair of strong arms wrapped around me. Warm and comfortable, I nuzzle my nose against his shirt and lay my head against his chest, letting the strong, rhythmic beating of his heart lull me in and out of consciousness. Finally, my mind alerts me to the fact that Devin's in my bed. I remember asking him to stay, and I vaguely recall each of us lying on our sides of the bed as we fell asleep. What I don't remember is how or when I ended up in his arms.

Not that I'm complaining.

It's ironic. I'm pregnant with the man's child, but this is the first morning I've actually awakened in his arms.

And to think, this time yesterday, I was still furious with him.

There's no denying it. After nearly a week of doing and

saying all the right things, the man finally wore me down. Little by little, I felt the wall I'd built between us starting to crumble. Holding my hair back while I puked—while highly embarrassing—is just another in the long list of sweet gestures that makes me wonder if I'd misjudged him. The man holding me in his arms right now is an entirely different creature from the man I met in the hotel piano bar.

Which one is the real Devin McAllister? Which one will wake up this morning?

"What are you thinking about?" he whispers against my hair.

I grin and look up to find him smiling down at me. "What makes you think I'm thinking about anything?"

"I can tell by the look on your face. You're deep in thought about something. Or someone."

"Hoping it's you?"

"I always hope it's me."

I laugh softly and try to remove myself from his grasp, but his arms tighten around me.

"Stay. Just a little while longer."

With a smile, I cuddle against his chest and close my eyes. "So, how did this happen?"

"You asked me to stay."

"Not that. *This*." I squeeze his waist. "I don't recall falling asleep in your arms last night."

He strokes my hair. "You didn't. I don't really know how this happened. Do you hate it?"

"No, it's nice, actually."

"I think so, too." Devin gently presses his nose against

my hair. "How is it possible that you smell so good first thing in the morning?"

I don't know what to say, so I just smile against his chest. We lay there in a comfortable silence, which is odd because we really shouldn't feel comfortable at all. We're virtually strangers—strangers who just happen to be bringing a baby into the world.

Yeah, that's not messed up at all.

"Devin, is this weird?"

"What do you mean?"

"Shouldn't this be a little awkward? We barely know each other."

"I guess it probably should be, but it's not awkward for me. Is it for you?"

"No . . . and that in itself is awkward. Isn't it?"

Devin laughs softly and kisses my forehead. "Let me guess. Even when there's nothing wrong, you tend to overanalyze a situation until you find something to worry about."

Am I that obvious?

Embarrassed to be pegged so easily, I bury my face against his chest.

"Don't do that. Don't hide."

Looking up, I gasp softly when he traces my bottom lip with his finger.

"I hide a lot. When I'm embarrassed. Nervous."

"Do I make you nervous?"

"No."

It's the truth. *He* doesn't make me nervous. It's my

reactions to him that make me nervous. My body. My mind. My heart. They're all at risk whenever he's around.

"I'm glad, Callie."

Just then, my stomach decides to growl.

"Hungry, Miss Franklin?"

How embarrassing. "Apparently."

"What sounds good?"

I consider this.

"Pancakes and bacon."

"You're in luck. I make awesome pancakes."

"You cook?"

"When forced. But I'll happily cook for you."

I wiggle out of his arms. This time, he lets me.

"I'd totally race you, but my very full bladder has other ideas."

Devin laughs and sits up in bed. "Go do what you need to do. I'll meet you in the kitchen."

"Do you have plans for today?" Devin asks.

I pour more syrup on my pancakes. He was right. The boy can cook.

"Not really. I have the rare Saturday free. Do you need to go in?"

"Nope. One of the perks of being the boss is I can take off whenever I want."

I grin and pass him the bacon. "Must be nice."

"It has its perks."

We eat in a comfortable silence. With each bite, I moan appreciatively.

Devin smirks. "I'm glad you have an appetite this morning."

"Me, too." *Let's just pray I can keep it down.* "So, you own your law firm? That's impressive."

"Thanks. It's small, but growing. My parents are big braggers. They love telling people their thirty-year-old son owns his practice. The truth is I'm just too stubborn to share my caseloads with anyone else."

The mention of his parents makes me think about mine.

"You know, I haven't told my folks about the baby. My mom's actually in town. Not to see me, of course. She's shooting a wedding at Belle Meade Plantation this weekend. I'm sure she'll want to stop by."

"You don't sound very excited about that."

"You don't know my mom."

"What about your dad?"

I smile. "Dad's great. He's a retired paramedic. Lives about three hours east of here in a little town called Brandywine."

"I've been rafting there. Pretty place."

"It is. He loves the mountains. He can hunt, fish, and sit on his porch all day long, and nobody bothers him."

"Is that where you grew up? In Brandywine?"

"Yeah. My parents divorced when I was fourteen. I split my time between them until Mom got remarried. Her new husband gave me the creeps, so I moved in with my dad. Mom's been bitter about it ever since. I think she's on husband number four now. Maybe five. It's hard to keep up, especially since we rarely speak. She lives in Atlanta."

"Does that bother you? I mean, it has to, right? The fact that you aren't close to her."

I shrug. "My mother's pretty toxic and impossible to please. Mom was seventeen when she got pregnant with me. The only reason my parents got married was because Grandpa insisted on it. Mom missed out on a lot, so she had really high expectations for me . . . so high it was suffocating. I was playing piano by the time I was five and speaking Italian by second grade."

"Wow, Callie. That's incredible."

"I guess. As I got older, the expectations became ridiculous. I just wanted to be a kid. Dad let me be one. He actually let me date, which is something Mom would never do. She was convinced I'd get pregnant and end up just like her."

Devin's face grows ashen. "Oh, she's going to *love* me."

I shrug. I stopped worrying what my mom thought about me and my life a long time ago. She can either be happy or not.

"It doesn't matter, Devin. I'm a grown woman. If I want to have a baby, I'll have a baby."

"Yes, ma'am," he says, grinning. "Speaking of which, would the baby like more pancakes?"

I groan in appreciation. After four pancakes, three slices of bacon, and two glasses of juice, I think I'm finally full.

"I'm done, but it was delicious, Devin. Thanks."

"Anytime." He grins and finishes the last of his juice. "So, now that you're stuffed, I'd like to ask you a question."

"Hmm, coercion through pancakes. I see how you are."

"You can say no, but I don't think you'll want to."

"Try me.

"How would you feel about having lunch with my family? It'd just be really casual at their house."

I've met his parents, so this is really no big deal, but I'd never been introduced to them as the *mother of their grandchild.*

"I should probably warn you," he continues, "they're ecstatic about the baby. Overjoyed is probably a more accurate description. And they absolutely love you, so there's nothing at all to be nervous about."

Well, in that case . . .

"I'd love to."

He smiles.

"What about your mom?" he asks. "Should we invite her, too?"

"Are you kidding? Absolutely not."

"We have to tell her sometime, Callie. And your dad. We should make plans to visit him soon."

Holy crap. Less than twenty-four hours ago, we weren't speaking to each other. Now, I'm having lunch with his family and he wants to meet my parents.

"You're a brave man. My dad owns lots of guns, you know."

"Most hunters do."

I glare at him.

"Look, Callie. We're adults. We're having a baby. We can't control how they're going to react to the news. It's like you said. What we do with our lives is none of their business."

I frown. "Did I say that?"

"You did. And no matter what happens, I'll be right here."

Callie

After helping me with the dishes, Devin heads home to shower and change. It's been such a good morning, so I decide to throw caution to the wind and reach out to my mom. I have enough respect for her work that I decide to send her a text instead of actually calling. I'd hate for her to have to deal with a pissed off bride all because of me.

Give me a call when you can.

Ten seconds later, my phone rings.

"Hey, Mom. I hope I didn't interrupt the pre-wedding madness."

"Callie, sweetheart. I was just getting ready to call you."

Sure you were.

We make idle chit-chat about nothing important, which

is pretty normal for us. It's only when she invites me to brunch that I remember what Devin said.

He's right. We have to tell her eventually.

"I've already eaten, but I was thinking maybe we could meet for lunch tomorrow before you head back?"

"My flight leaves late tonight."

How typical. She wasn't planning to spend time with me at all.

"I have some time this morning. Why don't I just drop by?"

Now? I glance around the apartment. It doesn't look too bad.

"Umm . . . okay. But can you give me about half an hour? There's someone I'd like you to meet."

"Oh?" Her tone immediately brightens. "A man?"

"Yes, a man."

"No one too serious, I hope. You know your focus should be on your career."

Well, that didn't take long. Instead of arguing with her like I normally would, I ignore her comment completely and tell her to drop by in an hour. As soon as we hang up, I text Devin to tell him my mom is on her way. Suddenly very anxious, I busy myself by making my bed and picking up around the living room. I've barely fluffed the sofa pillows when I hear a knock on the door.

He must drive like a maniac.

Secretly happy that I won't have to face my mother alone, I rush to let him in.

"That was qu—"

"Good morning, sweetheart," Mom says, smiling brightly as she makes her way inside. With a frown, she glances around, looking for imperfections. She's never liked my apartment and has no problem telling me so every time she visits.

I roll my eyes and kick the door shut. "You're very early."

"Honestly, Callie, you know how I feel about killing time." She kisses my cheek and heads to the couch. "Besides, I'm on a tight schedule today. I have to be at the plantation by noon."

"Can I get you something to drink?" I don't wait for her to answer before heading to the kitchen.

"Is this a new couch?" she asks.

"Nope. Same couch."

"Hmm. New pillows? Something's different."

Joining her on the couch, I hand her a bottle of water.

"Same pillows, Mom."

She eyes the fabric. "You know chevron's not my favorite, but you manage to make it work."

I smile tightly and drink my water. *What I wouldn't give for alcohol right now.*

"So, tell me about this wedding you're shooting."

"Tell me about this boy you're seeing."

"There's not much to tell," I mutter, already losing my nerve. *Why did I think this was a good idea?* "His name's Devin. He's a lawyer. His family's great. I met them at a hospital benefit. They're really nice people."

While I babble, Mom shifts around on the couch.

"What is . . ." she reaches around and pulls out a book

that's buried behind the pillow. My entire body freezes when I recognize the cover. Mom looks up at me, then back down at the book. "What is this?"

A knock on the door makes me jump.

"What is this, Callie?"

I ignore her question and head for the door. Devin's all smiles until he sees the expression on my face.

"What's wrong?" he mouths.

Shaking my head, I pull him inside and lead him over to the couch. Mom's holding the baby book and glaring at the man by my side.

"Mom, this is Devin McAllister. This is my mother, Kim Rhodes."

Always the charmer, Devin offers his hand. "It's nice to meet you, Mrs. Rhodes. Callie's told me a lot about you."

"Funny, she's told me absolutely nothing about you."

The two of us sit down, and Devin takes my trembling hand. Mom's forehead creases as she watches our fingers lace together.

"You're pregnant."

It's not a question, so I don't feel the need to confirm it. She knows. The lawyer, however, has other ideas.

"Yes, we are." Devin smiles and squeezes my hand reassuringly, as if this is just the most wonderful news in the world.

Mom's face turns various shades of red before she finally finds her voice again. "And you're getting married."

I shake my head. She shoots a glare in Devin's direction, as if it's his fault we're not planning a wedding.

"I see. And how far along are you?"

"About seven weeks."

Her face brightens. "Oh! Well, then, this is easily taken care of. You had me worried there for a minute."

I frown. "What does that mean?"

"You'll have an abortion, of course."

I feel Devin's body stiffen. This time, I'm the one who squeezes his hand.

"No, Mom. I'm not getting an abortion."

"You can't be serious, Callie. Your career is finally taking off. Trust me. They won't send pregnant journalists across the globe. You'll be chained to your desk. And this man won't even marry you."

"We don't have to get married in order to raise this baby."

Mom laughs bitterly. "You'll end up alone. You realize that, right? He'll leave you and you'll have to raise this baby by yourself."

Devin clears his throat.

"Mrs. Rhodes, with all due respect—"

She interrupts him with a steely glare. "You have knocked up my daughter and refuse to marry her, so I really have no interest in what you have to say."

"Mom, this isn't 1950. The world won't explode if we bring a baby into it without getting married. People do it all the time."

"Callie, you aren't listening to me. You have plenty of time for babies. Please don't let this baby ruin your life like—"

"Like I ruined yours." Angry tears trickle down my cheeks.

"That's enough," Devin snaps. "Mrs. Rhodes, I think it's time for you to leave."

"Excuse me?"

"I won't have you upsetting her."

Mom snorts. "I don't know who you think you are—"

"Well, then, let me introduce myself," he says as he walks over to the door. "I'm the father of this baby, and I won't have you upsetting her. You're going to be a grandmother. Congratulations. The choice is yours if you want to be part of its life."

"Callie, you're making a mistake. This man . . . and his baby . . . will ruin your life."

"Get out," I whisper, wiping my tears away. "Go to your wedding and then fly back to Atlanta and forget all about the daughter who ruined your life."

"Callie . . ."

"She asked you to leave." Devin opens the door.

My gaze remains on the floor as my mother walks over to him.

"You're just going to hurt her," she says coldly.

"I'm going to try very hard not to do that, but I can guarantee I'll never hurt her as much as you have today. Goodbye, Mrs. Rhodes."

I don't watch her leave. I rush toward my bedroom, slamming the door behind me.

To Devin's credit, he leaves me alone for a while, because I need time to get a handle on my emotions.

My mom's words had cut through me like a knife. I'd expected her reaction, but I hadn't been at all prepared for it. Not really. She'd been cruel, which isn't really new. Mom takes every opportunity to remind me what a mess I made of her life. But this time, she was talking about my baby.

Of course, my doctor and I had discussed my options. Abortion. Adoption. But I knew, deep in my heart, neither of those were options for me. Sure, this baby was unexpected and unplanned, and yes, I'd completely freaked out at first, but I never considered not keeping it. This is my baby, even if I end up raising it alone.

While Mom's words had been cruel, I have to admit she had a point. Devin's protective and sweet *now*, but will it last? Very soon, I'll be grumpy and hormonal and fat. He seems determined to be in my life, but what if he changes his mind? I have no idea if I can truly rely on him, so that means I shouldn't try.

I'm on my own. I need to remember that.

"Callie?" He knocks on my bedroom door. "I've tried to give you some space, but I'm losing my mind out here. May I come in?"

I wipe away the last of my tears. "Yeah."

Devin walks into the room and climbs into bed with me. He doesn't say anything. He just pulls me into his arms. I go willingly. Clinging to him, I bury my face against his chest while he strokes my hair.

"I'm sorry I made you go through that," Devin says softly. "I had no idea."

"I did. I knew. But it had to be done. At least she knows. It's over now."

He kisses my hair. "Callie, look at me."

Blinking away my tears, I lift my head. Devin gently strokes his fingers along my tear-stained cheek.

"I'm not going anywhere. You know that, right?"

My throat tightens.

"I know you don't believe me, and I can't blame you after the way I reacted last week. But I'm in this, Callie. I'm here and I'm not going anywhere. I want you to know you can depend on me."

I shake my head. "Please don't make me any promises. I don't expect you to. I don't expect anything. You seem like you really want to be part of the baby's life, and I'm glad. We'll work it out. Schedules and stuff. It'll be fine."

Sadness radiates from his eyes. "Unbelievable. She was here ten minutes and managed to destroy what little progress we've made."

"Yeah, she's good at that."

Devin sighs heavily. "Look, I know you're scared. I'm scared, too. And not just about the baby."

I close my eyes. "Please don't."

"I mean it, Callie. I have never, ever felt this way about

anybody."

I can't handle this. Not right now.

"Please don't be sweet. Please don't make me any promises."

"But I want to, Callie."

A fresh wave of tears wracks my body, and I bury my face against his chest.

"Can we please just take things one day a time? One hour at a time? I can't handle much more than that right now. My emotions are all over the place. I just want to get through morning sickness and the mood swings and try to figure out how to be a good mom. I have absolutely no frame of reference when it comes to that because . . . well, you met my mother. I really don't want to be like her."

Devin pulls me close. "You need to relax. All this crying can't be good for you or the baby."

Nuzzling his chest, I take deep breaths and try to calm down. Devin strokes my hair and whispers over and over that everything's okay. I close my eyes, letting the steady beat of his heart calm my worries.

"Are you always going to be this protective?"

He laughs. "Probably."

"That might be a problem. I'm used to being alone."

"I know, Callie, but you aren't alone anymore. I'm right here, and I'm not going anywhere."

Looking into his eyes, I can see he really means what he says. I just wish I could trust it.

"I know you don't believe me. That's okay. I'm just going to spend each and every day trying to convince you."

"More convincing? Aren't you tired of having to work so hard?"

"Worth it." Devin leans down and kisses my forehead. "Feel better?"

"Yeah."

"Good, because I'm getting ready to introduce you to the best parents in the world."

I grin and struggle to sit up. "We've met, remember?"

Devin chuckles and helps me climb off the bed. "Yeah, but this time you're meeting them as the mother of their first grandchild. Be prepared. They're a little excited."

"How excited?"

Are they really happy? Don't they have their doubts about me? About us?

Devin lifts my hand to his lips, placing a soft kiss against my palm.

"Almost as excited as I am to take you home."

Chapter 16

DEVIN

Her blonde pigtails whip in the wind as she glides through the air. She always gets mad when I push the swing a little too hard, but sometimes, an eight-year-old boy just doesn't know his own strength.

"Devin, it's too high!"

I grasp the chain-linked swing to slow it down.

"Better?" I don't want to scare her. It's my job to keep her safe.

"Better."

Shyann smiles softly, and with that smile, I can breathe again.

It's just one of a thousand memories that bombard me as I stare at the picture in the frame. This photo, specifically, always calls to me when I visit my parents. I love this shot because she's smiling in it. Of course, she was always smiling—even when she became pale and weak and so very ill.

There are thousands of photographs in the house, of course. Years of memories, protected in glass frames, family albums, and school yearbooks. Those pictures would stand the test of time.

My memories, however, are starting to fade.

I remember the important times. Birthdays. Holidays. Vacations. Those I can recall with startling clarity. It's the little moments that are beginning to slip away from me—the silly, inconsequential times in our life that would seem unimportant to anyone else. Like how she loved to lie in the grass and find shapes in the clouds. Or how she worshipped the Backstreet Boys and wouldn't shut up until I learned how to play "Shape of My Heart" on the piano.

I still can't stand to listen to it.

Callie's sweet laugh floats from the kitchen, effectively snapping me out of my memories. Mom had pulled her away from me as soon as we walked into the house, but I didn't mind too much. We'd had a hell of a morning. The fact that she's laughing at all is a miracle.

I know it's hypocritical, but I hate her mom.

When I first heard about the baby, my reaction had been less than ideal, too, but at least I'm trying to make it right. From what Callie's told me about her mother, I get the feeling Mrs. Rhodes won't be apologizing any time soon.

I sit down at the piano and hesitantly lift the cover. It's not like I'm going to play. I haven't played in fifteen years.

"Callie's lovely."

I look up to find my dad standing in the doorway.

"She is."

Dad sits down on the bench next to me. "Strong, too."

Yes, she's strong, but even that strength has limits. I saw it this morning.

"Have you told her about Shyann?" Dad asks, nodding toward the picture frames.

"Not yet."

"It's probably time to tell her, son."

"Tell me what?"

We both look up, and I can't help but smile. Callie's wearing my mother's favorite apron and covered in flour.

"Baking with Mom, I see."

She glances down and laughs as she unties the apron. "I'm told *someone* likes peanut butter cookies, so we've been experimenting."

My father grins. "Well, they smell delicious. I think I'll go steal a few."

As he walks by, he offers to take the apron back to the kitchen. I watch as my dad softly kisses Callie's cheek and whispers something in her ear. I can't hear a thing, but whatever he says makes her blush.

"Stop flirting with the mother of my child."

Dad chuckles. "She's all yours."

He walks out, and Callie joins me at the piano. I wrap an arm around her and pull her close to my side.

"Do you play?" she asks.

"I used to."

"Play for me. It's only fair."

"Fair?"

"I've played for you."

I smirk. "You certainly did."

Callie rolls her eyes and places her hands on the keys. A soft melody fills the air. It's hauntingly sad and beautiful.

"Your parents are great," she says. "My mom never taught me how to bake anything. She had this hideous blue apron she wore whenever she cooked. When I was in first grade, my teacher asked us to draw a picture of ourselves, showing what we wanted to be when we grew up. I drew a picture of me, standing in the kitchen and baking cookies. My apron was blue, just like Mom's."

She keeps playing, and I brush her hair away from her shoulder, watching as a strand slips through my fingers and down along her back. She's so pretty. I pray our child has her eyes.

"At the bottom of the picture, I'd written *Callie wants to be just like her Mom* in my very best handwriting. I couldn't wait to bring it home to show her. Mom took one look at the drawing and ripped it to shreds right in front of me. I was six years old, but I remember it like it was yesterday. It was the first time I realized my mother isn't a very nice person."

It's official. I hate Kim Rhodes.

Callie drops her head and closes her eyes as she continues playing the somber song. I need to say something . . . anything to erase the sorrow from her face. Leaning close, I gently slide my hand along her neck and pull her close to me.

"You're not her," I whisper against her ear. "You're going to be such a good mom, Callie. I know you are."

She sighs softly and tilts her face toward mine. I've never wanted to kiss someone so much, and if I'm being honest, I want to do more than just kiss her. I'm in unfamiliar territory with this woman, because kissing is usually the last thing on my mind. If she were any other woman, we would have done way more than just hand-holding last night. If she were any other woman, I'd lay her across this piano.

But we're in my parents' house. And she's not just any woman.

With a heavy sigh, I pull myself away from her and walk over to the fireplace, gazing at the pictures on the mantle. I trail my finger across the glass of a photo taken when we were both ten years old. The emerald frame perfectly matches our Halloween costumes. That was the year Shyann talked me into being Peter Pan. She was Tinkerbell.

She really could talk me into anything.

The day they lowered Shy into the ground was the day I vowed to never be emotionally bound to another human being. Instead, I focused on doing exactly what she told me to do—get my diploma, go to college, and graduate from law school.

Done.

I never wanted to put myself at risk to feel that kind of heartbreak ever again. So I didn't. And I *haven't*.

Until now.

Of course, it's different. Shy and I were bound by blood . . . our bond unbreakable.

Until life proved there was no such thing.

Distant and cold, I've spent the last fifteen years refusing to form any kind of connection with another living soul. I died that day, too, and I never wanted to come back to life.

Until now.

It terrifies me beyond all reason, but I want her. I want *this*.

"That's a cute picture of you," Callie says, suddenly standing right next to me.

"How'd you know it was me?"

"Those brown eyes? I'd know them anywhere. Hers, too."

I swallow down the emotion that threatens to choke me. Thankfully, Mom yells from the kitchen, announcing that lunch is ready. Callie keeps gazing at the picture, but she doesn't ask any questions as I take her hand and lead her to the kitchen.

"Mama Callie!" Owen shouts, swiftly lifting her into the

air.

Everyone laughs except me.

"Hurt her and you're a dead man."

He grins and places her carefully back on the ground. All of us take our seats at the table. Mom kept it simple . . . just soups and sandwiches. And of course, my peanut butter cookies.

Dad passes around the sandwich tray.

"Mom, do all of these have mayo?" I ask.

She frowns. "They do. I thought you said she couldn't eat mustard."

"No, I distinctly said mayo."

Callie reaches for my arm. "It's okay, Devin."

"I'm so sorry," Mom says. "I'll be happy to make you another—"

"Please, don't. I'm hoping that mayo thing was just a one-time occurrence. Honestly, I eat it all the time. It's fine."

"It's *not* fine." I walk over to the fridge and grab the turkey. "I don't want you to get sick. Mustard?"

"I won't get sick, Devin."

Ignoring her and her icy glare, I make her a new sandwich and bring it over to the table. My parents look at me like I've sprouted wings. My brother, naturally, can't resist giving me hell.

"Wow, Dev. I've never seen you so . . . domestic."

"Mayo makes her sick," I mutter.

Dad clears his throat. "So, I understand Uncle Owen has already gone on a shopping spree for his nephew or niece?"

"Nephew," Owen replies. "Gonna be a boy."

"I certainly hope so, since every piece of clothing you bought was blue," Callie says with a grin.

Everyone laughs. Out of the corner of my eye, I watch as she eats her soup and totally ignores my sandwich.

Stubborn woman.

Owen chuckles. "What if it's twins?"

Callie drops her spoon and glances nervously around the table. "Is that possible?"

Mom and I exchange a look.

"Are there twins in your family?" Dad asks.

"I . . . have no idea. I guess I should ask."

As my family continues discussing the odds of multiple births, I lean close and whisper in her ear. "Why aren't you eating?"

Her eyes widen as she looks down at her bowl. "What do you mean? I am eating."

"Five spoonfuls of soup is not eating, and you haven't touched your sandwich."

"You're *counting*?"

I shrug.

"You yelled at your mom for putting mayo on my sandwich. Now you're counting my spoonfuls of soup? What is wrong with you?"

"I'm just trying to take care of you."

"Well, stop it."

I sigh heavily and grab another cookie. Callie doesn't speak to me or even look my way throughout the rest of the meal.

But I still count. Sixteen spoonfuls in all.

And she never touches my sandwich.

After lunch, Owen and Dad pull Callie into the living room while I help Mom clean up the kitchen.

Mom hands me a plate. "I'm sorry about the mayo."

"I'm sorry I was such an ass about it."

She smiles. "It's okay. I haven't seen you that protective of anyone in a long time."

"She's pissed, though."

Might as well call the florist. Lord only knows how many roses it'll take this time.

"Yes, but you have to remember that she's been on her own for a long time. All this protectiveness is going to take some getting used to."

"Too much?"

Mom nods.

"But she's so stubborn. She didn't even touch that sandwich."

"You're both strong-willed. Your poor child has absolutely no chance whatsoever."

I grin. "You're excited about this baby, aren't you?"

"Ecstatic."

After she starts the dishwasher, we both sit down at the kitchen table.

"Thank you for being so cool about this. I met Callie's mom this morning. She was less than thrilled."

"Callie told me about that while we were making lunch. Her mother sounds like a horrible woman." I nod, and Mom tilts her head. "But something else is bothering you. What's wrong?"

I shrug. "I'm just nervous, Mom. I mean, I'm going to be a father. Do you know how unbelievable that sounds to my own ears?"

"Oh, I think I have some idea," she replies, laughing. "Can I just say that if you just had to get a girl pregnant, I'm so happy it's Callie. She's really wonderful, Devin. I think she's good for you."

Callie's laugh echoes from the living room. It makes me smile.

"Can I tell you a secret, Mom?"

"I love secrets."

"What I feel for her scares the shit out of me."

"Of course it does. You're in love with her."

I bow my head. "It's too soon to feel that way . . . isn't it?"

"I think the heart wants what the heart wants and it totally ignores logic. What does your heart want, Devin?"

Easy.

Her. My heart wants her.

"You know, Mom, I could really mess this up."

"You could. And you *will* if you don't stop watching her like a hawk when she eats."

"Sixteen spoonfuls, Mom! That's all she ate."

Mom laughs. "You counted?"

"Yes, I counted. Do you see what I mean? The woman drives me crazy."

"Short trip," Owen mutters from the doorway.

I flip him the bird.

"Be nice," Mom says with a frown.

Just then, Dad and Callie return to the kitchen.

"Mama Callie's ready for a nap," Owen says. Once again, he lifts her off the floor with a bone-crushing hug.

"Owen, I swear I'm gonna—"

Callie shoots me a glare, silently daring me to finish my threat. My mouth snaps shut.

Yep. It's going to take a lot of roses.

Chapter 17

Callie

The rest of the afternoon is quiet, but it's not a peaceful calm. The silence is filled with loads of tension because my baby daddy is apparently a controlling, overbearing Neanderthal and I want nothing to do with him.

Devin must sense this, because he's finally stopped apologizing for being a barbarian and is now pouting on the couch, pretending to watch the news. I'm at the kitchen table, pretending to work. Every few minutes, I'll catch him looking at me, and we'll both divert our eyes and pretend we don't notice.

I hope our kid is more mature than we are.

He's just being protective, my mommy subconscious whispers to me. She's been doing that a lot lately, but this time I ignore her because she's seriously getting on my nerves. I don't *need* his protection, and I certainly don't need him watching my portion sizes. Who does he think he is?

Your baby's daddy, she whispers again. I sigh loudly and tap my fingers louder against the keyboard, hoping to drown her out.

Bitch is really getting on my nerves.

I sit up a little straighter when he walks into the kitchen and opens up the fridge like he owns the place. Ignoring him, I continue researching the mayoral candidate I'm interviewing this week. The official website for Nashville real estate developer Dominic Barkley is full of pictures and biographical information. With his designer suit and phony smile, he looks like an arrogant ass.

Suddenly, another arrogant ass is waving a banana freezer pop in front of my face. The sly, overprotective jerk even unwrapped it for me.

"Truce?"

I glare at him. This is coercion. Pure manipulation.

I hold strong until he calls me by the name that always melts my heart and turns me into a stupid, stupid girl.

"I'm sorry, Songbird."

Damn him.

I snatch the freezer pop out of his hand and take great satisfaction in watching his eyes glaze over as he watches me eat it. Smiling innocently, I turn my attention back to my computer screen. After a few minutes, Devin lets out a groan and quickly heads back to the couch.

"Problem?"

"I just . . . can't watch you eat that anymore."

Good. He deserves to suffer after the way he treated me

today.

Still, I can't help but wonder just how sexually frustrated he might be. Chances are he's probably hooked up with someone since the weekend we met.

I, on the other hand, have not.

The baby book says my sex drive could increase as the pregnancy progresses. I really hope not. It's going to be hard to keep my hands to myself if Devin insists on spending every waking—and sleeping—moment with me.

Twenty minutes later, I have mercy on the poor guy and take my laptop to the living room. He's in the chair watching CNN, so I spread out on the couch and keep compiling my interview questions.

"Did you ever want to do broadcast news?" he asks.

"Nope. To be on television, you have to be eye candy and good at public speaking. I'm neither."

He turns toward me. "You don't think you're pretty enough to be on camera?"

"I know I'm not."

"You're wrong."

With a deep sigh, I save my work and close my laptop. I watch him stare at the television until I can't take it anymore. His eyes find mine as I walk over to the couch and climb into his lap. Devin's hands grip my hips as I run my fingers through his hair.

"I hope our kid looks like you."

"I hope the baby has your eyes."

"Compromise?" I murmur, pressing myself closer to him. "Your brown eyes and my blonde hair."

"Deal. See, we can get along."

"So it would seem."

Devin slides his hands along my back, pulling me tighter against him. With a shuddering groan, he buries his face against my neck and whispers my name.

"We're supposed to be apologizing," I whisper.

His blazing brown eyes find mine.

"I'm sorry for being an overprotective jerk."

"I'm sorry for being an oversensitive bitch."

"Apology accepted."

"Apol—"

Devin crashes his lips to mine, and in that moment, I'm lost. In his hands. His mouth. His moans. In the way he whispers my name when we come up for air. And in the way he wraps his hands in my hair and pulls my face back to his before we can even catch our breath.

He breaks our kiss and presses his forehead against mine. His gaze is reverent, and I nearly whimper when I see the emotion radiating in his shining, brown eyes. Slowly, I stroke his face, and he presses his cheek against the palm of my hand.

"Callie . . ." His voice is rough and low as it trails off, but he doesn't have to finish the thought. I can hear it. I can *feel* it. The unspoken, desperate plea that burns my skin and ignites my blood.

"Please."

Devin doesn't ask for an explanation. He doesn't need one.

With a low groan that radiates from his chest and deep

into my heart, Devin lifts us up, and I wrap my legs around his waist as he carries me to the bedroom.

I don't remember him undressing me. I can't remember undressing him. Yet here we are—naked and breathless on my bed, waiting for the other to finish what we'd both started.

Why isn't he doing anything?

Sliding my hands along his shoulders, I can feel the tension in his arms as he hovers above me. I arch against him, causing him to moan, but he still doesn't move.

"Devin, what's wrong?"

With a shuddering groan, his mouth captures mine. *Thank God.* If it weren't for his frantic kisses, I'd wonder if he wanted me at all.

"I can't do this," he says softly. "I just can't. I'm sorry."

He collapses against the mattress and shields his face with his arm. Stunned and breathless, I stare up at the ceiling and try to figure out what happened between the living room and my bed.

What had I done wrong?

Insecurity floods me. Pulling the blanket around me, I turn onto my side, away from him, and try to make sense of it all.

Devin wanted me, physically. But maybe his mind has other ideas. Or maybe his heart. It'd been fine the night at the hotel—when he didn't have to worry about attachments or consequences—but now that we're growing closer and I'm pregnant with his child, he just can't bring himself to make love to me.

It's completely humiliating.

A tear trickles down my cheek, and I angrily wipe it away.

"Callie, please don't cry. I'm sorry."

"I'm not crying."

Too bad my sniffle totally gives me away. He wraps his arm around me and pulls me close to his chest.

"I want you so much. Please don't doubt that." My stupid body trembles when his warm breath caresses my neck. "Everything about you turns me on. Your voice. Your smell. Your laugh. You drive me crazy. You have ever since the night we met in that bar. You're all I want. All the time."

"Then why did you stop?"

I turn over in his arms. My heart thaws a little when I see the absolute fear on his face. *He's scared? Why is he scared?*

With a sigh, he strokes my hair before pinning a strand behind my ear. "What if I hurt you? What if I hurt the baby? I don't know how to do this, Callie. I've never been . . . *gentle*. Tenderness means you care. I've never cared."

I smile. "So what you're saying is you care about me?"

"You know I do, Callie. You and the baby."

"That's really sweet, but Devin . . . our baby is like the size of a grape right now. All protected and safe and swimming in amniotic fluid. You can't hurt it."

I can tell by the expression on his face that I'm not convincing him.

"Remember that night at the hotel?" he asks.

I smirk. "Vaguely."

"I was rough with you."

"You weren't *rough*. You were . . . passionate. Big difference. And on that second night, you were almost tender . . . until I told you not to be."

"You said *don't be sweet*. I always wondered why."

"Because I felt . . ."

Unable to find the words, I close my eyes and bury my face against his chest. He pulls me close and kisses the top of my hair. Then he whispers against my ear.

"I felt it, too."

With tears in my eyes, I look up to find him gazing down at me.

"I didn't think I'd ever see you again. That's why I told you to not be sweet with me."

"I didn't think I'd ever see you again, Songbird. I guess fate had other ideas."

I'd never believed in things like fate and destiny, but I can't deny the chaotic series of events that have brought us here.

"Do you believe in that? Fate, I mean."

"I didn't use to. I think I do now."

He kisses me then . . . a sweet, toe-curling kiss that sends shivers up my spine.

"Did you ask the doctor about sex?" he asks softly.

"No. I mean, it wasn't really a priority at the time."

"Well, thank God for that. I'd hate to have to kill some bastard for putting his hands on you."

I roll my eyes. "You know, these caveman tendencies of yours are going to take some getting used to."

"I know. I'll try to keep him under control."

"I'd appreciate that."

We grin at each other.

"So, no sex?"

"Wow, you really have a one-track mind, don't you?"

I pout. Devin laughs and kisses my lips.

"I'd really like to wait until we talk to the doctor."

We'll see about that.

With a firm nod, I wiggle out of his arms and climb out of bed.

"Where are you going?"

"Getting dressed. I wouldn't want to be too tempting for you."

"Baby, I hate to break it to you, but you're just as tempting in clothes as you are without them."

"Hmm."

Very deliberately, I slowly slip the blanket off my body, letting it fall onto the floor. I hear his quiet groan as I take my time searching for something to wear. I grab a blue tank top and a matching pair of boy shorts and slip them on. I wear them around the house all the time, but then again, I'm used to living alone.

Which reminds me . . .

I turn to find him gazing at my body. I grin.

"Devin? I think you should go home tonight."

This gets his attention. His eyes snap to mine.

"Why?"

"This is what I normally wear around the house, and I wouldn't want you to be too tempted."

He playfully growls and jumps out of bed, but I'm too fast. We both laugh as I sprint out of the bedroom.

Devin did go home that night. He actually went home every night for the rest of the week, much to my dismay.

Operation Seduce Baby Daddy can't commence if Daddy refuses to play along.

We had met every night for dinner, though, and each evening ended with a heavy make-out session that did nothing but leave us both frustrated.

"It's ironic," Lorie says one day over lunch. "You slept together twice in one weekend, and now the guy won't even touch you."

"Oh, he touches me. He's insanely affectionate."

Megan places her fork on her empty plate. "Well, I think it's sweet. Simon says that you and the baby are all Devin talks about."

Lorie nods. "Owen says the same. I do believe our Callie has tamed the manwhore that was once Devin McAllister."

I roll my eyes. "Great. Could we possibly talk about something else? Anything else? And *where* is my dessert?"

The girls laugh. So what if I inhaled my grilled chicken sandwich, fries, and half of Lorie's salmon? I still want my cherry cheesecake.

While we wait, Megan shows us photos from her honeymoon. We're passing her cell back and forth when I feel my own phone vibrate on the table. Glancing at the screen, I smile when I see the message is from Devin.

> *I miss you, Songbird.*

> **How's your meeting?**

> *Boring. Entertain me, please.*

> **You should focus on your client, Mr. McAllister.**

> *I'd rather focus on you, Miss Franklin.*

I giggle. Lorie clears her throat. I glance up to find my two best friends smiling like idiots in my direction.

"Shut up. Both of you."

Megan grins. "We're just not used to seeing you so . . ."

"Happy," Lorie finishes. "It's nice."

"Thanks. It must be all those mommy hormones surging through me."

The waiter finally shows up with my cheesecake. I check the time. *Good thing I asked for it to go.* Reaching into my bag, I pull out some cash and toss it on the table.

"Love you both, but I have to get back to work."

We hug and promise to call each other later in the week.

I've barely stepped outside the restaurant when my phone rings.

"Callie Franklin."

"You left me hanging."

I grin and start the short trip back to the office. "I was having lunch with the girls. Besides, Devin, your client isn't paying you to text with your . . . whatever I am."

"That's a good point. We should probably give you an official title or something."

"If you start calling me your baby mama, I will have to seriously reconsider our upcoming road trip."

After much begging, Devin finally convinced me we need to visit my dad. I don't really mind—I enjoy my hometown and spending time with my father—but I'd be lying if I didn't say I was nervous. I don't expect Dad's reaction to be anything like my mom's, but I'm still not sure how he'll react to the news.

"Do you call me your baby daddy?"

Yes. "Of course not."

He laughs. "Well, I'll think of something."

We make dinner plans before hanging up. It's scary how natural this seems, as if we're just some ordinary couple when we're anything but. We've done everything backwards so far, but I get the sense that Devin is serious when he says he's determined to make this work. We're still getting to know each other—which is weird when you consider our situation—but it's easy to see how passionate he is about the family and the law. We've talked some about our childhoods, and I can always detect a sadness coming from him that I can't quite understand. I think a lot about that day at his parent's house and those pictures on the mantle. No matter how hard I try, I can't get Tinkerbell's face out of my mind. I don't know if it's my reporter's instincts or just women's intuition, but there's something there. An old girlfriend? A member of the family? More pictures of the girl are scattered throughout their house, but no one's mentioned her, and I just can't bring myself to ask. He'll tell me when he's ready.

I spend the rest of my afternoon preparing for my interview with the real estate tycoon turned mayoral candidate. It's a feature interview for our special election edition, and I'm thrilled Frank's giving me the opportunity. I'm just finishing up when I hear my name being called from the stairs. I look up to find Devin's delivery boy, holding a big bouquet of white roses. Devin had stopped with the daily dose of flowers, so this is definitely a nice surprise. I wave at the guy, who spots me from across the room before making his way over to my desk.

I grin sheepishly. "I'm sorry about this."

"Happy to do it, Miss Franklin. Besides, Mr. McAllister tips really well. Have a nice day."

After thanking him, I reach for the card, smiling brightly when I see Devin's handwriting.

I'm thinking your official title should be girlfriend.
Love,
Your Baby Daddy

Chapter 18

DEVIN

"There's a dog." Shyann giggles.

We're on our backs, looking up at the clouds.

I squint against the sunlight. "That's not a dog."

"Is too. See the tail?"

Concentrating hard, I look for the tail, or anything that resembles an animal. All I see are clouds. But I pretend to see whatever she sees, because it makes her happy.

"Dev, what's beyond the clouds?"

"Space."

"And then what?"

"Heaven."

"We'll go there someday. We'll go together. Promise we will."

"Of course we will."

I have no reason to doubt it. Shy and I do everything together.

A gentle breeze blows through the trees. I look up and smile. Shy would have loved the sky today. She was all about enjoying the simple things, and cloud-watching was one of her favorites.

Kneeling down, I place the white rose on Shyann's grave and trace my fingers over her name.

Shyann Hope McAllister
1985-2000

"Hey, Shy." I sit down on the grass and once again gaze at the sky. Darker clouds are starting to roll in. "I know it's been a while. I could make up a bunch of excuses, but that's all they'd be. Excuses. And none of them matter. There's no excuse for not visiting you more. I'm sorry."

I pick at one of the flower's petals. "I've been buying a lot of white roses lately. I think that's why I chose white, because they were your favorite. You always said red roses were pretty but totally unimaginative and lazy. A white rose showed you really put some thought into it."

A soft rain begins to fall. I lift my face toward the heavens.

"I've met someone, Shy. Her name's Callie. We're going to have a baby. She's beautiful and kind and has the sweetest laugh . . . besides yours, of course. She doesn't put up with my crap, and she makes me want to be better. A better lawyer. Better son. Better brother. A better man. We've only known each other for a short time, but I haven't felt this kind of connection with anyone since you passed away. It's *different*, of course, but just as strong. And it terrifies me."

It's been fifteen years since I've cried, so I'm surprised when a tear streams down my cheek.

"It's a fact of life. We live and die. It's the how and why that catches us by surprise. I didn't think I'd live through losing you, but I did. And then I swore I'd never love anybody else. I'd never risk losing someone else that meant so much to me. But I love her, Shy. I'm so in love with her. And I love our baby. But can I do this? Can I love her and be a good father? And can I do it whole-heartedly, without living in constant fear of losing them?"

A small ray of sunshine filters through the clouds.

I smile.

"I'm taking that as a yes, baby sister."

I'd only been five minutes older, but I still considered myself her big brother. Her protector. And she was my conscience. Shyann loved finding the beauty in things that weren't obviously beautiful at first glance. Like clouds, boy bands . . . and a twin brother who didn't go to Heaven with her like he promised he would.

Like I always do, I place a kiss on my finger and trace it over her name. After a visit to the cemetery, I usually feel dead inside, but as I walk to my car, I know that today's different. I feel lighter. Happier.

I've just started the car when I get a text. Pulling the

phone out of my jacket, I check the caller ID and smile.

Your baby misses you.

Which baby?

Both of us.

The words settle themselves in my heart, giving me even more confidence that I can do this. I *will* do this.

I miss you, too. On my way home.

The next couple weeks are so busy that I can't find a good time to tell her about my sister. We're both trying to get caught up with work so that we can enjoy our upcoming trip to see her dad in Brandywine. Between my late night meetings and early mornings in court, and Callie with her upcoming mayoral feature, we've barely had a waking moment together. And, if we do happen to find some time to spend together, I'm too focused on trying to keep my hands to myself to really think about anything else, because the woman has made it her life's mission to drive me completely insane with her short skirts, tall heels, and skimpy pajamas.

Being the responsible one sucks.

I'm probably being overly cautious, but until we talk to Callie's doctor, I'm just too nervous to have sex with her. Taking it as a personal challenge, she actually called the doctor to get his approval, but he was at some conference in Orlando. His nurse, however, assured Callie that sex during pregnancy was perfectly fine as long as there was no discomfort. My beautiful baby mama took this as a gigantic green light, but she's also sexually frustrated, so I'm not quite sure how much she can be trusted.

I just really want to talk to her doctor. Is that so wrong?

When the weekend finally rolls around, I'm more than ready to get out of Nashville for a while. It's a three-hour drive to Brandywine. Stupidly, I thought the pretty drive through the country—not to mention the fact that I was getting ready to meet her father—would squelch any mention of sex.

But no.

"Sex during pregnancy can be wonderful," Callie says, reading from the baby bible. "You can continue being intimate with your partner for as long as you and your partner are comfortable."

I roll my eyes and continue to drive. She's only been reading to me for the past two hours. There's actually a lot of information in there—and some of it's educational—but by the time we reach the mountains, I've had all I can take with the innuendos and flirting. Once we're officially out of civilization, I pull over to the side of the road, slam the car into park, and unbuckle my seat belt.

"Get over here."

Callie grins and swiftly climbs into my lap, groaning

low in her throat when her lips find mine. I hold her close, pouring every ounce of frustration and craving into the kiss. I won't be having sex with her today, but I never want her to mistake my willpower for lack of desire, because that's not it at all.

I kiss her until we're breathless. When she finally pulls away, her pretty blue eyes look a little dazed.

"Now behave yourself."

She smirks and crawls back into her seat. I'm unable to keep the smug smile off my face as we drive on. It's weird, but I'm excited about this weekend. A little anxious, but excited. This is the first father I've officially met, and the man owns guns . . . and knows how to shoot them. He seemed okay with the fact that she wanted to bring someone home. I just hope he's still cool with it when he finds out I impregnated his daughter.

Callie laughs. "You know, we've made really good time. We're almost there and *now* you're driving the speed limit. You aren't nervous are you, Mr. McAllister?"

"Nope. I'm just taking my time and enjoying the scenery now that you've shut up about sex."

"Poor baby." She laughs and points toward a brick house. "That's it. On the left."

Her laughter fades as we pull into the driveway, and I hear her take a deep breath. Reaching across the console, I take her hand in mine and give it a reassuring squeeze.

"Don't be nervous, Songbird."

"Can't help it. I'm thirty years old and you're the first guy I've brought home."

"And it's the first time I've been brought home, so we're both in unfamiliar territory. But we survived your mother. We can handle this."

"Dad's nothing like her. Promise."

I smile and lean over, kissing her softly.

"No worries. Okay?"

Callie nods and looks toward the house. It's small, with a porch swing and an American flag waving proudly in the breeze. In the driveway, there's an old Ford pickup and a red four-door sedan.

"I don't recognize that car. Wonder who it is?"

"Only one way to find out."

She nods slowly. "You know, Devin, it doesn't matter what he thinks. It's our life."

I get the feeling this little pep talk is more for her than for me, but I understand. No matter what she says, I know his approval is important to her, which means it's important to me.

"It's going to be fine, Callie."

I squeeze her hand once more before we step out of the car. After grabbing our overnight bags, I follow her to the front door.

She stops. "Umm . . . maybe you'd better wait here. Let me butter him up first."

"Callie, I don't think—"

"Please? Just give me a sec. Let me gauge his mood."

I chuckle and lower our bags onto the porch.

"Fine, Songbird. Go gauge his mood."

Callie kisses my cheek and doesn't bother knocking

before making her way inside. Sighing tiredly, I sit in the porch swing and gaze out at her neighborhood. It seems quiet. Peaceful. Across the road, a neighbor is watering his flowers. He waves in my direction, and I wave in return. It makes me smile.

Suddenly, the screen door swings open, and a pale-faced Callie rushes out onto the porch. Wide-eyed, she lets the door slam before sitting down next to me.

"What's wrong?"

She just shakes her head and stares straight ahead. Seconds later, a petite woman with short red hair steps out onto the porch. Her fingers work the top buttons of her blouse.

"Callie, I'm so sorry."

What the hell?

Before I can ask what's going on, a man appears in the screen door. He has Callie's blonde hair and piercing blue eyes. He looks apologetic . . . and a little embarrassed.

Were they . . .

"I should go," the woman says, blushing. "It's . . . so nice to you see again, Callie."

Callie clears her throat. "You too, Pam. I mean . . . I just saw much more of you than I ever thought I'd see, but yeah, it's good to see you, too."

I hide my grin. *They were.*

Callie's dad coughs nervously and nods in my direction. "You'll . . . take care of her? I'm gonna walk Pam to her car."

"Sure thing, Mr. Franklin."

Once they're out of earshot, I explode with laughter.

Callie punches my arm. "Stop that! I just walked in on my father and Pam Ford, my high school math teacher, having sex on his couch. That woman was straddling my father, much like I was just straddling you in the car, except *she* was naked and they were very much having sex!"

I can't stop laughing. "Way to go, Mr. Franklin."

Callie's head swivels in my direction. It's kinda scary.

"Keep laughing, Devin McAllister. And don't worry. I won't be trying to jump your bones for the duration of this trip. Maybe *ever*."

I grin.

Once Pam's gone, Mr. Franklin turns toward the porch, takes one long look at his only daughter, and bursts out laughing.

"You're both jerks!" Callie groans and heads inside the house.

I try to contain my laughter as Mr. Franklin makes his way up the steps. He grins and offers me his hand.

"Greg Franklin. How pissed is she?"

"Devin McAllister. I think she's traumatized, sir."

"Yeah, well, she'll get over it." He grins and opens the door. "It's good to meet you, Devin. Come on in. I bet you could use a beer."

"You have no idea."

Mr. Franklin gives me a fatherly slap on the back and leads me inside.

Chapter 19

Callie

It's true what they say. Men really do stick together.

Dad and Devin sit at the kitchen table, cracking jokes and laughing as if they've known each other for years. They drink their beer and make plans for all of us to go fishing this afternoon. I didn't even realize Devin liked to fish, but he's talking about the difference between a treble hook and a weedless hook, and it's totally impressing my dad. They've already called the local sporting goods store to see if they can buy Devin a one-day fishing permit. Seems silly to buy a license for one afternoon of male bonding and ass kissing, but what do I know?

"Callie never liked to fish much," Dad says, "but she loved baiting the hook."

"Is that right?" Devin smiles at me.

I shrug and continue licking my banana freezer pop—

Dad's peace offering and his way of apologizing for his own little taste of afternoon delight.

I'm an adult. Of course I don't expect my father to be celibate, but did I really have to see *Pam Ford* on top of my father? The woman who gave me *Ds* in Algebra out of the kindness of her heart? The teacher who encouraged me to embrace my creative side because there was no way I'd ever get a job as an engineer or accountant or anything that remotely involved numbers?

It's just weird.

After lunch, the three of us climb into Dad's pickup and head to the sporting goods store. I stay behind in the truck and play on my phone, thinking this whole license deal will only take a few minutes. Half an hour later, the two most important men in my life walk out with two new rods, dozens of multi-colored fishing lures, and a tackle box full of other crap I can't identify.

"What? No boat?"

Devin smirks. "I tried. He wouldn't let me."

"No sense paying full-price when they'll just go on sale in the fall," Dad says as he puts the gear in the bed. "We'll look then."

I roll my eyes. *Boys.*

Dad drives us to his favorite fishing spot on the Holston River. I spent most of my summers here when I was a kid. My dad did his best, but he didn't really know what to do with a girl all day, every day, and I liked to bait the hook, so it was a win-win for both of us. Sometimes we'd go out in his fishing boat, but we both preferred to stay on the shore.

Once the bait hit the water, I always lost interest. Dad didn't mind if I explored as long as I stayed within view. I collected rocks and shells, and when I got older, I started bringing my camera along. It's a peaceful place and one of the prettiest spots in our hometown.

The three of us walk the short path to Dad's favorite spot.

"I think I'll look around a little before we get started," Devin says.

Dad nods. "Stay on the trail, son."

Son. The word sends shivers up my spine and tells me what I already suspected. He's accepted Devin . . . already.

I hope he's still this accepting when he finds out we're having a baby.

"Want me to go with you?"

Devin shakes his head. "Nah. Spend some time with your dad."

He leans down and kisses my forehead before wandering off.

"Well, that was subtle," Dad says with a grin.

"I guess he thinks we needed some bonding time of our own."

"That's nice of him. You baiting?"

I nod and reach for his rod. Sure, they bought a bagful of pretty lures, but Dad says there's nothing like live bait. I'm just enough of a tomboy to agree with him.

He casts his line into the water. "Devin seems like a good man."

"He is."

"Kind of surprised how fast you're moving, though."

"Right back 'atcha, Dad. Since when are you and Ms. Ford such good friends?"

His ears redden. "We've actually been . . . friendly for a while now."

"Obviously."

"I really am sorry about that, Cal. Time just got away from us and—"

"It's fine. Not my business. If she makes you happy, then I'm all for it. I'd just rather not *see* it."

Dad chuckles. "Understood. And she does make me happy."

"Good. You deserve it."

"So do you."

We grow quiet as we watch his line bobble in the water. I know it's the perfect opportunity to tell him about the baby. *Should I wait for Devin?*

"Spit it out, Callie."

I sigh. He knows me so well. Still, I try to stall.

"Spit what out?"

"Don't misunderstand. I'm always happy to see you, but a spur-of-the-moment visit makes me think there's a little more to this weekend than just introducing me to your boyfriend. What's up?"

I look downstream. *Where is he?*

"There is something we'd like to talk to you about."

He nods. "I don't see a ring on your finger, so I'm guessing you haven't eloped."

"Nope. No elopement."

"Should I be worried?"

Before I can answer, Devin reappears and sits down next to me. Happy to have a distraction, I grab his rod and bait his hook. He casts his line and then leans over to kiss my cheek. Out of the corner of my eye, I see my dad watching us, and I see him smile.

"Callie, why don't you take a walk? I'd like to talk to my new fishing buddy here. Guy stuff. You wouldn't be interested."

Looking between the two of them, I wonder if this is such a good idea, but I do want them to have the chance to get to know each other before we drop our baby bomb. Maybe some more male bonding between the two of them will make the news a little easier to hear.

"I saw a snake on the trail, so stay close, okay?" Devin says.

Normally, his request would make me cranky, but snakes are no joke.

"I'll just walk upstream a bit. Look for some shells." I kiss both guys on the cheek. "Don't kill each other."

They both grin as I walk away.

Chapter 20

DEVIN

As an attorney, I'm a cynic by nature. I prepare for the worst and hope for the best, which is pretty much how I approached this weekend with her dad. I've only been fishing a few times, but Mr. Franklin seems impressed with what little I know, and I'm happy to learn. Honestly, I'd do just about anything to get this man's approval, and if that means an afternoon of fishing in the blistering sun, then that's what I'll do.

There's little to do while fishing except talk and watch your line, but I'm having trouble doing both because Callie's standing upstream, with the legs of her jeans rolled up to her knees. She's walking through the water, her blonde hair glistening in the sunlight, looking content and peaceful and beautiful. I wish I'd brought my phone just so I could take a picture.

"You could have a hundred-pound bass on your line right now and you wouldn't even notice."

I look over to find Mr. Franklin smiling at me. I laugh.

"You're right, I wouldn't."

He watches his daughter wading before sighing quietly and turning his attention back to his rod.

"You love her."

Just like that. No fanfare. No threat of bodily harm. No rifle pointed at my face.

"Yes, I do, Mr. Franklin."

"Greg."

I nod.

"Does she know you love her?"

"I . . . haven't actually said the words, no."

He stares out at the water. "I see. So, it's okay to get her pregnant, but it's not okay to tell her you're in love with her."

Holy shit.

"I got a very interesting phone call from her mom a few days ago. The woman never calls me, so I knew it was serious."

Fantastic.

"We wanted to tell you together. That's why we're here."

"I figured as much."

"I don't mean to be disrespectful, but that ex-wife of yours is a piece of work."

"Why do you think she's my ex-wife?"

We grow quiet, and I know he's waiting for me to continue, but what am I supposed to say? I mean, this afternoon proves the man is cool with premarital sex, but I wonder if his outlook on the subject might be different when his daughter's involved.

"Callie's mom was . . . difficult," Greg says quietly. "We got pregnant and married too young, but back then, that's what you did. If you got a girl in trouble, you married her. No questions asked. From the moment we got married, Kim was pissed and bitter about having to give up college and a career. I didn't ask her to give them up, but the truth was we couldn't afford for her to go to school. I had two jobs—flipping burgers during the day and working as a paramedic at night—and it was just barely enough for us to get by. She was so tough on Callie . . . putting all these bullshit expectations on her and expecting her to be this little adult when she was just a kid. I understood why. Kim wanted more for Callie. That's what all parents want. So, yeah, I understood the logic. I just hated the way she went about it."

"I get it, too, but she actually demanded we abort the baby. I'm not sure I'll ever be able to forgive her for that."

"Which just proves to me how much you love my daughter. Don't worry about Kim. She rarely shows her face, and when she does, it's like a tornado. Fast and furious."

"And destructive."

Greg nods. "Can you handle that?"

"I can handle it."

Looking across the water, I see that Callie's walked deeper into the river.

"She's okay. The water's shallow there."

I breathe a sigh of relief.

"You're very protective. I bet she loves that."

"Oh, she hates it."

We laugh, and after a few minutes of silence, Greg suggests we check our lines. Neither of us is surprised to find our bait gone. It's not like we're really paying attention.

"Wanna try a lure this time? We only bought about a hundred of them."

"Sure." I chuckle.

We attach the lures and cast our lines back into the water.

"Devin, I could give you the whole *what are your intentions toward my daughter* speech. I heard it from Kim's father, and I remember every word of it. But Callie is a grown woman. You seem to really care about her, which makes me think the two of you will be just fine. So, I won't ask your intentions, but I will say this. If you hurt my daughter, her crazy-ass mother will be the least of your worries. You take care of her, and take care of my grandchild, and you and I will have no problems."

"Yes, sir."

Callie starts walking back to us. She gives me a questioning look, but I just shake my head and adjust my fishing rod.

She pulls her knees up to her chest. "Everything okay?"

"We are. Wish I could say the same about the fish," Greg says, glancing down the shore. "I think I'll move downstream for a bit."

Greg reels in his line and makes his way down the shore.

"What was that all about?"

"*That* was about your dad already knowing you're pregnant."

Her blue eyes widen. "What? How?"

"Your mom told him."

"He knew all along?" She sighs deeply and stares out at the sparkling water. "Well, he brought you to his favorite fishing spot, and he didn't drown you, so I guess he approves?"

"It would seem so."

"And he's really cool with it?"

I reel in my line. Nothing's biting, anyway.

"He said as long as I take care of you and the baby, he'll have no problem with me."

Callie smiles.

The sky begins to darken, and Greg shouts that a storm's coming. The three of us quickly pack up our gear. Callie takes my hand as we head back to the truck.

The rest of the night is just as nice as the afternoon. After dinner, the three of us sit out on the back porch and watch the storm while Greg shares stories about Callie's escapades as a kid. Much to her embarrassment, he even pulls out some old family photo albums. Greg adores his daughter, and it's obvious the feeling is mutual.

Around midnight, Greg says goodnight. Sleeping arrangements aren't discussed, but with only two bedrooms in the house, I assume I'm on the couch, and I'm fine with that. This is her father's house—and we aren't married—so I figure respect should be paid. Callie disagrees but doesn't put up much of a fight. We both realize he's been cool about all this. The last thing we want to do is rock the boat.

So the couch it is.

With the rain pounding on the metal roof and the uncomfortable couch, I don't do a whole lot of sleeping. I've nearly dozed off when I hear someone come down the stairs. I look up to find Greg standing at the bottom, dressed in bright yellow rain gear.

"Didn't mean to wake you," he murmurs. "I just got a call on my cell. Big maple tree fell down on a neighbor's house."

"Anyone hurt?"

"Hope not. I'm gonna go see if they can use some help."

"That's nice of you. I thought you were retired, though."

"I am, but this is a neighbor. You take care of your neighbors."

I nod. Just another reason why I love the mountains.

"I can go with you," I offer.

"Nah. Just stay here and take care of my girl."

I nod and lean back against the pillow. "Will do. Be careful out there."

"I will." He starts to walk away but then turns back around. "You know, it's ridiculous that you're down here on my lumpy sofa. I mean, she's already pregnant. What's the worst that could happen?"

I chuckle. "Goodnight, Greg."

"Night." As he walks toward the kitchen, I hear him say, "Hundred bucks says you won't be on the couch when I get home."

I wait until his truck starts before sitting up and reaching for my wallet that's on the end table. When I confirm that I do, indeed, have a hundred dollars in cash, I waste no time in sprinting up the stairs.

"You're a brave, brave man," Callie whispers in the darkness.

With a grin, I crawl beneath the blanket and wrap my arm around her, pulling her close to my chest.

"Just missed you. Besides, that couch is shit for sleeping."

"Dad and Pam seemed to enjoy it."

"Yeah, because they weren't *sleeping*."

"Don't remind me." Callie laces her fingers with mine. "Did I hear the truck start up?"

"Yeah. A tree fell through a neighbor's house. Your dad went to help."

"Once a paramedic, always a paramedic. I used to hate when he had to work in weather like this. It's so dangerous."

I kiss the skin along her shoulder, causing her to wiggle against me.

"Behave," I whisper against her ear.

With a deep sigh, she turns around in my arms. The lightning in the window briefly illuminates her face, making it impossible for me not to kiss her, letting my lips linger along the corner of her mouth.

"And you said you couldn't be tender."

"I'm learning."

"I think you've been tender all along. You just hide it well."

"I've been hiding for the past fifteen years, Callie. And I was content with hiding until I met you."

She gently strokes my face. "You don't want to hide anymore?"

"Not from you."

It's not the ideal setting for this conversation, I know. A torrential storm is battering the house and it's the middle of the night. But she's smiling at me, her eyes hopeful and alive, and I find myself eager to finally tell her every blissful and heartbreaking detail of my life.

"I want to tell you about Shyann."

With the lightning flashing through the window, I can see the confusion that suddenly appears on her face. I smile softly and play with a strand of her hair.

"Shyann was my twin sister."

Her eyes flash with surprise. "*Was?*"

"She died when we were fifteen."

"Oh, I'm so sorry, Devin." She squeezes my hand. "Was she the girl in the picture? Tinkerbell?"

I nod. "Halloween. We were ten years old. I got the shit kicked out of me at school the next day for wearing that costume, but I didn't care. It was worth it to see the smile on her face."

"You sound like an amazing brother." Callie lays her head on my chest, her fingers ghosting along the front of my

T-shirt while my hand drifts along her spine. "Will you tell me about her?"

"She loved the Backstreet Boys and Britney Spears. She was a natural brunette but liked to dye her hair depending on her mood. Purple. Pink. Blue. Nothing was off limits. She loved to take pictures. She had this shitty, cheap-ass camera, but she loved it so much and wouldn't even discuss replacing it. Shy would take pictures of the most ordinary, mundane objects . . . clouds, food, insects. Everything interested her. Everything was beautiful in her eyes."

"Did you guys have that twin connection? You know, reading each other's minds and finishing the other's sentences?"

"Not really, but we were very in tune to each other's moods. Her happiness depended on mine, and vice versa. She was my best friend."

We grow silent as the rain crashes against the window. Suddenly, a flash of lightning and a deafening crash of thunder shakes the house. We'll probably lose power soon.

"What happened to Shyann?"

I pull the blanket tighter around us.

"Shy loved to dance. She took ballet lessons for a while. When she was thirteen, she started complaining of pain in her joints. My parents assumed she was just overdoing it in class, but it wasn't long before they started to notice other symptoms. She began to bruise really easily. Kept getting colds that never really went away. Started losing weight because she had zero appetite."

She closes her eyes. "Cancer."

"Leukemia, yeah. She was diagnosed a week before Christmas. It felt like I'd been punched in the stomach. She'd always been so lively and happy, and suddenly, she was pale and fragile. Shyann was a tough chick . . . ready to hit it head-on. And she tried. Countless tests and doctors and treatments, and none of it mattered. Nothing made a difference. I felt guilty, like it was my fault. I mean, I was her brother. I'd always protected her."

My voice starts to break, but it feels good to talk about it. To actually say it out loud when I've kept it bottled up for so long.

"She died two years after her diagnosis. After that, our entire family fell apart for a while. Owen started picking fights at school. Dad stopped working. Mom cried day and night."

Callie holds me close. "And what about you?"

"I became the asshole you met that night in the hotel bar. Arrogant. Cold. Unable and unwilling to have any kind of normal relationship because I was too afraid of loving someone and losing them. I think Shy knew how low I'd spiral, so she made me promise to graduate from college. It forced me to focus on something besides my grief. Otherwise . . . I really don't know what would have become of me, because I simply did not care about anything."

Callie looks up at me, her eyes filled with tears. "But your family's so strong now. So are you."

"It took a long time, but yeah, we're better now. They say time heals. I don't know if that's true. Maybe you just get used to the pain. I'm still a mess, in so many ways. That's why I *dated*—if you can call it dating—women like me. Professional women with their own money and their own lives who were perfectly content with no strings attached."

She smiles softly. "You sure got more than you bargained for with me, didn't you?"

"In the very best of ways, Songbird." I kiss the top of her head and slide my fingers through her hair. "I'm still afraid, Callie. I never wanted to be close to anyone, but I don't have a choice now."

"Devin, I don't want you to be with me out of . . . obligation."

"That's not what I meant. I don't have a choice because I'm so crazy about you, and I've felt that way even before I knew you were pregnant. I couldn't get you out of my head, no matter how hard I tried. I couldn't even look at another woman without thinking about you. So please, never think I'm here just because of the baby. I want to be with you."

"I want to be with you, too."

I brush her lips gently with my own, letting my hand drift down to the small of her back. Before I can stop myself, I'm pulling her on top of me, groaning when the heat of her body collides with mine. In the back of my mind, I think about the baby and my fears, but the house is empty, and she's so warm, and she's grinding against me.

There's only so much temptation a man can take.

Suddenly, a noise in the hallway makes us both jump.

"What was that?" Callie whispers.

"It's your father." Greg laughs from behind the door. "Someone owes me a hundred bucks. I'll be expecting my money, along with bacon and eggs, first thing in the morning. Goodnight, you two."

We wait until we hear the slam of his bedroom door before throwing the blanket over our heads and laughing hysterically.

Chapter 21

Callie

It's still raining when I wake up the next morning, but the storm has passed. Devin's still asleep, and I hate to wake him, so I gently kiss him before wiggling out of his arms. He mumbles my name, which makes me smile because I am *such* a girl, and then I head to the shower. Dad's probably still asleep, but I want to get breakfast started. After all, penance must be paid for our sleeping arrangements. Interestingly enough, the make out session in my childhood bedroom wasn't the highlight of my evening.

Last night, Devin bared his soul to me.

His sister's story certainly explains his family's devotion to cancer research and the Children's Hospital. And now, I know that Devin's protective streak isn't about controlling me. He's truly afraid of losing me, and now I understand why.

I get dressed and make my way downstairs. Dad's usually

an early riser, but he'd had a late night. I start the coffee and grab what I need from the fridge. While I cook, I can't help but wonder about my baby. I can't even imagine having one newborn, but two? Devin's a twin. Could I have twins, too? And what about leukemia? Is that genetic?

I make a mental note to google my questions later.

I'm so lost in thought that I don't hear Devin sneak up behind me. I jump when he rests his chin on my shoulder.

"Does your dad like extra, extra crispy bacon? Because it's black."

I quickly look down at the pan. "Crap!"

With a groan, I toss the charred strips down the garbage disposal. Thankfully, the eggs look much better. Devin laughs and offers to set the table while I start a new batch of bacon.

"Something smells . . . scorched," Dad says as he makes his way into the kitchen.

"You know what? Both of you can kiss my—"

Devin silences me with a kiss.

"Good morning. Isn't it a beautiful day?"

I shoot him a glare and turn my attention back to the sizzling pan.

"I don't know about beautiful, but it's certainly calmer than it was last night," Dad says, pouring himself a cup of coffee.

"How's the neighbor's house?" Devin asks as he joins him at the table.

"They'll need a new roof, but luckily no one was hurt."

I bring the rest of the food over to the table. That's when I notice the crisp one hundred dollar bill next to Dad's plate.

I still don't know what that's about.

After breakfast, Dad heads to the living room to watch some football game. Devin offers to help me clean the kitchen, but honestly, I'd rather he spend time with my father. It's scary how comfortable they are around each other. It makes me wonder if Dad feels like he missed out on anything by not having a son. Now that I'm older, it's easy to see why my parents' marriage didn't survive because they are completely different people. Sometimes opposites attract, and while the attraction was probably there in the beginning, that's not enough to sustain a relationship, especially when they were forced into their marriage vows. It makes me sad . . . for both of them, and it makes me wonder if Devin and I stand any chance at all. We're not talking marriage, but we've made the decision to raise this baby together. What if things don't work out between us? Will my child grow up like I did—splitting time between two homes until he or she finally picks her favorite parent?

I don't want that for my kid.

"You're very quiet today, Songbird."

I drop the frying pan in the water. "You have got to stop sneaking up on me like that."

"Sorry." He wraps his arms around my waist and presses a kiss to my neck. "Want some help?"

"I'm nearly finished. I thought you were watching the game? And what's with the hundred bucks?"

He laughs. "I'll tell you later. I think your dad would like to spend some time with you, without the boyfriend around. I'm going to invent an excuse to drive into town."

I grin. "The boyfriend, huh?"

"Is that okay?"

I dry my hands before turning around in his arms.

"It's great."

"Really?"

I nod.

Suddenly, the most beautiful smile stretches across his face. He looks so happy and boyish, and all I want to do is kiss him until I can't breathe. Unfortunately, my father chooses that moment to refill his coffee cup, effectively derailing my plans.

"So, you're making me a grandpa."

I curl my feet under me and get comfy on the couch. "I am. How do you feel about that?"

Dad grins. "I think I'm way too young to be a grandfather, but I guess I'm not. The more important question is how do *you* feel about it?"

"A little freaked out. A little excited."

He nods. "That's normal. I hear your mother was less than supportive."

"Would you expect anything less?"

Dad reaches for the remote and mutes the television. "Cal, when you were a kid, I always tried to say nice things about your mom . . . because she's your mom. But you're an adult now, and I think it's important that you understand some things about our marriage."

"Such as?"

"Kim loved you. *Loves* you. It's me she resents. Always has. She blames me for getting her pregnant. For marrying her. For turning her into a housewife. I didn't ask her to give up the idea of college and a career, but the truth is we couldn't afford for her to go, and we couldn't afford daycare. I had to two jobs and we were still barely making it. She wanted more for you. So did I."

"But my situation is so different."

"It is, absolutely. But to your mom, you're still her little girl. I'm not saying it's right. I'm just saying I'm not at all surprised by her reaction. And I'm not defending it. I just . . . I don't know. I guess I hate to see you completely cut your mother out of your life. She'll come around. Once the baby gets here, I bet her tune changes."

"I don't know if I even want her anywhere near my baby."

"I understand that, too."

We spend the rest of the afternoon in the living room watching movies on cable. It's a true testament to his love for me that he's willing to sit through *The Notebook*. He doesn't really know what to do when I bawl like a baby as the credits roll.

I must cry myself to sleep, because my phone's ringtone jerks me awake. Groggy and blurry-eyed, I find Dad fast asleep in his recliner. I reach for my cell on the end table and try to focus on the screen. It's a message from Devin.

Do you know how happy you make me?

And just like that, I'm bawling again.

I could blame my crying jag on hormones, or the sappy movie, or the great weekend with my dad. I could even blame it on the fact that, last night, Devin shared a side of himself with me he'd never shared with anyone else. But I know I'm really crying because I'm happy. Genuinely, totally happy for the first time in my life.

And the reason for that happiness just pulled into the driveway.

I race through the kitchen and fling the door open just as Devin walks up the steps. His eyes widen when he sees me.

"Callie?"

Without a word, I leap into his arms and bury my face against his neck. He wraps his arms around me and carries me inside. Devin sits down at the kitchen table and gathers me into his lap, holding me close.

"Callie, what is it?"

I wipe away my tears and gaze into his worried, handsome face. There's so much I want to say to him, but I'm not brave enough. Not yet. Instead, I smile and gently stroke his cheek.

"You make me happy, too."

Chapter 22

Callie

"Back to reality," I mutter, gazing wearily at the line of traffic. "You know, Oliver, sometimes I hate living in the city."

My photographer and I are now fifteen minutes late for my interview with real estate mogul and mayoral candidate Dominic Barkley.

Oliver grins. "You say that every time you come back from your father's house. By the way, does Daddy approve?"

"Daddy does indeed. To be honest, I think Devin's the son my father never had."

He laughs. "Awesome. It's always nice to have the support of the parentals. I hope to experience that myself someday."

I smile sadly. Leo and Oliver have had an uphill battle with both sets of parents since they moved in together. Apparently, the fact they're now sharing an apartment made it officially official that their sons were gay. The guys try to make light of it, but I know it bothers them . . . just like it would've bothered me if Dad hadn't accepted Devin or if his parents hadn't welcomed me with open arms.

"They'll come around someday, Ollie."

He doesn't look convinced, but he smiles anyway.

When we finally reach the campaign headquarters of Dominic Barkley, I try not to roll my eyes at the god-awful red, white, and blue streamers that welcome us as we step inside. We're greeted by his campaign manager—a fiery redhead named Jocelyn. According to the tabloids, Mr. Barkley recently left his wife of twenty years for a curvy, voluptuous woman, and Jocelyn definitely fits the bill. My suspicions are confirmed when she leads us to his office. Oliver and I hang back while Mr. Barkley finishes his phone call. Jocelyn walks over to his desk and whispers something in his ear. She smiles and bats her eyelashes while he continues his call and slides his hand along her ass.

So disgusting.

"The man is running for elected office," Oliver murmurs. "Don't they know they're supposed to do that stuff behind closed doors and *not* in front of the press?"

"I guess not. What are you waiting for? Take a picture."

With a grin, Oliver lifts his camera. Who knows? Maybe someday Jocelyn will get tired of being manhandled by her boss. If she files a sexual harassment suit, we'll have the evidence . . . and the scoop.

"Sorry to keep you waiting," Mr. Barkley says, standing up from his desk and walking over to us. He flashes his phony, pearly-white grin and shakes our hands.

"Dominic, this is Callie Franklin from the *Journal*," Jocelyn says.

"And this is my photographer, Oliver Grant. Thank you for making time for us, Mr. Barkley. We apologize for running late. Traffic was horrible."

"No apology necessary. And please, call me Dominic."

His gaze rakes over me, and my skin instantly crawls. Jocelyn clears her throat and offers me a chair. I place my phone on the edge of the desk.

"I prefer to record, if that's all right?"

"Of course."

Jocelyn offers to give Oliver a tour of the office, but he must detect my unease because he politely declines and sits down next to me.

The interview takes about thirty minutes. Dominic's answers, while articulate, are well-rehearsed and purposely vague. Politicians like to do that. On the off-chance they're elected, they don't want their responses, or their campaign promises, to come back and bite them in the ass.

"A few photos?" Jocelyn asks at the end of the interview.

"That would be great. Thanks."

She suggests using the fireplace as a backdrop. I step back and let Oliver do his thing while making a few additional notes in my phone. When I look up again, I find Dominic's eyes fixed on me.

Creep.

Once pictures are over, I'm more than ready to get back to the office.

"Would you like a quick tour of the headquarters?" Dominic asks as we head to the door.

"We've taken enough of your time, Mr. Barkley. Maybe some other time."

"Yes, Dominic. You have a meeting downtown," Jocelyn says, her tone clipped and cold. Clearly, the woman's unhappy with the amount of attention her boss is showing me. "When should we expect to see the feature in the paper, Miss Franklin?"

"Next Friday. Mr. Barkley will be included with the rest of the candidates in our special election edition."

"I certainly look forward to reading it," Dominic says, his gaze roaming down my legs.

Note to self: No more skirts.

I thank them for their time before grabbing Oliver by the arm and ushering him toward the exit. I hear Jocelyn's shrill voice screaming at her boss before the door slams.

"Creepy," Oliver mumbles. "Did you see the way he was looking at you?"

I nod and dig for my keys. "Thank God I'll never have to see him again."

"Don't count on it. He's leading in the polls."

"Well, I'm not voting for him. The man's disgusting."

"Agreed, but I must say you do look hot in the skirt. You're all glowy, too. That sweet country air must do a body good."

I grin and climb into the car. Oliver slams the passenger-side door and reaches for his seat belt.

"By the way, don't tell Devin," he says.

"Don't tell Devin what?"

"About the creepy bastard and how he couldn't keep his eyes off you."

I frown. "I hadn't even thought about telling him. *Should* I tell him?"

"Did you hear what I just said? No, you shouldn't. If someone looked at Leo the way that man just looked at you . . ."

"You'd be jealous? Seriously?"

"I'd be *pissed*."

We're quiet on our way back to the office. In my mad dash to work, I'd skipped breakfast, so when my stomach growls, Oliver insists we stop at the deli for lunch. He places his order while I check out the condiments.

What will it be, Baby? Mayo or mustard?

I smile at the girl behind the counter. "Turkey and cheese with . . . extra mayo. And banana peppers!"

I've never eaten a banana pepper in my life, but right now, my body's *craving* it.

Oliver wrinkles his nose. "Gag."

"It's what the baby wants."

I'm starving by the time we get back to the office. I don't even turn on my computer before digging into my sandwich. I've nearly finished stuffing my face when Leo peeks over my cubicle.

"Oh, Callie . . . ugh, what is that smell?"

"Shut up. It's delicious."

"You're insane. That disgusting smell will kill the pretty flowers!"

"What flowers?"

Leo grins and nods toward the stairs. Standing there is a delivery boy holding a vase full of tulips.

"Ooh, your favorite! Are those from Oliver?"

He rolls his eyes. "I wish. But no, stinky breath. They're for you."

For me? Tulips?

Leo waves the teenage delivery boy to my desk. He's not Devin's usual guy, and these definitely aren't Devin's usual embarrassing display of white roses.

"Callie Franklin?"

"That's me. Thanks."

He places the vase on my desk and tells me to have a nice day. Leo reaches for the card.

"Are you cheating on me and Devin with some guy named . . . Dominic?"

I frantically snatch the card out of his hand.

> Looking forward to reading your interview.
> Perhaps next time we can talk about you.
> What about dinner on Friday? ~Dominic

Shit. My stomach lurches.

Something tells me I'm going to regret those banana peppers.

"You're quiet tonight."

Devin and I are in the living room. He's on the floor with his back pressed against the sofa, checking his email. I'm stretched out on the couch, letting my fingers wander aimlessly through his hair while I try to figure out what to do.

"Sorry. It was just a long day."

I'm not considering the invitation. Not at all. What I'm trying to decide is which, if any, of today's crazy events I'm going to share with Devin. When Oliver saw the tulips and the card, he changed his tune quickly, insisting I tell Devin about the creepy asshole's behavior during the interview.

Is it harmless flirting? Is it borderline stalkerish?

Will Devin laugh it off? Will he be jealous? Pissed?

I can't be expected to make a sound decision when there are so many questions and just as many potential outcomes.

"Oh, how was your interview? Is Dominic Barkley still an asshole?"

"Yes," I mutter.

Devin's fingers freeze on his keyboard. "What happened?"

"What do you mean?"

"What happened, Callie?"

Pissed. He's gonna be pissed.

"He's just really arrogant. And creepy."

He eyes me carefully. "Creepy how?"

"How do you know him?"

"I've met him at a few charity functions. He has a problem keeping his hands to himself."

"Some used to say the same thing about you."

"Completely different. I was at least nice to the women I slept with. Dominic chews them up and spits them out. Rumor has it he left his wife for his campaign manager."

"Pretty sure that's not a rumor." Taking a deep breath, I decide to test the waters. "Devin, would you say you're the jealous type?"

He sets his laptop aside and turns toward me.

"I'm not sure. I've never really been in a relationship where I actually cared enough to be jealous."

"Well, let's say, hypothetically, that someone hit on me."

His eyes darken. "Did Dominic Barkley hit on you?"

"Hypothetically . . ."

"Callie—"

"So you *are* the jealous type."

Devin sighs heavily. "I honestly don't know. I mean, the thought of another man putting his hands on you makes me want to punch a wall."

Fantastic.

"But I know that's completely hypocritical because you're a beautiful woman. Men are going to notice. As long as you're not uncomfortable with the attention—and as long as the guy doesn't disrespect you or cross the line—then I suppose I can live with it."

I nod. "That sounds . . . fair."

Sending me flowers was completely weird, but was it disrespectful? I don't think so. Maybe if I just pretend it didn't happen, the entire thing will blow over. Dominic will take my silence as refusal and quietly go away. Besides, he has far more important things to think about right now. Like his campaign.

Devin pulls me down onto the floor and kisses me softly. "I don't want anyone else looking at you because I'm a selfish man. But I'm too pretty to go to jail, so it's probably not a good idea for me to kill every asshole on the planet who looks at you."

I grin. "Good point. Besides, who'd help me raise the baby?"

"Exactly. But, if anyone ever makes you feel uncomfortable, I want you to tell me. I won't let anyone hurt you, Callie."

"I know you won't."

His eyes burn with emotion. I slip my hand around his neck and pull his lips to mine. Our gentle kisses quickly turn frantic, and just as I'm getting ready to rip of his T-shirt, he suddenly pulls away.

"Banana peppers?"

I laugh and cover my mouth. *Oops.*

"With turkey and mayo. *Extra* mayo. I told you that vomiting deal was a one-time thing."

Devin grins and kisses my neck. "Can the banana peppers be a one-time thing, too?"

"Shut up. They made your baby very, very happy."

"Good. I want both my babies to be happy."

"We are. Blissfully and completely happy. Except for one tiny, little thing."

His face grows serious. "What tiny, little thing?"

"You'll figure it out."

I kiss him quickly before wiggling out of his arms and running to the bathroom.

The next morning, I'm awakened by the feel of soft, wet lips against my bare shoulder. Warm hands find their way beneath my tank top, and the moan that escapes me is almost embarrassing.

Almost.

"Devin?"

He trails kisses along my neck and up to my earlobe, stopping briefly to give it a gentle tug with his teeth.

"Dev—"

"Shh," he murmurs. I whimper when his tongue flicks across the shell of my ear. "I'm taking care of you."

I told him to figure it out.

He figured it out.

Devin's hand slips lower as his mouth latches onto my neck once again. Reaching behind me, I grab his hip and wiggle my bottom against him. He groans my name while his fingers slide and explore. It doesn't take long before we're both trembling, breathless, and totally shattered.

"Talk about a quickie," Devin whispers against my skin.

"And whose fault is that?"

He chuckles. "Mine. All mine."

I turn around in his arms and grin lazily.

"All yours."

Devin brushes his nose with mine.

"Good morning."

"I'll say."

He grins.

After quick trips to the bathroom, we climb back under the covers and snuggle into each other's arms. We both must fall back to sleep because, an hour later, a loud banging on the door sends us both jumping out of bed.

"What the hell?" Devin asks, glancing at his watch. "It's not even seven."

I try to wipe the sleep from my eyes and look down at my bare legs. "I'll go. I'm . . . partially dressed."

"Put on some jeans!" Devin groans when the bedside alarm goes off. He slaps at it and throws the blanket back over his head.

I find my robe and tie it around me as I race to the living room. I don't even bother looking through the peephole before opening the door.

"Who the—?"

"Good morning, Miss Franklin. Sorry to wake you."

It's the pimply-faced flower delivery guy from yesterday, holding a monster bouquet of pale pink lilies.

Shit. Shit. Shit.

"It's seven o'clock in the freaking morning! Why the hell are you beating on my door and waking up my neighbors?"

"Just following orders, Miss Franklin."

"Well, you can tell your boss I don't want them. Do not deliver any more flowers to me. Do you understand?"

The kid shuffles his feet. "You'll have to discuss that with Mr. Barkley, ma'am."

"Take them back!" I look over my shoulder to find Devin rubbing his face as he makes his way into the living room. Lowering my voice, I glare at the kid. "I'm serious. Take them back to your shop."

"Miss Franklin, I can't take them back. I'll get fired."

Devin appears at my side and frowns when he sees the flowers in the kid's hands.

"I don't want them," I whisper.

My heart begins to beat erratically as Devin reaches for the bouquet. The relieved delivery boy hands him the vase and runs for the elevator.

I kick the door shut and count to one hundred.

When I turn around, Devin's sitting on the couch. The flowers are on the end table, and the card is in his hand. I take a deep breath and join him. Reaching for the card, I gently pry it from his fingers.

> Hope you enjoyed the flowers I sent yesterday. I look forward to dinner on Friday. ~Dominic

I rip the card to shreds and toss it onto the floor.

"Devin . . ."

His eyes blaze. "I was wrong."

"Wrong about what?"

"I'm most definitely the jealous type."

Chapter 23

DEVIN

I've been consumed by jealousy and rage a few times in my life. When I was nine, a stray dog wandered up to our house and preferred Owen far more than me. I was a little pissed when Simon scored two points higher than me on the LSATs. And I'm always livid on the rare occasion I lose a court case.

None of those situations compares to the fury I feel right now. It's unnerving—this powerful, Neanderthal-like urge to find Dominic Barkley and punch him in the face for even thinking he might have a chance with my girl.

That's right. *My* girl.

Mine.

"Devin," she whispers gently, like she's talking to a wild animal . . . which is exactly how I feel. "Devin, look at me."

When I don't respond, she climbs into my lap and takes

my hands in hers, placing them on each side of her beautiful face. Callie frames my face with her own hands, forcing me to look into her bright blue eyes. Under the intensity of her stare, I feel my blind rage start to ebb.

"Better?"

I nod.

"So, you *are* the jealous type. I was afraid that might be the case. Which is why I didn't tell you about it last night."

Suddenly, it all became clear. The hypothetical questions last night weren't hypothetical at all.

"Tell me now."

With a sigh, Callie gently caresses my face. "During the interview yesterday, Dominic was . . . weird. He just kept staring at me. Oliver even noticed and refused to leave me alone with the man. He didn't touch me. He didn't say anything inappropriate. It was just obvious the man is a sleaze. I did my job and got out of there as soon as I could. About an hour later, flowers were delivered to me at the office. Tulips. From Dominic. Inviting me to dinner on Friday night. I gave the flowers to our sixty-year-old receptionist. She just lost her husband. I thought they might brighten her day. That's it."

"Where's the card?"

"In my desk at the office."

"Why did you keep it?"

"I'm a reporter, Devin. I keep everything." She glances down at the torn card on the floor. "Well, almost everything. I'm a big believer in hoarding, especially when it comes to politicians. You never know when you might need evidence."

"How very Lewinsky of you."

I feel her stiffen.

"If you mean *smart*, then yes. And how dare you even compare the two situations. It's nothing like that. The man sent some flowers and asked me out to dinner. That's *all*. I thought ignoring the first card would be sufficient, but I guess not. I'll handle it."

"You'll handle it?"

"Yes. I'll just send a message to his campaign manager and decline the invitation. She'll *love* that, considering he couldn't keep his hands off her. Jocelyn will have evidence he's a creep, and I'll never have to speak to him again. Two birds. One stone. Problem solved."

She sounds so strong. So convinced. As if a message will stop him.

It wouldn't have stopped me.

I remember the night we met and how I debated approaching her at the piano. Then she started to sing, and my decision was made. From that moment, I was determined to get her into my bed. If she'd refused, I would've pursued her mercilessly until she finally gave in. I don't know Dominic Barkley that well, but I know the kind of man he is. It's the same kind of man I used to be. I wouldn't have taken no for an answer. I'm betting neither will he.

"I have to get ready for work. Are we okay?"

I nod. "I don't want you to see him, okay? Send an email. Call. Whatever. But do not talk to his man in person."

"Devin . . ."

"No, Callie."

"What do you mean *no*?"

I sigh. *Of course that'd piss her off.*

"Just . . . please don't. Okay?"

She wraps her arms around my neck and presses her lips to mine. "You have no reason to be jealous, Devin. I'm all yours."

"All mine."

Closing my eyes, I let her soft lips and sweet touch consume me and soothe the jealous beast that reared his ugly head in what was otherwise an incredible morning.

"I won't lie," she whispers against my ear. "You're really sexy when you're jealous. I knew you were crazy about me."

"You have no idea how crazy I am about you."

Her eyes search my face before she presses her forehead against mine.

"I'm crazy about you, too. I think about you all the time."

I smile. "What do you think about?"

"I think about the future."

"So do I."

"You do?"

"Of course. Speaking of which, I have something for you."

Callie shifts onto the couch, and I race to the bedroom, digging in my jacket for the box tucked securely inside the pocket. I return to the living room, and her eyes widen when she sees the jewelry box in my hand.

"Haley's Jewelry Store? That store's in Brandywine. When did you . . ."

I smile and offer her the gift box. "Remember when I

drove in to town to give you and your dad some time alone? I did a little shopping."

She grins and tugs on the bow. "At the most expensive jewelry store in town. I bet Ms. Haley saw dollar signs when you walked in."

"She did seem very happy to see me. Just open it."

Callie takes a deep breath and opens the box. She gasps as she trails her finger along the sterling silver bracelet with a heart-shaped charm.

"It's the baby's birthstone. I know you don't wear a lot of jewelry, but this is small, and I just wanted to give you something to show how much you mean to me . . . and something that symbolizes our future."

Callie's eyes fill with tears. "It's so pretty, but it's too much, Devin."

"It's not nearly enough."

How could a tiny, overpriced piece of silver adequately signify how important she is to me? I carefully remove the bracelet from its box and fasten it to her wrist.

"Thank you. I love it so much."

"I'm glad." I kiss her softly before glancing down at my watch. "Okay, since we're both officially late for work, do you want to get some breakfast on the way?"

She smiles. "I'd love that. And you'll let me handle Dominic?"

"Yeah. Send your message. But no more secrets. Any small, inconsequential contact he makes with you, I want to know about it. Deal?"

"Deal. See? We *can* compromise."

With a wicked grin, she climbs out of my lap and takes my hands, pulling me off the couch. "I think we should compromise one more time before we leave for work."

"Oh?"

"Race you to the shower."

Callie winks and laughs as I chase her into the bathroom.

Chapter 24

Callie

Today's the big day.

Finally.

"Here you go. Aren't 3D ultrasounds great?"

Dr. Clifton hands each of us a grainy image from today's ultrasound.

"And we're sure there's just the one baby?" I ask, examining the picture closely.

The doctor smiles. "Just the one. The mother carries the twin gene, so the fact that Devin's a twin doesn't really matter at all. And since you don't know of any twins in your family, the chances were slim."

"It's too bad Baby McAllister was feeling shy," Devin says.

I grin. He'd really been hoping we'd learn the gender today. Dr. Clifton had offered to do some kind of blood test if we were really desperate to know, but we've decided to wait and try it again next month. There are just too few *good* surprises in life, so we're content to stay in the dark for now.

Throughout the appointment, Dr. Clifton has been amazingly patient while Devin quizzes him on everything from my weird banana pepper cravings to my slightly elevated blood pressure.

"We'll definitely want to monitor it. Are you feeling particularly stressed, Callie?"

Yes, Doc. I think I'm being stalked by a crazy mayoral candidate while trying to convince my baby daddy that it's all good.

"There's just . . . a lot going on."

The doctor nods. "I know it's easier said than done, but try to relax. The ultrasound looks great, so no worries there."

Devin clears his throat. "Dr. Clifton, my twin sister passed away due to leukemia."

"I've been expecting this question," he says kindly. "I've known your father for a long time. Unfortunately, we know very little about what actually causes leukemia. Naturally, if a family member has cancer, your chances increase, but truthfully? It's cancer. We're *all* susceptible, so I'm afraid I can't offer you any real assurance about this. For now, let's focus on a healthy pregnancy and a safe delivery."

I squeeze Devin's hand.

"Any other questions?"

Devin smirks. "Well, there's one more, yes. Is it safe to have sex during pregnancy?"

Dr. Clifton turns to me. "Are you feeling any discomfort during or after sex?"

"I wouldn't know."

"I'm sorry?"

"We haven't had sex since . . . well, conception. Devin's concerned that it's dangerous for the baby."

Dr. Clifton smirks. "No sex since conception? No wonder you're stressed out."

"I know, right?"

Devin rolls his eyes.

"That's actually a very real fear for most first-time parents," the doctor says. "Devin, let me assure you. Sex during pregnancy is completely safe. Of course, if Callie feels any discomfort, or if there's any bleeding or cramping, then that could be a concern and you should call me immediately. Otherwise, you're good to go."

We grin at each other. *Finally!*

"And I'm guessing that's your last question," Dr. Clifton says with a chuckle as he leads us out.

We thank him and stop by the receptionist to confirm my next appointment before making our way out of the building. Instead of walking straight to the car, Devin abruptly grabs me by the hand and pulls me around to the edge of the building. He presses my back against the wall and levels me with a look so possessive and loving I nearly whimper. Before the sound can escape my throat, Devin crashes his mouth to mine. With a moan, I wrap my arms around his neck, pulling him close while memories consume me, reminding me of the weekend that's changed my life forever. We've kissed many times since then, but he'd always been careful. Reserved. Sweet. Apparently, being given the green light by the good doctor was all Devin needed to finally let go. I'm breathless and trembling when he finally pulls away.

"Take me home," I whisper.

Devin gives me one last bone-melting kiss before leading me to the car.

My fingers fumble with the key as I struggle to unlock my door. Devin's making it impossible, with his chest pressed against my back while he kisses my shoulder.

"Unlock the door, Callie," he whispers against my ear.

I mutter a curse and finally manage to get the key in the lock. We're barely inside the apartment before Devin's kicking the door shut and lifting me into his arms. Wrapping my legs around him, I drop my bag and lift my shirt over my head as he carries me to the bedroom. We laugh as zippers unzip and buttons unbutton, but our laughter fades when he lowers me onto the bed and places soft, reverent kisses along my stomach.

"I love everything about you, Callie. I love that you're pregnant with our baby. I love that there's this little person inside of you, and he or she's going to be the very best parts of you and me. And I don't care if it's a boy or a girl, as long as it's healthy and looks just like you."

I smile and run my fingers through his hair. Goosebumps

erupt across my flesh as his mouth blazes a trail up along my collarbone. He presses himself into me, making me moan, and I shift my hips in quiet invitation. Devin lifts his head, his eyes burning with intensity and desire as he gazes at me. Making me feel wanted and worshipped and—

"I love you, Callie."

And then he starts to move. Slowly, torturously at first, with deep, wet kisses and soft, gentle moans that build and build until I'm sure I'm going to explode. Wrapping my legs around his waist, I whimper his name and hold on tight as his movements become frantic and desperate. It's too much, too fast, and just like that first weekend, I'm unable to control my body's reaction to his. He tells me he loves me again, and I cry out his name as I shatter into a million pieces beneath him. His groan vibrates through me as he buries his face against my neck, leaving him breathless and trembling in my arms.

I run my fingers through his hair as we try to get our rapid heartbeats and breathing under control.

"Did you mean it?" I whisper.

Devin lifts his head and smiles at me.

"You know I did. I love you, Callie."

My eyes fill with tears as I gently stroke his face. We have so much to learn about each other. I don't know his middle name or where he was born. I don't know where he went to college or the name of his favorite movie.

But I know he loves me.

"I love you, too, Devin."

His face breaks out into the most beautiful smile I've

ever seen.

And now he knows I love him, too.

"Best day off *ever*. Do we really have to go back to the real world?"

Devin mutters something from the bathroom. I grin. We're not particularly thrilled with the fact that we have to be sociable today. Spending hours upon hours in bed yesterday has made us very lazy.

I could really get used to lazy, especially if Devin can be lazy with me.

With a resigned sigh, I check my reflection in the full-length mirror. We're running late, so it's not like I had a lot of time to do anything elaborate. I grabbed the first dress I found in my closet, threw it on, and then pulled my hair into a ponytail.

Devin rushes back into the bedroom. "Unfortunately, we do. You have a story to write, and I'm due in court. The judge is going to chew my ass. I've never been late to a hearing. You, Miss Franklin, are a very bad influence."

He stops griping long enough to look in the mirror. "You're gorgeous and particularly glowy this morning."

I smile. "Wonder why?"

Devin grins and kisses my shoulder. "Need some help with that zipper?"

"Please."

He zips me up before taking a long look at the two of us in the mirror.

"Damn, we're a good looking couple." Suddenly his eyes widen. "Is that . . ."

I look down in a panic. "Is that what? There better not be a stain—"

"Callie, turn to your side."

"What?"

"Turn to your side and look at yourself in the mirror."

"Devin, this is—"

"Just do it!"

With a heavy sigh, I turn and try to find whatever's caught his attention. It must be a big deal, considering how late we are.

"I don't see any—"

"Look down, Callie."

And that's when I see it. Maybe it's just the clingy fabric of the dress, but that doesn't matter. It's small, but it's there.

I place my hand on my stomach. *Hello, baby bump.*

Devin wraps his arm around me and places his hand on top of mine.

"Best morning ever," he says softly.

Chapter 25

Callie

After spending the morning chained to my desk, I finally submit my article to Frank and head out to lunch. I need some fresh air, and that turkey, mayo, and banana pepper sub is calling my name.

I pick up my lunch and walk to the nearby park to find my favorite bench. The sandwich is delicious, *again*, and I inhale it while thinking about how perfect the day has been. In fact, the only unpleasant aspect of my morning was the email I'd sent to Jocelyn, asking her to relay my regrets to Dominic Barkley that I'd be unable to meet him for dinner. Between the upcoming mayoral debate and dealing with his probably very pissed-off campaign manager and bed buddy, I'm hopeful Mr. Barkley will have plenty to keep him busy for a while.

I toss my trash in a nearby container before glancing at

my phone. As I check my messages, I can't help but notice the sun reflecting off my pretty bracelet. It's so simple and pretty—something I would totally have picked out for myself. I don't wear a lot of jewelry, but this is far too beautiful and meaningful to sit in a jewelry box. It's my little constant reminder that there's this tiny person growing inside of me, and that I'm in love.

It's a first for me. I've never been in love before. Not like this. And while his overprotective tendencies still drive me a little nuts, I understand them a little better now. I need to keep reminding myself that Devin's not trying to control me. He's trying to protect me. Because he loves me.

I don't know why, but that makes it a little more tolerable.

I've just replied to an email when I feel someone's gaze on me. Glancing up, I see a jogger and some guy walking his dog, but otherwise, the park looks pretty deserted.

Weird.

"I'm losing it," I mutter.

Grabbing my bag, I head back to the office. Frank probably has some notes for me, and I'll need most of the afternoon to edit and rewrite before the article finally goes to press. As I walk along the street, I still get the feeling someone's watching me. Or following me. I look over my shoulder but don't really see anyone suspicious.

You've got to relax, Callie.

I'm desperately in need of a distraction, so I pull my phone out of my bag and call the best distraction I know.

"I was just thinking about you," Devin answers.

I smile and take the crosswalk leading to our building.

"Oh yeah? What were you thinking about?"

"Thinking I'd like to take you to lunch."

"Ah, I just ate. I had a lovely sandwich in the park."

"Did my child demand banana peppers again?"

"Your child did demand it. It's like he *knows* me."

"Or *she*."

"Heaven help us. Something tells me you'd be one of those gun-toting fathers if she's a girl."

"And what's wrong with that?"

"Nothing. Nothing at all."

He laughs.

"The sandwich *was* delicious, by the way, but I promise my breath will be minty fresh by the time you get home."

"I'd kiss you anyway."

"You'd better."

Devin sighs heavily. "The real world sucks. I could really get used to staying in bed with you all day. I don't like it when you're so far away from me."

"You're silly. I'm just across town."

"That's too far. A mile's too far. An inch is too far."

"Oh, you're very sappy today. I love it."

"I love you."

I smile every single time he says it.

We make plans to order take-out for dinner as I make my way inside the building. When I reach the newsroom, I toss my phone into my bag just as Frank yells from his door, asking me to come into his office.

"Close it," he says.

Crap. Crap. He rarely asks us to close the door. He likes

for the entire newsroom to hear him when he barks at one of his reporters.

He sits down behind his desk. "You look like you're gonna puke. You'd better not puke in my office."

"I won't puke." *I hope.*

"Have a seat and calm down. It's a good article, Callie. I just have a few notes."

I breathe a sigh of relief.

"Election coverage seems to agree with you. Why don't you cover the debate tomorrow night? Take Oliver with you."

This day keeps getting better and better.

"Awesome. Thanks, Frank."

He takes off his glasses and cleans them with the bottom of his shirt. "Just one thing. Be sure not to let your personal opinion influence your reporting. You're not writing editorials."

I frown. "I don't know what you mean."

"Look, we're all tax payers, and we're all registered voters. Or at least we should be. It's natural to have an opinion about the candidates. It was subtle, but I've been doing this a long time, and I can tell you're less than impressed with Dominic Barkley. I don't care why. Not my business. My business is this newspaper and what we print. Reporters are supposed to remain neutral. Do you understand what I'm saying?"

I thought I had been neutral. Apparently, my contempt for Dominic Barkley seeped into my article.

"I understand. Should I edit?"

"Nah. Like I said, it was subtle. Just be careful in the future."

I nod. He's finally giving me the chance to cover actual news. The last thing I want to do is screw it up. I thank him and head for the door.

"Oh, Frank. I should probably tell you I'm—"

"Pregnant. I know. Leo's been grumbling about some nasty sandwich and your freaky pregnancy cravings."

I laugh and head back to my desk. I don't get it. The banana peppers smell like heaven to me. I don't understand why they smell so awful to everyone else. I'm still pondering this when I sit down at my desk. My phone vibrates, and I dig it out of my bag to check the screen.

> *Let's take tomorrow off.*

I grin.

> **No can do. I'm covering the debate tomorrow night.**

> *The mayoral debate?*

Oh no. I hadn't even considered the fact that I'd have to be in the same room with Dominic Barkley. Could be awkward.

> **Yes.**

> *I'm going with you.*

> **Oliver is going with me.**

Great. He can ride with us.

I sigh and try to figure out how to handle this. The debate will be held in a college auditorium and crowded with voters and reporters. The chances I'll even have to make eye contact with Dominic are slim. This is work. Devin's just going to have to ignore his caveman tendencies for one night and let me do my job.

Before I can reply, I get another message.

Don't even try to talk me out of it. I'm going. End of discussion.

Is he serious? End of discussion?

I don't even bother with a reply. It can be the end of discussion—for now.

But just wait until I get home.

I'm prepared for a fight when I walk into the apartment later that afternoon. Instead, I find Devin sitting on the couch, staring daggers at a fresh bouquet of orange tiger lilies. My stomach drops.

"Where did those come from?

"Did you have lunch with Dominic today?"

"Are those from *him*?"

"Answer the question, Callie!"

"Don't you dare yell at me! And are you seriously asking me that question? I told you I ate lunch in the park."

He tiredly rubs his face and exhales a heavy sigh.

"Believe it or not, I was hoping you lied to me."

"I . . . don't understand."

Devin reaches for my hand. Despite my anger, I take it and let him pull me toward the couch.

"I'm sorry I yelled."

"Okay . . ."

"Did you see Dominic anywhere today? Maybe in the park? Or on the way back to the office?"

"No, Devin. I didn't see him anywhere. Why are you interrogating me?"

He hands me the card.

> You looked beautiful at lunch today. I love banana peppers, too. ~Dominic

My stomach lurches, and I leap off the couch and race to the bathroom.

Devin paces the living room with his cell phone against his ear, alternating between barking and whispering orders to someone on the other end. I'm on the couch, nibbling on a banana pop and praying my stomach calms down. Every few minutes, Devin takes a break from his frenzied pacing and sits down next to me. He squeezes my hand, kisses my forehead, cups my cheek . . . anything to comfort me.

They say a reporter should always trust her instincts, but today, I'd ignored them when it came to my personal safety. I *knew* someone was following me. To have it confirmed has totally sent me over the edge with a million different emotions, but the overriding one is fear.

I'm afraid.

But I'm not afraid for me.

My hand rests on my stomach. It's intense—this protective intuition that's consuming me. I can't help but wonder why it's so overpowering for me and yet my own mom seems to lack the same mothering instinct. Protecting my baby has suddenly become the most important thing in my world.

Devin finishes his call and drops to his knees in front of me. I watch with teary eyes as he leans close to my stomach. His trembling fingers lift the hem of my blouse, and he places a soft kiss against my skin.

"I won't let anything happen to you. Either of you."

"I know you won't."

A knock on the door makes us both jump.

"It's just Owen. Don't get up."

"No problem."

But it's not just Owen. Walking in behind him is a massive, broad-shouldered man with deep ebony skin who looks like he can bench press a Buick. The guys shake hands before they all turn their attention to me.

"Callie, this is Malik. He's a former Navy SEAL and now works in personal security. He's a friend of Owen's."

"It's nice to meet you, Miss Franklin."

The towering man offers me his hand. I'm almost afraid to shake it, but his grip is surprisingly gentle.

"Nice to meet you, too. And you can call me Callie."

He smiles, which makes him look a lot less scary.

Owen sits down next to me and gives me a hug. "Don't worry about a thing. We're going to take good care of you and my nephew."

"*We* are? Who's we?"

"I've hired Malik for your protection," Devin explains.

"You hired a bodyguard?"

"*Bodyguards*," Owen says with a grin. "You're gonna get so sick of me, Mama Callie."

"Don't you have a job?"

Owen nods. "That's why you have two. One of us will be with you at all times."

Unbelievable. My eyes flicker to Devin, who looks as if he's bracing himself for a fight. Normally, he'd get one, but any irritation I might feel is overshadowed by this all-encompassing mothering instinct that's desperate to protect her child. I have no reason to believe Dominic could be violent, but the fact is I'm obviously being followed—if not stalked—and that puts my baby in danger. Are two burly bodyguards complete overkill? Probably. But the mother in me can't find it in myself to care.

"Please don't fight me on this," Devin says, his tone soft

and pleading.

"I won't fight you."

He sighs with relief and leans down, kissing me softly. I then watch as he takes the orange tiger lilies—vase and all—and dumps them in the trash.

Chapter 26

DEVIN

"I have more security than the mayoral candidates," Callie mutters as we make our way into the auditorium.

Owen shoots me a grin. To my enormous surprise, she hadn't fought me when it came to the bodyguards, but that didn't mean she was happy about it. And that's fine. She can complain all she wants. With Malik on one side and Owen behind us—and her photographer leading the way—I couldn't ask for better protection.

I refuse to let that stalking asshole within a hundred feet of her.

The stage is simple, with a blue backdrop and two podiums. We take our seats as the moderator welcomes everyone and introduces the candidates. The men take their places at the mics, and the host informs them about the debate rules and time limits. My eyes narrow as I watch Dominic and his fake smile. Callie gives my hand a reassuring squeeze before opening her tablet to take notes.

As the debate flows from question to question, I sit and stew. I should've handled him myself, but Callie wanted to deal with it. I hadn't expected a polite email to change his mind. It wouldn't have changed mine. As a matter of fact, she'd told me to go to hell, and I kept sending her flowers. I even camped outside her door night after night.

Maybe I'm a stalker, too.

Callie must feel my eyes on her, because she glances up from her tablet and smiles at me.

"I love you," she mouths.

She loves me. Despite my stalkerish, overprotective tendencies.

When the debate ends, I watch as the candidates leave the stage and navigate their way into the crowd.

I lean over and kiss her temple. "I'll be right back."

Callie nods without looking up from her tablet. I give Owen a pointed look that he understands immediately, and he slides in next to Callie as I head for the lobby. It takes me a grand total of thirty seconds to find Dominic. His hand's on the back of a busty redhead who he introduces to everyone as his campaign manager. Typical. Dominic Barkley is rarely found without an attractive woman on his arm.

It wasn't that long ago that someone would have said the same thing about you, McAllister.

I shake off that irritating thought and make my way to his side. Dominic plasters on a smile when he sees me.

"Devin McAllister! It's been a long time."

I offer him my hand. "It has. I know you're busy, but I was wondering if I could speak with you for a moment. Alone."

"Anything for a voter. Especially an influential one."

No doubt he's thinking he can pump me for a photo op or campaign money. Poor bastard doesn't have a clue what he's in for.

He whispers something into the redhead's ear before his security detail leads me toward a conference room. His bodyguard closes the door behind us. Dominic waves me toward one of the chairs surrounding the table.

"I won't take much of your time, Dominic."

He sits down beside me. "I should be thanking you. It's nice to get away from the crowd for a few minutes. What can I do for you, Devin? I haven't seen you in months. Charity events aren't your scene anymore?"

"No, I've found a new scene."

He grins and loosens his tie. "Can't say I'm disappointed. Just means more women for me."

"That's what I'd like to talk to you about."

"Oh?"

"I've fallen in love with a wonderful woman. We're expecting a baby."

"Is that right? A woman's tamed Devin McAllister?"

I nod.

"I never thought I'd see the day. Congratulations, I guess, if that makes you happy."

"Thank you. And yes, I'm very happy. Except for one thing."

"What's that?"

"I'm gonna need you to stop stalking her."

His smile fades. "I'm . . . not sure I understand."

"Her name's Callie Franklin."

Dominic's face turns ashen.

"I'm going to say this as politely as I can. I assure you it will be the only time I'm civil when it comes to this request. Stop having her followed. Stop sending her flowers."

He grins and leans back lazily in his chair.

"She's a beautiful woman, McAllister."

"That she is."

"You aren't up for a little healthy competition?"

I try desperately to keep a tight grip on my temper. "Have a little class, Barkley. She's pregnant. You're frightening the woman I love. I'm politely asking you to let it go. If not—"

"And here comes the threat."

"Not a threat. It's a promise. You're in the middle of a campaign. The last thing you need is to be arrested for stalking."

"I'm not following Cal—"

"No, I'm sure you don't have time to stalk her and run an efficient mayoral campaign at the same time. But you're having her followed. Your last love note confirmed it. You know she works for the *Journal*. You're running for office. The last thing you need is a sexual harassment scandal making front page news."

He chuckles. "You're bluffing. You can't prove a thing."

I pull the handwritten card out of my pocket and place it on the table. "See this? I have the evidence—right down to the banana peppers reference. Do not test me on this,

Barkley. I will ruin you. Are we clear?"

Dominic regards me coolly before nodding his head.

I stand up from my chair and put the card back in my pocket. "Good. Contact her again and I'll call the police."

With a cocky grin, he rises from his chair. "You seem to forget that I'll be in charge of the police when I'm elected mayor."

I take a step closer. "Fine. Contact her again and I'll kill you. Better?"

His eyes flash with anger, but he nods firmly.

"I'm glad we understand each other. Good luck with the election."

I turn on my heel and head for the door.

"Can I count on your support?" he asks as I turn the knob.

"Not a chance in hell."

And with that, I step out into the hallway, letting the door slam behind me.

The month following the debate is filled with lots of physical and emotional changes for Callie—some of which aren't enjoyable at all. The good news is, with the Dominic situation finally under control, Callie's blood pressure is back in the normal range. The bad news is she's on a rollercoaster of emotions now that she's midway through the second trimester. No matter how hard I try, I can't seem to do anything right. What makes her happy one day can make her furious the next.

Dad tells me to get used to it.

At night, we've started reading to each other from the baby bible. Yesterday morning, when I reminded her not to wear high heels because—according to the book—they could strain her back, Callie dissolved into tears. The banana pepper craving ended as quickly as it started, and now, the mere mention of mayonnaise sends her running for the toilet. The return of the nausea, combined with the mood swings, has brought our amazing sex life to an abrupt halt.

It's been three weeks since we've had sex.

Three very long weeks.

But I'll take it. I'll take it all. The mood swings. The crying jags. I'll take it . . . because I love her.

After a crappy day in court, I decide to grab a pizza for dinner, because both of us could use a nice, relaxing night at home.

Home.

Callie's apartment has truly become my home. I even have a key. Despite that, she hasn't officially asked me to move in with her. It seems the next logical step, but just because I spend every single night with her doesn't mean she's ready to live with me. I'm saving that discussion for later—when her emotions are on a more even keel. Besides, our lives have changed so much already. I'm hesitant to add one more life-altering event to the mix.

I can be patient.

When I step inside the apartment that evening, the first thing I hear is Callie crying from behind her bedroom door. Normally, this would cause me to panic, but these days, it doesn't take much to cause a meltdown. I place the pizza on the kitchen table before heading to her room. I don't even bother to knock, and when I open the door, I see my beautiful girl lying across her bed, crying softly into her pillow.

With a quiet sigh, I slowly climb up on the bed and reach for her. She comes willingly, burying her face against my neck when I wrap her in my arms.

"What's wrong, sweetheart?" I whisper against her ear.

She sniffles and lifts her head.

"I'm ugly."

We've only had this same discussion three times this week. Very gently, I slide my fingers across her wet cheeks.

"You are not ugly. You are so beautiful, Callie."

"Whatever. You just like that my boobs are getting bigger."

I fight back a grin.

"You know, I think you're even prettier now than on the night we met, and I thought you were gorgeous then."

"You're such a liar, Devin McAllister. I'm fat and getting fatter. I have heartburn from hell. Nothing fits. And I have a zit!" She points to her forehead, and sure enough, a tiny pimple is starting to form. "I haven't had a zit since high school!"

"Sweetheart, the book said your skin goes through changes and that pimples were a possibility. Besides, you have bangs. Nobody's—"

"*Everybody* will see it. This whole pregnancy thing sucks. They say you're supposed to be glowing and happy, but all I feel is undesirable and moody. I have to pee all the freaking time. I *cry* all the time. And today, Frank sent me home from work early because I told the copy editor to kiss my ass. I'm being such a bitch to everyone and I hate it."

I kiss her temple and hold her close. "You know this won't last forever. Your body's just adjusting to the fact that you're growing a human being inside you. You're allowed to be hormonal."

She sniffles quietly and wipes at her nose. "Why do you put up with me?"

"Because I'm crazy in love with you. Besides, I don't feel like I'm putting up with anything. I just wish I could make you feel better."

"You always do." Callie sighs and leans in, kissing me gently. "I'm sorry."

"It's okay. Feel better?"

She nods.

"I brought pizza."

"With mushrooms?"

Please, God, let her still like mushrooms. I nod hesitantly.

"That sounds delicious!"

Callie kisses me one last time, and I can't help but laugh as she jumps off the bed and races to the kitchen.

Chapter 27

Callie

It's official. Devin McAllister is a saint.

Not only is he putting up with my crazy, hormonal ass, but he's actually being sweet about it. He never loses his temper and never makes me feel anything less than beautiful and loved. I know I'm not the easiest person to live with right now, and I'm being a bitch to everyone.

Leo told me so.

Devin, however, just takes it all in stride, which makes me feel even worse. But it's not like I can control my emotions. Thankfully, he knows this, and he doesn't hold it against me.

I've felt better this week, to be honest. I'm not nearly as moody and my crying jags have dwindled. I still don't feel normal, but at least I can walk into work without biting someone's head off.

It's a good thing, too, because the newsroom is a zoo

because of the mayoral election next week.

The flower deliveries have stopped and my new bodyguard hasn't been around, so I'm guessing Devin had a conversation with Dominic. I haven't asked, and I won't, because I don't care. I'm just glad the man's out of my life.

For now, anyway.

Dominic's leading in the polls, which means I'm probably going to have to look at the man's face in the mayor's office for the next four years. I'm not particularly thrilled about that, but I'm a professional. I'll deal.

"Doughnut?"

Glancing up, I find Leo smiling down at me. He's holding a box of glazed in his hands. I happily reach for one, take a bite, and moan happily.

"Mommy seems to be in a better mood this week."

"Sorry I've been such a bitch."

"You can make it up to me. There's a new Italian place I want to try."

I grin. "It's a date. Now, if only I could think of a way to make it up to Devin. He's been so patient and sweet."

Leo swallows the last bite of his doughnut. "Surely you aren't having trouble thinking of ways to show him some gratitude."

"Well, what do you get the man who has everything?"

"You give him you."

"He already has me."

Leo shakes his head. "You're overthinking this, Franklin. We men are simple creatures."

"Meaning?"

"Sex!" he shouts, causing every head in the newsroom to turn.

"A little louder. I don't think Frank heard you."

I glance down at my desk calendar. *One week. Two weeks. Three weeks. Four . . .*

"Wow."

"What?"

"It's been four weeks."

"*Four* weeks? You've slept next to that man every night and you haven't—"

"I haven't felt like it, Leo! And it's not like he's tried . . ."

"Of course he hasn't tried! You've been an insane pregnant woman with your crazy mood swings and that gigantic pimple on your forehead."

"Hey!" But Leo isn't listening to me. He's powering off my laptop and grabbing my bag. "What the hell are you doing?"

"You are leaving right this minute. Go over to that man's office and show him some appreciation." Leo reaches for my ponytail and loosens my hair. He immediately starts ruffling it with his fingers. Satisfied, he then looks at my clothes. "The skirt's good. Heels would have been nice."

I roll my eyes. "Sorry, I wasn't planning to seduce anyone today. Besides, Devin won't let me wear them. The baby book says not to, and in Devin's world, that book is gospel."

Leo's face softens. "He really loves you."

"I know." I smile.

"Go!" Leo pulls me by the arm and leads me to the exit. "And I want details!"

"Not a chance." I grin and kiss his cheek. "Thanks, Leo."

I've never actually been to Devin's office, so I'm surprised when his secretary greets me by name. Sure, we've spoken on the phone a few times, but we've never met.

"It's nice to finally meet you, Alicia. I'm curious. How'd you know it was me?"

"Your picture's on his desk. And on his screensaver. You make him very happy."

Suddenly, Devin curses loudly from behind his office door.

"He doesn't sound too happy today."

Alicia winces. "For the past few weeks he's been . . . on edge. I was just getting ready to take him some coffee. *Decaf.*"

I grin. "Is he . . . umm . . . busy for the next hour or so?"

"Actually, his schedule's clear for the next two hours. I'm headed out to lunch."

"And how long is your lunch?"

"How long do you want it to be?"

We smile at each other.

Once she leaves, I softly knock on Devin's door. He mutters something unintelligible when I walk into the room.

"Alicia, forget the coffee," he snaps as he looks down at his phone. "I think I'll go to the gym for lunch. Work off some steam. Call and see if my trainer is available."

Guilt consumes me. He looks so stressed out, and it dawns on me that this wonderful man who's been so calm and patient with me is actually at his wit's end.

"I can think of a much better way to work off some steam."

Devin's head snaps up. Reaching behind me, I lock the door. His gaze never leaves mine as I make my way over to his desk.

"Hi, baby," he says softly. "I'm sorry. I thought you were Alicia."

With a nod, I turn his chair around before reaching for the buttons of my blouse.

"Alicia's gone to lunch. A very long lunch."

His eyes glaze over as I strip slowly, letting my blouse fall to the floor.

"Why would she be taking a long lunch?"

I unzip my skirt and let it pool at my feet before climbing onto his mahogany desk. Devin's eyes rake over my body, and for the first time in weeks, I don't feel fat or unattractive. I felt beautiful and powerful and desired.

"I asked her to. I thought you and I could use some privacy."

Devin rises from his seat and stands between my legs. Leaning in, his lips gravitate to mine, but I dodge his kiss in order to make quick work of his shirt and slacks. They fall to the floor, and I wrap my legs around his waist, pulling him closer.

"Have you ever had sex in your office?"

He shakes his head.

"Do you want to?"

His mouth collides with mine, and with that, I have my answer.

Chapter 28

Callie

"Today is an important day," Devin murmurs softly against my stomach. "We get to find out if you're a boy or a girl. It's very important you aren't shy this morning."

I laugh and slide my fingers through his hair. "Devin, I don't think—"

"Hush. I'm negotiating with our child."

I stifle my laughter as he promises to buy the kid a car for his *or her* sixteenth birthday, if only they'll cooperate today. I love seeing him happy and totally in love with our baby, so I let him continue his silly discussion until Dr. Clifton walks in. The man barely gets the door closed before Devin's on his feet.

"We can do the ultrasound today, right?"

Dr. Clifton grins. "Good morning to you, too."

"Sorry, Doc. Devin's a little excited."

"Well," the doctor muses, and I swear I can see a twinkle in his eye. "We can certainly try. Let's just hope Baby McAllister isn't feeling shy today."

Devin shakes his head and sits back down beside me. "Not gonna happen. We just had a very long talk."

"Oh?"

"Devin and the baby have a deal," I explain. "If the baby gives us a peep show today, Devin buys him or her a car when they turn sixteen."

Dr. Clifton laughs. "Well, that sounds like a good deal to me. Let's give it a shot."

Moments later, Devin excitedly squeezes my hand as Dr. Clifton slides the transducer across my stomach. The three of us watch the blurry screen with anticipation.

"There's the heartbeat," the doctor says, pointing to a rhythmic thumping on the screen. "Still just the one, by the way."

I sigh with relief. Not that twins wouldn't have been great. It's just the idea of one baby is overwhelming enough.

"What's that? It looks like a long string of pearls." Devin asks softly.

"The baby's spine."

I don't trust myself to speak. I'm too mesmerized by the sight of our baby on the screen.

"There's a leg," Dr. Clifton murmurs.

Our eyes follow the shape of the leg until we find—or *don't* find—what we're looking for.

"I guess she's getting a car when she turns sixteen," Dr. Clifton says with a chuckle. "Congratulations. I'll just give you guys a minute."

Tears swim in my eyes as we watch our daughter on the black and white screen. Devin sighs contently and presses a kiss to my cheek.

"Look at her, Songbird."

All I can do is look at her, and in that moment, I'm suddenly seized with fear. She's tiny and defenseless, and I certainly haven't had the best of role models when it comes to mothers.

"Can I do this?"

Devin squeezes my hand. "Of course you can do this. You can do anything. *We* can do anything."

"Why aren't you scared? How can you be so optimistic?"

Devin chuckles. "Are you kidding? I'm scared to death. But she's ours, Callie. We'll love her and protect her, because that's what good parents do. We'll figure it out. I can't wait to figure it out."

I marvel at the sincerity in his voice and pray he's right.

After our appointment, we call our family and friends with the news. With the gender revealed—and happily announced to anyone within earshot—Devin decides it's time to hit the baby superstore.

"Do we really need a bassinette?" I ask while Devin examines the safety ratings on the box. "I mean, isn't the crib enough?"

"Well, the good thing is that the bassinette is portable. So, if the crib is upstairs but we're downstairs, we wouldn't have to carry the baby up just so she can take a nap."

Someone's obviously further along in the furniture chapter of the baby book.

"But we don't have stairs."

"I know, but we might someday."

"Oh really?"

Devin shrugs and heads over to the car seats. One model has so many snaps and buckles I'm pretty sure it could be used on the space shuttle.

"You don't like my apartment?"

"I like your apartment just fine. We just might want to buy a house someday. Something with a yard."

"Oh."

Do I *want* a house?

Yes, I think I do.

Happiness fills me as Devin tosses various baby products into the great big blob of pink that's become our shopping cart.

Poor Uncle Owen's going to be so upset. He really had his heart set on a nephew.

"Umm . . . Devin, I don't think we need teething rings just yet."

He just grins and keeps tossing stuff into the cart.

"What do you think about breast feeding?" he suddenly asks, nodding toward a pump.

"I think it sounds incredibly painful." I wince as I

examine the contraption. *Do I even want to breast feed?*

Devin must sense I'm feeling overwhelmed, because he puts the pump back on the shelf and points the cart toward the cribs. My eyes brighten when I see that each "nursery" is arranged by theme, complete with bedding, furniture, and decorations.

"That's a lot of pink."

"You don't like pink?"

"I . . . not really. Are there rules in Babyland? Does everything have to be pink just because she's a girl?

Devin looks around. "You're right. We need help."

The salesgirl must've heard him, because she's immediately by our side. When Devin asks her to show us something girly but *not* pink, she steers us toward some mint greens and lilacs that I love immediately.

"This is my favorite theme, and this crib is a great choice," she says. "It's convertible. As the baby gets older, it converts into a toddler bed and then to a twin. It comes in cherry, oak, and pearl white."

While Devin quizzes her on the safety stats of the crib, I glance at the price tag on all the furniture and nearly faint. *Are we seriously buying all this stuff today?* I mentally calculate how much it costs and quickly compare it to my bank account balance.

Holy crap. It's just wood, right?

"Do you like it, Callie?"

I blink. "Yes, but—"

Devin notices my apprehension and asks the girl to give us a few minutes.

"What's wrong?"

My eyes ghost over the nursery. "It's all beautiful. I'm just a little overwhelmed, I guess. I thought we'd pick out some clothes, some diapers . . ."

"And I've gone overboard. I'm sorry, Callie. We don't have to do all this today."

I sigh with relief. "Thanks. I love it, honestly. I just can't afford it all. Not today."

His forehead creases with confusion. "Is that what you're worried about? The money?"

"Well, yeah. I'm just a reporter, Devin. I live paycheck to paycheck like most Americans. I have some savings, but—"

With a grin, Devin leads me toward the nursery's rocking chair. He sits down and pulls me into his lap. "Sweetheart, I didn't expect you to pay for any of this. I'm happy to do it."

"But . . . we're partners in this. Equals."

"Of course we are, but don't you see? Everything I have is yours."

"Including your money?"

He shrugs.

"Devin, that's not true at all. And if it is, it shouldn't be. It's not like we're married."

"An issue I would be happy to rectify. Just say the word."

"Don't try to change the subject."

"I'm not trying to change it. I'm trying to figure out what you're so upset about. Are you mad because I'm offering to buy bedroom stuff for our kid? Or are you mad because we aren't married?"

I take a deep breath. "I'm not mad. I'm just . . . not used

to this. I don't like not being able to afford what I need. And I *can* afford it. I just can't afford it all today."

I can tell by the look in his eyes he doesn't get it, and that's not his fault. Devin was raised with money. Now he's a successful lawyer. My dad was a paramedic. Mom didn't work until after they divorced. Growing up, I had everything I needed, but there wasn't a lot of money left over for frivolous things. My salary's decent, but I can't just spend thousands of dollars in one day without charging it, and I really hate to use my credit card unless it's an emergency. *This* isn't an emergency.

Devin sighs softly and kisses the side of my neck. "Callie, I want to do this. I love you. I love our daughter. I know you have this independent streak, but we're a team now. Partners, like you said."

Tears sting my eyes. "I love you, too, but it's too much, Devin."

"Nothing is too much. Not when it comes to you and our baby."

"I want to pay for half."

Devin chuckles. "God, you're so stubborn."

"I'm just—"

"Overwhelmed, I know."

I nod. We just found out we're having a daughter. And now, Devin's talking houses and backyards and breast pumps and thousands of dollars of baby furniture. My life is just one big rollercoaster, and while most of it's wonderful, it's also scary as hell. Will I ever just feel settled and calm?

Devin kisses the hollow just below my ear. "And I didn't

help with an impromptu shopping spree to Babyville. I was just excited, I guess. I'm sorry."

"Don't apologize. I'm glad you're excited."

"I am, but this stuff can wait. We have time."

"No, you're right. We're already here. We might as well make a decision."

He smiles. "I know it's expensive. Let me buy this for our baby. Nothing would make me happier."

I glance around us. I really do love it. It's only the price—and my feelings of inadequacy—that make me hesitant.

"You can buy the furniture. I'll buy the accessories."

"Deal." Devin grins brightly. "Look at that. Another compromise. We're getting good at this."

I kiss him sweetly. "We are. Thank you. You're so good to me."

"I love you," he says simply, as if that explains everything. Maybe it does.

After making the sales girl's day, we decide to order take-out and spend a quiet night at home. We watch the local news, and both of us are disheartened to learn that Dominic now leads his opponent in the polls by nearly twenty percentage points. With the election less than a week away, it's safe to assume I'll be reporting on Dominic Barkley for the next four years.

Devin's unusually quiet for the rest of the night, and while it'd be easy to blame his subdued mood on Dominic, I know I have to accept my share of the blame. I'd soured our happy day with my insecurities, and those insecurities were just a by-product of growing up with a mom like Kim. All my life, she'd drilled into my head not to rely on a man. To make my own money and my own life so that I'd never have to depend on someone else. And, more importantly, so I could support myself in case my relationships turned out just like hers.

I love Devin, and I know he loves me, but I also have to be smart.

When we finally climb into bed, Devin pulls me close to his chest. His soft rhythmic breathing against my ear nearly lulls me to sleep, but then he whispers my name in the darkness.

"Hmm?"

"Callie, I've been thinking about what we were talking about at the store. About being partners. Equals. You *are* my equal. I just don't think being equal has anything to do with money. Money doesn't buy happiness. If it did, my sister would still be alive." His arm tightens around me. "I never thought I'd be this happy. You make me this way, and money has nothing to do with it."

"I know. You make me happy, too. Happier than I've ever been. My emotions are just all over the place. So much has happened so fast, and it *keeps* happening. I wish life could be still for just a second, but that's not going to happen anytime soon."

"It's been a crazy few months. We should run away. Take a vacation or something."

That sounds nice. It's also impossible with both of our jobs, but it's nice to dream. I play along.

"Where would we go?"

"Where do you want to go?"

I laugh softly. "Surprise me."

"I can do that."

I smile. *Will I ever get used to his ability to grant my every wish?*

"Devin, I'm going to have a very hard time letting you buy me things. I'm just stubbornly independent. I always have been. I'm not completely destitute, but news reporters don't make bank. I have to manage my money. My savings account is decent, but it's all I have."

"I understand, but when it comes to the baby, I need you to understand something, too. I *want* to take care of her. That means I'm going to buy whatever she needs . . . and probably a lot of things she won't need at all. She's going to be spoiled, and I'm sorry about that, but I can't promise I'll be able to control it. And if *we* don't spoil her, trust me when I say her grandparents will."

I grin. "And don't forget Uncle Owen."

"And your dad. Remember when we called to tell him it's a girl? He said he'd taken the hundred bucks he made off me and started her a college fund with it."

We laugh.

"Callie, I don't want you to worry about money. I'm a decent attorney and I've made good investments. Money should never be an issue for us."

"But that's just it. It's your money."

"It's *ours*. What's mine is yours, remember?"

"That's a nice sentiment, Devin, but it's not true."

"It would be true if we were married."

"But we're not."

We grow quiet, and just as I'm falling asleep, I hear him whisper against my ear.

"I want to marry you, Songbird."

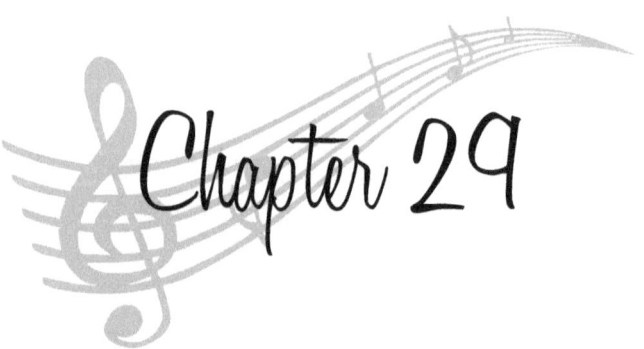

Chapter 29

Callie

Did he mean it?

The question has rattled around in my brain all day.

Shaking my head, I lean back on the park bench and try to enjoy what's left of my lunch break. It's a beautiful, cloudless fall day, and the leaves are just starting to change colors. After a few minutes, the ducks arrive, so I tear off a couple pieces of bread from my leftover sandwich and toss it onto the ground for them to fight over. They'll migrate soon, and I'll miss seeing them at lunch. When they return in the spring, I'll be a mother.

Will I be a wife, too?

Apparently, Devin assumed I was asleep when he whispered his nighttime proposal in my ear. He hadn't mentioned it this morning at breakfast, and I certainly didn't bring it up. He knows I'm an emotional mess right now. Why would he say something like that?

And did he mean it?

I close my eyes and raise my face toward the sun, willing its warmth to soothe my frazzled nerves. Suddenly, I feel someone sit down next to me. I open my eyes and nearly jump out of my skin when I find Dominic Barkley sitting by my side.

"It's nice to see you again, Callie. Pretty day, isn't it?"

I take a deep breath and toss more bread onto the ground. A couple of mallards gather around us, happily snatching up piece after piece.

"Still having me followed, I see."

"Actually, I called the news office. A very chatty receptionist told me you liked to come to the park for lunch. So I took a chance."

"I'll be sure to mention that to Human Resources. She should be fired."

He chuckles.

"What can I do for you, Mr. Barkley? Or should I say Mayor Barkley?"

He smiles. "Let's hope. And call me Dominic, please."

"What do you want?"

"I'd like to apologize. I see now that I came on a bit too strong. I'm sorry. I had no idea you were involved with someone, and I certainly didn't know you were pregnant."

"Your investigator would have figured it out sooner or later."

"I apologize for that, as well. I met a beautiful woman and I wanted to know more about her."

"That's a creepy way to get to know someone."

He nods. "Agreed. Politicians tend to go overboard sometimes. We have many resources at our disposal, and sometimes, we use them when we shouldn't. I'm sorry if I frightened you."

I nod and continue watching the ducks.

Dominic chuckles lightly. "I have to say, I am a little surprised. You aren't Devin's usual type."

"What's Devin's usual type?"

"Beautiful—which you are. And rich."

"Money doesn't buy happiness, Mr. Barkley."

"No, but it makes life a little easier, doesn't it?"

"I wouldn't know."

"True. A news reporter for a local paper couldn't know much about that. Which is why I have an offer for you."

"What kind of offer?"

"Well, Callie, I don't know if you follow the news at all . . ."

It's a joke. We both know it's meant to be. But I just can't muster the energy to laugh. He sobers quickly and clears his throat.

"If the polls are to be believed, I am going to be the next mayor of Nashville. Naturally, I'd like to replace most of the current staff. I want to be ready, so I've been conducting interviews. I'm going to need a communications director."

"Which is what? A fancy name for a speech writer?"

"*Senior* speech writer, but yes. Your work is exemplary. I think you would make a fine addition to my administration. Interested?"

"Hmm. And what would Jocelyn have to say about that?"

"Jocelyn will be my press secretary. She'll have plenty to keep her busy."

I smirk. With him as mayor? I'm sure she'll have her hands full.

If this job offer came from any other mayor-elect, my answer would be a no-brainer, but this is Dominic Barkley, and he's a creep.

"Callie, I know your first impulse is to say no, but I think you should know the base salary is six figures."

I blink. *Six figures?*

Dominic hands me a card. "Think it over. Call this number to speak with Jocelyn. She can give you more information about insurance benefits and such. That's important with a baby on the way."

I stare at the card in my hand as he stands to leave.

"I hope you can accept my apology, and I hope you give serious consideration to my offer. I look forward to hearing from you."

Dumbfounded, I gaze at the words and numbers on the card until my eyes finally cross. With a heavy sigh, I toss the card into my bag and rest my hand on my baby bump.

Baby girl, your mom is on a roller coaster ride that never ends.

I spend the rest of the afternoon at the paper trying to work on an article, but it's a waste of time. Between Devin's whispered proposal and Dominic's job offer my concentration is completely shot.

Glancing around, I wonder just how much I'd miss it. The deadlines. The hustle. The working my way up the ladder. Dominic Barkley just offered me the whole ladder—complete with affordable benefits, a 401K, and a six-figure salary.

But he's a creep.

Granted, most politicians are, but this particular man had me followed. Investigated. All because he thought I was hot? It's overkill, for sure, but he backed off. And now, he's offering me a dream job. I could truly be Devin's equal. I could bring something to the relationship besides me and our baby.

I'd be nuts not to consider it.

You aren't Devin's usual type.

Recalling Dominic's comment makes me open my web browser and type *Devin McAllister's girlfriends* into the search engine. Several images pop up, and most include Devin with his arm wrapped around some beautiful woman that isn't me. Because I'm a glutton for punishment, I click on one of the pictures of him and a gorgeous woman with long black hair. According to the caption, her name's Nina Drummond. The picture had been taken at a benefit he attended after Megan's wedding but *before* I told him I was pregnant.

Still, I want to know more about her.

A search for Nina Drummond reveals that she's an attorney with a firm in Memphis. A graduate of Harvard Law, she's obviously intelligent, certainly beautiful, and most definitely wealthy.

Dominic's right. I'm not Devin's usual type at all.

Irrational jealousy consumes me.

I close the browser.

Stop this. He loves you. You are having his baby. He said he wants to marry you.

But can I keep him?

And more importantly, do I deserve him?

Shaking my head, I reach for my cell. I know I'm spiraling into a jealous, insecure rage, and there's only one person who can snap me out of it.

Ice cream emergency. Meet me at the mall?

I hit send.

"Have those pregnancy hormones deprived you of your

common sense? You can't be seriously considering working for that man."

I should have called Megan.

With a heavy sigh, I dip my spoon into the gigantic sundae in the middle of our table.

"This thing needs more caramel," I mutter.

"Don't ignore me, Franklin."

"Yes, Lorie, I'm considering it. It's an amazing opportunity."

"If it were any other mayor, I'd agree with you. But *this*? This is a terrible offer, and to be quite honest, I'm having a hard time believing you don't *see* that it's a terrible offer. The man *stalked* you, Callie. Something is clouding your judgment and I'd like to know what it is."

Lorie's world is very black and white. Right and wrong. Good and evil. I don't know why I thought she'd understand.

"Is he blackmailing you?"

"No."

"Then explain it to me. Give me one good reason why taking this job would be a good thing?"

"I can give you *one hundred thousand* good reasons."

"So it's the money."

I nod.

"Have you forgotten your baby daddy is filthy rich?"

"I'm not worried about us having enough money, Lorie."

"Then what is it?"

"I'm bringing nothing to this relationship."

Lorie eyes me skeptically. "You're bringing *you*. You're bringing that baby. What else do you need to bring?"

I sigh deeply and place my spoon on my napkin. "I'm assuming the whole family has money. Including Owen. Right?"

"So?"

"So doesn't that . . . intimidate you?"

She shakes her head. "Not at all, and you know why? Because they're good people. They've welcomed us both into their family, and I know for a fact they're crazy about you. Devin is apparently a changed man since he fell in love with you *and* you're giving them a grandbaby. Thanks for that, by the way."

"What do you mean?"

"Oh, I just have to live up to Saint Callie. No pressure there."

"Bite me."

She winks. "Seriously, where's all this coming from?"

"Devin and I went baby shopping. It was just . . . very eye-opening. And Devin wanted top-of-the-line furniture, nothing but the very best—"

"The *nerve* of that man."

"We split the bill, but only because I insisted. He planned on paying for every bit of it. Every diaper, every blanket, every—"

"I get it, Callie. What I don't get is why this is a problem."

"I want to be his equal, Lorie."

She regards me thoughtfully.

"Why do you let her do it?"

"I . . . don't know what you're talking about."

"Your mother. The woman lives four hours away and

she still has this amazing ability to make you feel like you're undeserving and unworthy. All that *don't-be-dependent-on-a-man* bullshit she drilled into your head since you were a little girl. It's ridiculous, Callie."

I start to argue, but it's no use. She's right.

"Has Devin made you feel less than his equal? Ever?"

"No."

"Do you love him?"

"You know I do."

"Are you carrying his child?"

I roll my eyes and point to my swollen belly.

"You will never be his equal. And he will never be yours."

My eyes narrow. "Meaning?"

Lorie picks her up her spoon and dips it into the caramel. "Don't you see? You are bringing his baby into the world. He can't do that. What *can* he do? He can buy the baby expensive shit for the nursery and worship the ground you walk on. *That's* what he can do. And he's doing it. Let him do it. In return, you carry and nurture the little girl that's growing inside you, and you love Devin with all your heart. Money will never make you equal. Love makes you equal."

Her words sink deep into my soul, and I wipe away the tears that start to trickle down my cheeks. She's right, of course, and I'm surprised by Lorie's gentle words and quiet demeanor. She's never this philosophical and soft-spoken. It's kind of nice.

"But this Dominic Barkley bullshit? Devin's never going to let that happen."

And just like that, the real Lorie's back.

"This is my decision, Lorie."

"Actually, it's not just yours. You want to be equals, remember? Your decisions affect him and vice versa. Devin will tell you not to take this job, because a good man protects the woman he loves from slime balls like Dominic Barkley, especially when his woman loses all common sense and considers a job offer from her former stalker. Are you insane?"

After my verbal lashing from one of my best friends, I take a walk through the mall to clear my head. It's just October, but some of the stores are already decorating for Thanksgiving and Christmas. It makes me wonder how the McAllisters celebrate the holidays. Do they have a big dinner and watch football on Thanksgiving Day? Do they open presents on Christmas Eve or Christmas morning? Those weren't my Christmas traditions, of course. Growing up, Dad worked most holidays, which didn't matter because Mom wasn't much of a cook. After they divorced, I shuttled between the two of them until I got old enough to rebel against the custody agreement and stayed with Dad full-time. We started our own traditions. Like opening gifts on Christmas Eve just so we could sleep in the next day. Or making snow angels in the backyard and snowmen in the front. It actually felt like the holidays when I was with my dad, and it had nothing to do with the presents under the tree.

Money doesn't buy happiness.

That's what I want for our baby. I want her to have the love and security I never really felt, and I know with Devin, his family, and my dad, she will. She would be spoiled rotten and hopelessly adored. Even if we never get married, our kid would never be forced to live with me in one city and with her dad in another because we would never, ever let that happen. Even if things don't work out between us, we would stay close for the sake of our daughter.

Of this, I'm positive.

I just wish I could be as certain about everything else in my life.

"Hi, sweetheart. Doing some window shopping?"

I turn to find Devin's mom standing right next to me.

"Just taking a walk. Clearing my head." I nod toward the multitude of bags in her hands. "I see you've been busy."

Valerie laughs—a warm, motherly laugh that curls my toes and makes me ache for my own mother who rarely laughed that way.

"Rumor has it I have a granddaughter on the way. I hope you like pink."

This is a good mom. I want to be a good mom.

"Pink's . . . great." I smile, but my voice breaks a little. Of course she notices, because she's a good mom.

"Bad day?"

"No, just . . . an emotional one, I guess."

She nods. "I remember. Those mommy hormones wreak

havoc, don't they?"

"Yeah."

Valerie smiles kindly. "What can I do?"

I wipe my eyes and offer her the best smile I can muster. "You can take me home."

Chapter 30

Callie

Half an hour later, I'm sitting with Valerie in her kitchen. She sips her tea while I ramble on about my crazy life.

I hadn't needed to clarify when I asked her to take me home. She knew.

Valerie listens with rapt attention while I talk about the baby. Her eyes shine with happiness and pride when I tell her about Devin's bargaining tactics with our daughter during the ultrasound and the shopping spree that followed.

"Life sounds pretty wonderful. So why isn't Mommy happy?"

"Because Mommy is feeling inadequate and undeserving."

To my surprise, she nods in understanding.

"It's overwhelming, isn't it? You have this beautiful baby growing inside you and a man who would move heaven and earth to make you happy."

When she puts it like that, I feel guilty. How many women can't have babies? How many women have asshole boyfriends?

"I know I'm lucky."

"You are, but I understand it. William was finishing up med school when I got pregnant. Then we found out we were having twins. By the time Devin and Shyann were born, he was working full-time at the hospital. I was alone a lot. William's mom and dad moved closer just to help us with the kids. They were retired and more than happy to dote on their grandchildren on a permanent basis."

I smile. "I bet that was a relief."

"Oh, it was. I know a lot of people complain about their in-laws, but not me. Mine were amazing people. It did take some time for me to feel comfortable around them. I hadn't grown up with the same luxuries as William and his family, so I felt . . . insecure. Undeserving. Unworthy."

Valerie pours herself another cup of tea and offers me more cookies.

"No, thanks. Can I ask you a question?"

"Sure."

"How did you overcome it? The insecurity, I mean."

"It took time, but I finally accepted that just because we came from different backgrounds didn't mean I was unworthy of his love . . . or his family's love. I was a good mother and good wife. That's all I needed to be. In the grand scheme of things, that's what really mattered."

The phone rings from the living room, and Valerie excuses herself to answer it. She's gone for a while, so I head to my favorite place in the house—the room with the piano. Sitting on the bench, I slowly lift the lid, letting my hands wander aimlessly along the keys as I start to play. My mood has always dictated the movement of my fingers, so the song is haunting and sad. While I play, I glance at the picture frames on top of the piano. One's of Devin, decked out in a cap and gown. He looks young, so I can only assume it's from his high school graduation. Most graduates are all smiles, but not him, and it's easy to understand why.

He graduated without his twin by his side.

Tears spill down my cheeks as I finish the song, and suddenly, a pair of warm, strong arms encircle me and lift me off the bench. Devin's smell surrounds me. I bury my face against his neck as he carries me upstairs.

We enter a bedroom, and he lowers me down onto the bed. Our eyes lock, giving me a glimpse of the mixture of love and fear he's feeling right now. I smile softly and brush my fingers across his cheek as he slowly undresses me. Devin pulls his shirt over his head and pushes down his slacks, and within seconds, he's pressed against me. I don't think about the fact that his mom's just downstairs. I don't even think about whose bed we're in. I just whisper his name against his heated skin and hold on tight to the man I love.

"I really hope this is a guest room."

"It is now. It used to be my bedroom." Devin sighs softly and kisses the side of my neck. "You scared me to death, Callie."

I lift my head. "Why?"

"I got a call from Malik. I'm sorry Dominic got that close to you. It won't happen again."

My body tenses, prompting Devin to hold me close.

"He won't bother you anymore."

I have to tell him. I'm going to have to tell him eventually, anyway.

"Devin, he wasn't bothering me. He . . . offered me a job on his mayoral staff."

He bolts up in bed. "You've got to be kidding me."

"As his senior speech writer."

He tiredly rubs his face. "The nerve of that bastard. What was his reaction when you told him to go to hell?"

"I . . . didn't. I mean, I haven't decided yet."

A deathly silence hangs in the bedroom. After a few tense minutes, Devin gently turns my face toward him.

"Don't tell me you're actually considering this."

"My salary would be six figures, Devin."

"I don't give a shit if it'll make you a billionaire, Callie!"

"Stop screaming. Your mom will worry."

"Mom left as soon as I got here. She called me because she thought I needed to know you were . . . what's the word she used? Oh yeah. *Emotional.* I assumed it was because Dominic cornered you at the park, but I guess I was wrong. You're upset because you're considering this job offer, and you know I won't let you do it."

"You won't *let* me?" I swiftly climb out of bed and reach for my blouse. Who does he think he is? "I don't suppose we can talk calmly and rationally about this?"

"No, because there's nothing to talk about, Callie. Have you forgotten that the man stalked you?"

"He apologized."

"Well, as long as he apologized . . ."

"Stop it, Devin."

He watches me get dressed. "This is about the money, isn't it? You think just because you'll be making six figures that you'll be happy? He's an asshole, Callie. He wants you, and he doesn't give a shit that you're mine and pregnant with my child."

"I'm not yours."

Devin slowly climbs out of bed and walks over to me. If it were any other man, I'd be afraid of the intense look in his eyes. But he loves me. I love him. And I'm not scared.

My back presses against the wall as his body leans close to mine. He trails his nose across my cheek before kissing the edge of my mouth.

"You are mine . . . body and soul, and you know it. I love you so much I can barely breathe."

My body trembles when his lips slide along my neck.

"What's your plan, Devin? Kiss me into submission?"

He takes a step back.

"Callie, do you honestly think for one second that I'm going to let you put yourself and our baby at risk by working for him?"

"I don't want to fight with you, and I didn't want to keep it from you. I'm simply telling you that he made me an offer. I'd be crazy not to consider it."

"No, Callie."

"We'll see."

"Over my dead body."

His eyes blaze, but I hold my head high and stare right back at him. I won't let him boss me around. No matter how much I love him.

"I love you, Devin."

"Do you?"

I know he doesn't mean it, but it breaks my heart anyway.

"You know I do. But I've been making my own decisions for a long time."

"Things are different now. It's not just about you anymore."

"I know."

I walk around him and head for the door. He's not rational right now, and to be honest, neither am I. We both need some space.

"Don't walk out on me, Callie."

"Don't treat me like a child."

"Don't act like one."

I step out into the hallway and slam the door behind me.

My silent phone rests in my hand. Not a call. Not a text. Nothing.

He's not coming home.

I stare at the clock on my cell, the numbers taunting me. With every passing minute, I'm reminded I'm all alone.

I walked out, and he didn't chase me.

Selfishly, I admit that's what I expected because that's how we are. We fight. We say things we don't mean. We make up. It's what we do. Because no matter how mad I am, or how mad he is, we always find our way back to each other. He always comes back to me. To us.

He's not coming back tonight.

I've finally done it. I've pushed him away. My desire to be an equal provider for our daughter has brought me here—to this cold, dark place where I'm all alone.

No amount of money is worth this.

I throw back the covers and sit up in bed. I'm hungry, but I can't eat. I'm exhausted, but I can't sleep. Desperate to talk to him, I send him another text. He hasn't replied to any of them so far, and he's not answering his phone, but I send it anyway. I tell him I won't take the job, and I mean it.

Screw my stubborn independence.

Lorie's right. Even from hundreds of miles away, my mom has this insane power over me. Her voice still rattles around in my brain, telling me to focus on the wrong things for all the wrong reasons. Feeding on my insecurities to the point that I actually considered accepting a job offer from a man who makes my skin crawl.

You're so stupid, Callie.

Pulling my knees close to my chest, I wrap my arms around my legs and start to cry.

Nothing new. I've cried all night.

Earlier tonight, I'd given the delivery boy from the baby store a heart attack when he arrived with the furniture. As he brought the boxed crib into the nursery, he told me the store would have been happy to assemble it for us, but Mr. McAllister had been adamant about putting it together himself.

I'd dissolved into tears right then and there.

The guy quickly brought in the rest of the furniture, and as soon as I signed my name, he was gone in a flash. Through teary eyes, I gazed at all the baby furniture and then quickly closed the nursery door.

It's so beautiful I can't even look at it.

My rocking becomes frantic as my exhausted and emotional mind begins to spiral into a pit of anxiety. In my head, I can hear my mom, telling me that, just as she predicted, I've ended up alone. I hear Lorie's warning that Devin would react this way. And I can hear him screaming at me and calling me a child.

My chest tightens and my heart pounds as their taunting voices start to mingle.

I can't breathe. Why can't I breathe?

The bedroom spins in and out of focus.

Something's wrong with me.

Something's wrong with the baby.

My phone's still in my hand. I tap a number. I have no idea which one until I hear Valerie's voice.

"Callie? What's—"

"Can't . . . breathe."

She doesn't ask any more questions, and the next thing I know, Devin's parents are there.

"Callie? Callie, what's wrong?" Valerie sits down on the bed next to me. "Where's Devin?"

I just close my eyes and try to will my body to stop shaking so much.

The next thing I know, William is cradling me to his chest and carrying me out of my apartment.

Chapter 31

DEVIN

I place the glass against my temple. "Make it a double."

The bartender shoots me a look but pours me another drink anyway. My head pounds, and the bright lights of the club don't help. Shit's sliding in and out of focus, but it's preferable to the hell that's been playing in a continuous loop inside my head.

It's been twelve hours since she walked away from me. Twelve hours since I screamed at her. Twelve hours since the woman I love more than anything turned into a complete stranger right in front of my eyes.

Obviously, I hadn't been clear enough when I told Dominic I'd kill him. I'll rectify that . . . just as soon as I can walk out of this bar.

Callie had left me, and I'd let her. I won't chase her. Not this time. She can bat those beautiful eyes all she wants, but this is the one time I'm not giving in.

There's no way in hell she's working for that man.

I down my drink.

Money.

It's the root of all evil and the death of so many marriages.

Marriage.

I asked her to marry me. Had she heard me? Did she even care?

And what is this sudden fixation with money? Did she not realize my family's loaded? Doesn't she understand money will never be an issue? Of course, we'd never really talked about that.

We haven't talked about a lot of things.

I wave at the bartender, but he finally man's up and cuts me off. That's okay. There's not enough booze in this place to make tonight any better.

"You look like hell," a smooth voice whispers in my ear. "Rough day at the office?"

I look to my right to find Nina Drummond sitting on the stool next to me. She smiles before ordering herself a drink.

"Hello, Nina."

She looks like sin, of course, in her skin-tight blouse with the top two buttons undone. With her long pencil skirt and stilettos, she's every man's fantasy.

Every man except me.

"I detect a slur, counselor. Just how much have you had to drink?"

"Not nearly enough. What are you doing in town?"

"Working on a merger. Remember? With Spellman

Communications? I told you about it."

I don't remember, but I pretend I do. We make small talk for a while before my eyes finally begin to grow heavy.

I have to call a cab. Or Owen.

"You look tired, baby," Nina coos in my ear. "I'll be in town for the next two days. Why don't you and I take this pity party back to my hotel?

I try to focus on her face. When I do, I'm reminded how easy it used to be with Nina. No strings. No expectations. No emotion. No heartache.

No Callie.

I reach into my wallet and throw some cash on the bar. "I don't think so, Nina. I'm just gonna call myself a cab and head home."

I manage to climb off the stool, but walking isn't so easy. Nina takes pity on me and does her best to hold me up. She loops her arm through mine and helps me out of the bar.

"Just . . . get my cell out of my pocket and call my brother."

Nina waves to someone, and the next thing I know, there's a guy wearing a chauffer's hat helping me into a long black car. The two of us pile into the backseat, and I mutter a curse when the car starts to move.

"Just close your eyes," Nina whispers softly, lacing her fingers with mine. "I'll get you home. Just relax and let me take care of you."

I'm too tired and too drunk to argue.

Besides, if Callie can do something stupid, why can't I?

Rays of light stream through the blinds. With a groan, I curse the sun and throw the blanket over my head.

Worst hangover ever.

Then I recall my bender from the night Callie told me she was pregnant.

Correction. *That* was the worst hangover ever.

Still, this one's rough, and the constant vibration of my cell isn't helping. I ignore it for what seems like forever until I finally give up and reach for it on my nightstand. I blink my eyes until I can focus on the name on the caller ID.

"What do you want, Owen?"

"Where the hell have you been?"

"I . . . don't know. Here, I think."

"Where's here?"

"My apartment."

He sighs. "The one place I didn't look. We've been trying to call you all night. Why haven't you been answering your phone?"

"Because Callie and I got into a fight and then I got drunk, okay?"

"God, you're an idiot," he mutters tiredly. "Listen, you need to get to the hospital. I don't know what's wrong. I just know that Callie called Mom, and Mom and Dad took her to the ER."

I bolt out of bed. "The hospital? Owen, what's—"

"I don't know. I just got here. Something about Callie's blood pressure being through the roof. Just get your ass here."

The line goes dead.

Time stands still.

The world stops turning.

And then I scream.

I've never been a religious man, but during my frenzied drive to the hospital, I find myself bartering my soul.

"Please let them be okay," I whisper. "I'll do anything. Give anything. Do anything. Just tell me what you want. Tell me what I need to do."

Surely God isn't this angry with me. He won't take them away from me. He won't rip my heart and soul out of my chest. God wouldn't do that. Not again.

Would He?

Divine intervention must take the wheel, because suddenly I'm at the hospital. I rush through the emergency room doors and immediately crash into my brother's iron chest.

"Whoa . . ." Owen grabs my arms and holds me steady. "Calm down."

"Where is she?"

"You have to calm down."

My voice is a pained whisper. "For the love of God, Owen, please tell me she's okay."

Tears run down my cheeks. The last time I cried was fifteen years ago.

I won't survive it again. I can't.

"She's okay," he says, and I feel relief course through my veins.

"And the baby?"

"Baby's fine, too."

I exhale a shaky breath and slump against the wall. "What the hell happened?"

"From what I understand, Callie was waiting up all night for my asshole brother to come home. When he didn't— and when he refused to answer his phone after about the hundredth call—she had a complete meltdown that led to an anxiety attack. She called Mom. The panic attack made her blood pressure spike. I don't know the difference between a systolic and a diastolic, but apparently, it wasn't good. It's better now."

"I want to see her."

"I'll take you, but if you wake her up, Mom will kick your ass into next week. She's *pissed*."

"I know, okay? Just tell me the room number."

"No, you *don't* know!" Owen's irate voice echoes down the hall. "The mother of your child needed you and you weren't there. I thought falling in love would straighten your ass up, but you haven't changed a bit."

"That's . . . not true."

I *am* a changed man. Nina Drummond can attest to

that. She'll never speak to me again, and that's fine. She never liked to be ignored or denied, and I'd shattered her ego once again by refusing her invitation last night. She and her driver had helped me inside, but when she offered to stay, I politely asked her to leave. Because even in my drunken stupor, she wasn't what I needed. She wasn't *who* I needed. And she wasn't who I wanted for the rest of my life.

But I also know I don't deserve a medal for resisting temptation last night. My ass should have been home with my girl.

Owen sighs heavily and places his hand on my shoulder. "Couples fight. If you get drunk every time you guys have an argument, you're going to be a raging alcoholic. Grow up, McAllister."

I nod.

"Second floor. Room 212. I'm going to work now, but if you upset her, I will come back and kick your ass."

"If I upset her, I'll let you."

When I step into the room, the first thing I see is my mother. She's sitting with her back to the door, but I can see that she's holding Callie's hand.

"It's about time," Mom whispers.

"I know."

I sigh heavily and walk over to the bed. Callie's sleeping

peacefully, but seeing her in a hospital bed, with her blonde hair splayed across the stark white pillow, conjures images in my head that I've blocked out for more than a decade.

"Here," she says, offering me her chair. "You look like you're about to pass out."

"I'm okay. It's just . . ."

Mom places her hand on my shoulder. "I know. Which is why I'm not going to tell you how disappointed I am. I'm going to assume that this will never, ever happen again."

"It won't, Mom."

"Good."

Leaning over the bed, I kiss Callie's forehead before placing another kiss on her stomach. With a heavy sigh, I crumble into the chair. When I reach for her hand, Callie sighs softly in her sleep, and with that small, insignificant sound, I feel my body finally start to relax.

"Her blood pressure's better now?"

"Yes. Dr. Clifton thinks he may keep her overnight, just to be safe. He also mentioned bedrest, which she won't be happy about, so be ready for a fight."

"No. No more fighting."

She nods. "Are you okay?"

"I am now."

Time passes slowly. At some point, Dr. Clifton arrives to talk to us. He tells us that Callie's blood pressure has improved and the baby is perfectly fine. He does want to keep her for observation, and if her vitals are still good, she can go home in the morning.

"What about bed rest?"

"Not yet. But I do want her to come see me once a week so that I can keep an eye on it. When you get back home tomorrow, have Callie call to schedule an appointment."

"I will. Thanks, Dr. Clifton."

After he leaves, Callie's nurse comes in and kindly but firmly reminds us about visiting hours. Mom takes the hint and gives me a hug, with the promise that she'll call in the morning.

"And as for you, Mr. McAllister," the nurse says. "Dr. Clifton says you'd like a cot?"

I breathe a sigh of relief. I'm glad the doctor realized I wasn't leaving her side. Not for a minute.

"I would. Thank you."

She smiles and tells me she'll be right back. I sit down next to Callie's bed and reach for her hand once again.

"Devin?"

My head jerks up. Her eyes flutter open.

"I'm right here, Songbird."

She squeezes my hand and smiles.

"Is the baby okay?"

"She's fine."

Tears fill her eyes.

"Are *we* okay?"

I lift her hand to my lips. "We're perfect."

"You have to forgive me."

"There's nothing to forgive, Callie." I lean over her and kiss her softly.

"I was so stupid, Devin. I'm sorry."

"I'm sorry, too." I wipe away her tears and smile. "I'm

sorry for the stupid fight and I'm sorry I wasn't there last night."

The bed's small, but I have to hold her, so I pull back the blanket and climb in next to her. Callie snuggles close to my chest, and I hold her close. She melts into me, and for the first time since I stepped into this hospital, I feel the tension drain from my body.

"Say you forgive me," she whispers.

"Only if you forgive me."

She nods.

"Now try to relax. They'll kick me out of here if you get upset."

"Okay." Her eyes close, and I brush away what's left of her tears.

There's so much more we need to say, but it can wait. With a tired sigh, I press my lips to her hair, and we drift off into a peaceful sleep.

Chapter 32

DEVIN

The next morning, Callie's discharged from the hospital, with strict orders to take it easy and to cut back on her hours at the newspaper. I'm due in court, so Mom offers to help Callie get settled in at home. On the way to the courthouse, I call my secretary and tell her to make sure my calendar is clear for the weekend, because Callie and I are turning off our phones and spending the next two days hibernating at home.

But first, I have to tell her about Nina.

It's a conversation I'm not looking forward to, for very obvious reasons. But, if there's one thing I've learned, it's that the truth always comes out eventually. Regardless of the fact that nothing happened with Nina, I know it's important to be upfront about my whereabouts last night.

When I get home later that afternoon, I find Callie on

the couch, wrapped up in a blanket and watching television.

"Hi, baby. I'm happy to see you're following doctor's orders."

She flips through the channels. "Did you know daytime TV sucks these days? There's like . . . four soap operas on the air. It's just talk shows and reality stars. Where did all the soaps go? I used to love *Guiding Light*."

With a grin, I loosen my tie and join her on the couch. "Bored are we?"

"You have no idea. If Dr. Clifton puts me on bedrest I will seriously die."

"We have eight hundred channels, Callie."

"And they all suck. But yes, I am following orders and taking it easy."

"I'm very happy to hear that. Are you hungry?"

Callie turns off the television. "Yes, but first . . . could we just talk about all the things we need to talk about so that we can get it out of the way and enjoy the weekend?"

I smile. My Songbird has zero patience.

"I know we need to talk, but I don't want you getting upset."

"I'll stay calm. Promise."

"What about your blood pressure?"

She nods toward the digital monitor on the end table. "Your mom insisted on stopping at the pharmacy on the way home. I've been checking it every few hours."

"And it's good?"

"Yep."

"Okay, let's talk."

Callie smiles and snuggles close to my side. I nuzzle her hair and breathe her in, thankful she's in my arms and safe.

"I'm sorry I didn't come home."

"Where were you?"

"At a bar, drinking myself into a stupor. That's what I do when my entire world comes crashing down around me. It's only happened a few times in my life."

"But twice because of me," she says softly. "You went on a bender the night you found out I was pregnant, too."

"But that's not your fault. Like Owen said, if I get drunk every time we have an issue—"

"You'll be an alcoholic."

I nod.

"You were so mad at me, Devin."

"I was scared for you. Why, Callie? Why would you want to work for that man?"

She sighs. "I didn't. Not really. I have this deep need to bring something to our relationship and to provide equally for our little family. Dominic dangled this huge carrot in front of my face. I just thought I should consider it."

"But working for him isn't the answer. You have to know that."

"I do, and truthfully, I don't think I would have accepted it. But when you start giving me orders, I get defensive. Telling me I can't isn't the answer, either. We have to be able to talk about stuff like this."

"I understand. But you also have to understand that if I think you could potentially get hurt, I'm going to do everything in my power to make sure that doesn't happen."

"You can't protect me from everything, Devin."

I kiss the tip of her nose. "Watch me."

Callie smiles.

Taking a deep breath, I pull her close. "As long as we're being honest, I need to tell you what happened at the bar."

"Okay . . ."

"I ran into an old . . . I don't know what you'd call her. Girlfriend's not the word. A former hook-up, I guess."

"A woman."

"Yes. Nothing happened. She and her driver took me home. When she asked to stay, I declined, and then I passed out until Owen called me the next morning."

"Was it Nina Drummond?"

The question surprises me. I didn't even realize she knew Nina.

"It was. How do you—"

"The Internet is an amazing place. You just type *Devin McAllister's girlfriends* and all these gorgeous women pop up." Callie stares down at her knotted fingers. "Nina's a lawyer. And beautiful."

"She's not important."

"Why did you turn her down?"

"Because she's not you." I trail my fingertip from her temple to her chin. "All I want is you, Songbird. For the rest of my life."

Callie sighs softly. "Speaking of that, I have a confession, too."

"Okay."

"I heard you say that you wanted to marry me."

"I wondered." With a grin, I bring her hand to my lips and kiss it gently. "What do you think about that?"

"I think you should know I'm not opposed to living in sin."

I chuckle. "I bet your father would have other ideas."

"Oh, please. I seem to recall some hundred dollar bet between the two of you. Plus I'm pregnant. He *knows*, Devin. Besides, he owes me. Seeing Dad with my math teacher has given me years of ammunition."

"Very true. So, you'd say no if I proposed?"

She considered this. "Do you know two out of three marriages end in divorce?"

"I'm well aware. Why do you think I'm such a successful attorney?"

She rests her hand on her stomach. "I just don't want to end up like my parents."

"We won't, Callie. We'll end up like mine."

I lean close, kissing her softly. What I really should do is drop to my knees and beg her to marry me, right this minute. But I don't want to propose without a ring, and I don't want her thinking the only reason I'm proposing is because we had a fight. The timing's just not right, but someday, it will be.

Someday soon, the timing will be perfect.

I slide my hands along her waist and pull her into my lap. "Callie Franklin, you are the love of my life, and I am going to propose to you. You need to be prepared so you'll be ready with the correct response."

She smiles and wraps her arms around my neck. "And

the correct response would be?"

"Yes. A thousand times yes."

Later that night, when we're in bed and I can hear her soft snores in the darkness, I hold her close and whisper a silent prayer, thankful that I didn't screw up the very best thing that's ever happened to me.

I've never been a religious man, but tonight, I am.

Chapter 33

Callie

"Audrey?"

I shake my head. Devin marks the name off the list. We're nestled on the couch—me with the baby name book in my hand and Devin with a legal pad filled with potential baby names.

He tries again. "Katherine? Elizabeth?"

"Hmm. I'm sensing a pattern here. Do you have a thing for old Hollywood movie actresses?"

He mutters something before crossing both names off the list.

I feel a twinge of guilt. "Okay, I don't *hate* Elizabeth."

"Really?" Devin looks down at the paper. "Elizabeth McAllister. That's a lot of name for a little kid. What about Beth?"

"Beth McAllister." I let it roll off my tongue. "I think I

like it."

He grins and writes it down on the legal pad. "Middle name?"

I actually have an answer for this one. I've been toying with the idea for a while.

"I was thinking . . . Shyann."

His pen freezes on the page. "Really?"

"Elizabeth Shyann McAllister. What do you think?"

Devin tosses the pad aside and lunges for me. My laughter is swallowed by his kiss.

"I think I love it," he says, his voice filled with emotion. "And I love you. Thank you."

"I love you, too."

"Our daughter has a name," he whispers against my lips. "You know what this means?"

"We can get stuff monogrammed now?"

Devin grins.

"Not exactly. It means we need to give you a name, too."

I play along. "But I have a name."

"A new name."

"Hmm. I guess it does." I sigh heavily, as if this is just devastating news.

"Marry me, Songbird."

I press my forehead to his.

"Is this your official proposal?"

His face falls. "No. I mean, I *want* to. But I don't have the ring. I mean, I *have* it. It's just getting engraved."

Ooh! "Engraved with what?"

Devin smiles and glides his nose against mine. "It's a

surprise. But I won't propose without a ring. You're gonna love it. At least, I hope you love it. I think you'll love—"

I silence him with a kiss. Devin McAllister's so sentimental. Who knew?

"I'll love it."

The cemetery is peaceful and serene, just as you'd expect a cemetery to be. It's actually kind of beautiful, with pink and yellow wildflowers growing between the marble stones. Devin's planned the entire day, and while this stop along the way had been a definite surprise, I can see by the expression on his face that this moment is important to him. Therefore, it's important to me.

Today, I get to meet Shyann.

Devin gazes down at the grave. I watch silently as he kneels and traces the letters of her name.

"Hey, Shy. I know it's been a while. Life's been . . . insane, but I want to introduce you to Callie."

He holds my hand as he tells his sister all about us and the baby. I'm sincerely happy to be here, even though I can't help feeling that I'm intruding on a sacred moment between brother and sister. But when I try to step away to give him privacy, Devin just pulls me into his arms and keeps talking about everything that's happened and is still happening to us. He tells her about my blood pressure scare and how I've cut back on my hours at the newspaper. And how Megan is now coming three times a week to do yoga and meditation with me. I stand there quietly while he shares the inconsequential events in our life together, and the sentiment only makes me love him more.

Once we're back in the car, Devin's quiet as we head toward the interstate.

"Thank you for bringing me to meet her."

He squeezes my hand and drives on. It's not an awkward silence at all. I know he's just lost in memories, so I sit quietly and hold his hand as we head to the first of three houses we're viewing today.

House hunting hadn't been a priority until we took a good look at all the furniture we bought and realized it won't fit in my apartment. After much discussion, we both agreed we wanted a house just outside the city, with a big backyard for our daughter. Devin contacted a realtor and gave her a budget, only to learn that the Nashville real estate market is ridiculous and anything decent in a good neighborhood is going to cost us. So far, we'd viewed four homes, but none of them had everything we're looking for.

"Maybe we should just build," Devin says as he exits the highway. The city fades into countryside, and I'm immediately reminded of my hometown.

"Maybe we should. We'd still have to look for land."

He sighs tiredly. "I know. Maybe we'll get lucky today. Ellen seemed excited when she called about this one."

Ellen, our realtor, has been nothing but patient. Of course, she would be, since she wants to get paid.

A few minutes later, Devin takes a right and we enter the neighborhood of Bridle Trails. Million dollar homes surround us. My mouth drops open when Devin parks the car in front of one of them.

"You've got to be kidding."

He turns off the ignition. "I know it looks big, but it's actually very homey and comfortable inside. And it's in our price range."

"You've already seen it?"

"Just the pictures online."

"It's so beautiful, Devin."

He smiles. "Good. That's half the battle. Want to check it out?"

I nod, and the two of us head toward the front door. Ellen's right there to greet us. She excitedly opens the door and waves us inside.

"Did you have any trouble finding the place? I know it's kind of hidden."

Devin shakes his head. "Not at all. Thanks for showing it to us on such short notice."

"Oh, it's my pleasure." Ellen smiles at me. I had loved her immediately. With her sweet smile and beautiful gray hair, she kind of reminds me of my grandma. "How are you feeling, Callie?"

"I feel great, thanks. And this place is gorgeous."

"Isn't it?" Ellen leads us through the family room. With the pleasantries out of the way, she's suddenly all business. "Four bedrooms. Four baths. A den and remodeled kitchen, with cherry cabinets, granite countertops, and new stainless steel appliances. There's a hot tub. Of course, that'll have to wait until after the baby's born, but it's a wonderful feature of the house. Oh, and there's a tennis court out back."

As we follow her upstairs, I whisper to Devin. "Do you play tennis?"

"Nope."

We smile at each other as Ellen continues her sales pitch. The master bedroom is gigantic. While the other bedrooms aren't as large, they're definitely bigger than the ones in my apartment. I can see Devin mentally measuring.

"This room's perfect for the nursery," he says.

I grin.

Smelling a sale, Ellen grins, too.

She finishes her spiel by telling us about the great school district and friendly neighborhood, but it's unnecessary. I love it, and by the look on Devin's face, he loves it, too.

"I'll give you guys some time to talk." Ellen says, giving us a bright smile before making her way downstairs.

Devin wraps his arms around my waist. "So, what do you think?"

"*This* is honestly in our price range?" It's a legitimate question. The house has a tennis court, for crying out loud.

"That's not what I asked. Tell me what you think and then I'll tell you how much it costs."

"I love it. I just don't know if the tennis court's necessary."

"It's not. We can have it removed."

Of course we can. "Well then, I think it's perfect."

"Good. And yes, it's in our price range. But is this really what you want? That's what's most important."

My eyes ghost along the hardwood floors and the French doors of the master bedroom. It has everything I could ever want in a house—minus the tennis court, of course.

I turn my attention back to the man I love and see the excitement in his eyes.

How can I possibly say no?

"I want it."

Devin's smile makes me weak in the knees.

"Then it's yours."

After my nightly blood pressure check—110/70 thank you very much—the two of us climb into bed. We have a little ritual. I lie on my back for as long as it's comfortable while Devin's head rests on my stomach as he reads to the baby. Tonight's story is *The Velveteen Rabbit.* Closing my eyes, I run my fingers through his hair as his soft voice washes over me.

"Real isn't how you are made," said the Skin Horse. "It's a thing that happens to you. When a child loves you for a long, long time, not just to play with, but REALLY loves you, then you become real."

"Does it hurt?" asked the Rabbit.

"Sometimes," said the Skin Horse, for he was always truthful. "When you are real you don't mind being hurt."

I smile softly and gaze down at the man I love. The man

who wants to be my husband. We have so much to learn about each other, but I know enough. The important things.

The *real* things.

Devin loves me. He loves our baby. I have a feeling he'll be like my dad. Laid back but protective. Firm but loving. He'll never make our daughter feel like a burden, or a mistake, or a nuisance.

Suddenly, a fluttering in my stomach makes me gasp, and he jerks his head away from my stomach.

"Was that—"

Tears fill my eyes. Even though the baby book says most mothers feel the baby move by the twentieth week, I'm well into my second trimester and haven't felt a thing. Dr. Clifton hadn't seemed concerned when I mentioned it.

"What did the book say?" Devin asks. "That it would feel like a quickening . . . or butterflies. Right?"

"That's exactly how it felt."

I gasp again, and this time, Devin's hands are all over me. "Where?"

With laughter bubbling from my lips, I take his hand and position it right where I felt the butterflies. His smile takes my breath away.

"She's really in there," he whispers in amazement. "I mean, I *know* she's in there, but—"

I lace my fingers with his. "I know. She's just more real now."

He grins. "Have you felt her move before?"

"Not that I've noticed. Maybe she liked your story."

"Then I'll have to read it every night."

For the next hour, we lay quietly with our fingers pressed against my swollen stomach, but the baby apparently decides she's done entertaining us for the night because the feeling subsides. I can't be disappointed, though, because I know this is just the first of so many amazing moments.

Real moments.

And I get to share them all with Devin.

It's long past midnight, but I can't sleep. Instead, I sit by the window and gaze at the flickering street lights, letting the sound of Devin's snores relax me while I think about the one thing that's been weighing heavily on my mind for the past few nights.

My mom.

Maybe it's because of how quickly Valerie came to my rescue and how she continues to mother me, but I've been wondering how much my relationship with Kim might have been different if she'd been more . . . motherly. More understanding. Compassionate. Encouraging. That's the type of mom I want to be for our daughter. Already, I feel this intense protectiveness for my baby, and she's not even here yet. Had Mom ever felt that way about me? Or have I always been a living, breathing reminder of her lost dreams?

Lifting my gown, I run my hand over my stomach. The skin's taut and I can already see stretch marks, but I don't care. Our baby is going to be surrounded by family and friends who love her.

Isn't that what every little girl wants?

Isn't that what every big girl wants, too?

As my due date draws closer, I find myself wanting to get everything in my life in its proper order. *Nesting*, the baby book calls it, and there will be plenty of it when we start moving into the house. But I also want to get my personal relationships on solid ground before the baby arrives, and that means I need to try to mend my relationship with my mother. At the same time, I have to let go of the shame she instilled in me and stop letting her poison my thoughts with her constant negativity.

Glancing at the bedside clock, I wonder if it's too late to call. Mom's a night owl like me, so I decide to take my chances. I grab my phone off the nightstand and head to the living room couch. Taking a deep breath, I dial her number.

"Callie?"

"Hey, Mom."

"Are you all right?"

"Yeah. I hope I didn't wake you."

"You didn't. I'm just editing some photos. How are you?"

I smile. "I'm good. Great, actually."

"That's wonderful. I guess the baby is coming soon?"

"In a few months, yeah. We're having a girl."

"And where will you live?"

"We've bought a house."

She's interested in the home's details. I can tell she's impressed by the square footage and the tennis court. Of course she is. It's expensive.

"Sounds gorgeous. It's not really your style, though, is it?"

"I know, but it's actually really cozy and comfortable. We hope to close later this week."

"And Devin's buying it, right?"

Here we go.

"No. We're buying it. Together."

"On your salary?" Mom laughs coldly. "Oh, Callie, it's perfectly fine to admit that Devin's the breadwinner in this relationship. I *am* glad to see you're embracing it. He won't marry you, and he won't stay once the baby's born, but at least you're letting him lavish you with gifts in the meantime. I knew I raised a smart girl."

I can tell her the truth. I can tell her Devin wants to get married and that he'll never leave me. I can tell her I'm going to get the happily ever after she never had.

I could say all of that, but I don't.

The truth is, she did raise a smart girl, because I'm seeing clearly for the very first time. My unplanned arrival turned my mother into a bitter person, but that's her problem, not mine. She chose to give up on her dreams. She decided money and material possessions were the most important things to her. And she's the one who gave up on her marriage.

Choices . . . every one of them.

I choose to not be like my mother.

"Your granddaughter will be here very soon. She will be loved and adored and never be made to feel like she ruined my life. She'll have a father like mine—one who is kind, generous, and loves her for who she is. And she'll have a family who will do everything in their power to love and protect her. It's up to you whether you want to be part of that."

Mom says nothing in response. I take her silence as a sign that our conversation is over.

"Goodnight, Mom."

With my mind filled with a contentment I've never known, I make my way back to bed. Devin's arms immediately find me and pull me close to his chest.

"Devin?"

He sighs softly and kisses the side of my neck. "Hmm?"

"Will you marry me?"

Chapter 34

DEVIN

This girl—this beautiful, incredible, amazing woman—is literally going to be the death of me.

"What did you say?"

She turns over and slides her arm along my waist.

"Will you marry me, Devin?"

I've wanted to ask her to marry me for weeks now. I've just been waiting on the ring so that I could plan and execute the most romantic proposal ever known to woman or man. I even have a speech prepared. But now, my plans have been blown because she just proposed to me.

Wait.

Callie just proposed to me.

"Don't tease me, Songbird. I don't think my heart could take it."

She traces my mouth with her fingertip. "I'm not teasing.

I want everything in its proper order before Beth arrives. I love you, you love me, and we love our kid. We're getting ready to move into our big, beautiful home. We should be a family—officially. It's time."

She sounds so sure, and my mind begins to race with possibilities. Screw the sentimental engraving. I'll book a flight to Vegas and marry her tonight. Today. Right now. What time is it? Does it even matter?

Nope. Doesn't matter at all.

I gaze into the eyes of the only woman who could bring me to my knees with just a touch. "I should be upset that you're raining on my parade, but I'm not."

"I want to be your wife before the baby arrives."

"I want to be your husband before the sun sets tomorrow."

Surprise flickers across her face, quickly replaced with a slow grin. "Really?"

"Really."

"Our parents would kill us."

"You're bringing their first grandchild into the world. They'll get over it."

Callie laughs and places my hand on her stomach. "Beth apparently likes the idea of eloping, too. Feel that?"

Sure enough, our daughter is kicking the crap out of her mom's belly. Our little girl, who's going to have me completely wrapped around her finger from the moment she's born. Many years from now, I'll walk her down the aisle and straight into the arms of a man who won't be anywhere near good enough for her.

Greg Franklin's face immediately pops into my mind.

No matter how much I want this *right now*, I can't take that moment away from Callie's dad.

"We should do this right. You deserve it."

Her forehead creases. "You mean . . ."

"Yep. Dress. Flowers. The whole thing."

"But—"

"Callie, nothing about us has been traditional. You should have a wedding, and your father deserves the chance to walk you down the aisle. I won't take that away from him, because I wouldn't want anyone to take it away from me."

Her eyes glisten with tears. "Wow."

"Is that a good *wow*?"

"It's a great *wow*. There's only one problem."

"What's that?"

"You didn't accept my proposal."

I smile and bury my face against her neck.

"Yes, Songbird. A thousand times yes."

After that night, time seemed to start moving at warp speed. Ellen, the realtor, knew we were anxious to move into the house as soon as possible, and with the homeowners more than ready to sell, we closed on the house later in the week. We hired movers and decorators and anyone else she'd let me pay to ensure that Callie did as little as possible. To my surprise, she wasn't at all interested in choosing furniture and drapes, so I gave Megan and Lorie my credit card and told them to go nuts. Simon and Owen had warned me those words were dangerous, but I didn't care. By the end of the week, we were moved in and the house was fully furnished. Most importantly, it'd been accomplished without adding one ounce of stress to my fiancée's life.

But now there's a wedding to plan.

And a crib to assemble.

That's my job, and it's proving difficult.

"Screw this *Slot A* into *Slot B* bullshit. Just give me the sideboards."

Simon laughs and hands me the directions. "I know we're guys, but maybe that's why it says *READ THIS FIRST* right here at the top."

I never imagined I'd be sitting with my brother and my best friend in the middle of a nursery, trying to assemble a crib. The instruction manual's the size of Callie's baby book.

It's just a rectangle. How hard can it possibly be?

Owen points to the red label on the wood. "That's *Slot C*, Devin. No wonder it doesn't fit."

With a groan, I toss the pieces back onto the carpet. "Why didn't I just let the store put it together?"

Simon flips through the pages of the manual. "Because this is part of the whole daddy experience."

Owen nods. "Plus, it's good practice for me. I'll be needing your help with this very same project in about seven months."

Stunned, I drop my screwdriver. "Seriously?"

He grins. "Yep. Lorie's pregnant. We found out last week."

"But you just met her!"

Simon chuckles. "Umm . . . actually, he met her at my wedding. Which is the exact same weekend you met Callie."

Oh yeah.

"And if I recall correctly," Owen says, "You knocked up Callie the first night you met her, so . . ."

"It could have been the second night," I mutter.

"Exactly, so save your indignation and just be happy for me."

I grin. "Are *you* happy?"

"I'm ecstatic."

"Then I'm happy for you. Getting married?"

"Not for a while. Lorie says one wedding is enough right now."

I can't disagree, because the girls are downstairs right now, making lists and setting up appointments with bakers, caterers, and bridal shops. Like a good groom, I once again handed over my credit card, and the three of us had made ourselves scarce by hiding out in the nursery.

For the next few hours, we work on the baby furniture. Now that we're actually reading the instructions, the crib starts to take shape. We then move on to the changing table and dresser, and before long, we have everything assembled and in its proper place, just like Callie wanted. All that's left are the curtains.

Owen and Simon sit down next to me in the middle of the floor while the three of us admire our handiwork. As I gaze around the room, I am amazed that *this* is my life. I'm a grown man, sitting on plush carpet, surrounded by pastel-painted walls and cherry baby furniture.

What was once in pieces is finally whole.

Just like my life.

Just like my heart.

"There you are," Lorie says. "Proud of yourselves?"

The three of us look to up to see our lovely ladies standing in the doorway. The smile on Callie's face tells me she loves it.

"Actually, yes," Owen says. Simon and I nod in agreement.

Megan snaps her fingers. "On your feet, McAllister. There's more work to be done."

I stand up and grin. "Yes, ma'am?"

"We'll get this cleaned up. You guys need to get down to the courthouse and apply for your marriage license."

"And the engraver called, so you can go pick up the rings," Lorie says.

I wind my arms around Callie's waist. "Anything else?"

Megan nods. "You need to call Callie's dad, get his blessing, and get him *here* next week."

"Done." I'm actually happy to have an excuse to escape the insanity for a while. If the look on Callie's face is any indication, she feels the same way.

I grab her hand and lead her downstairs, both of us happy to have some time ourselves.

"Wow," Callie says with a grin as we walk out of the courthouse. "Are you sure I'm worth ninety-eight bucks?"

I slip the marriage license into my jacket pocket before pulling her into my arms. "I would have paid a million dollars to marry you."

She rolls her eyes at my ridiculous sappiness, but she lets me kiss her anyway. Suddenly, a throat clears from behind us. Callie looks over my shoulder, and her eyes widen. When I turn, I find myself face-to-face with the only asshole who could possibly ruin my perfect day.

"Dominic."

He nods. "Devin. Callie, you're absolutely glowing."

"Thank you. If I'm glowing, it's because I'm happy. Devin and I just applied for our marriage license."

Have I mentioned lately how much I love this woman?

Dominic smiles politely. "Is that so? Making an honest woman out of her, McAllister?"

"That's right."

"Well, congratulations to both of you. I must say I'm still surprised. Never saw you settling down."

"Life is full of surprises. Like you becoming mayor."

Dominic smiles tightly before turning to Callie.

"I'd still love to have you as part of my administration. Perhaps after the baby arrives we could sit down and—"

"No, thank you."

"No? You don't even want to discuss it?"

She shakes her head. "I won't be working for you. Not now. Not ever. Now, if you'll excuse us, we have a wedding to plan. Have a good day, Mayor."

Dominic's eyes narrow, but it'd be political suicide to cause a scene right here on the front steps of the courthouse. Clearing his throat, he nods and congratulates us again before heading inside.

"That was fun," she says with a grin.

"Indeed. Ready to see your ring?"

"I am."

Callie loops her arm through mine as I lead her to the car. Once we're on the road, I decide to complete one more task on my to-do list. I call Greg Franklin and put him on speaker.

"Hey. Mr. Franklin. How are you?"

"Devin? Everything okay with Callie and the baby?"

"Hi, Dad," Callie says. "We're in the car and you're on speaker. Everything's great."

He breathes a sigh of relief. "That's good to hear. What's going on?"

"I just thought you should know I'm officially proposing to your daughter today."

He chuckles. "I guess it's not a surprise, since she's right there with you."

"No surprise at all," Callie says. There's a happy giggle to her voice. "We just applied for our marriage license."

"Well, I guess I could say it's about time, but it's been

what? A week?"

Callie huffs. "Seven months, thank you very much."

I grin. "So, do we have your blessing?"

The line grows silent, and Callie and exchange anxious looks. *What if he says no?* He should. I'm nowhere near good enough for his daughter.

"You love her?"

He knows I do, but I understand he has to ask. It's his job.

"I do, sir. More than anything."

"You'll take care of her and my granddaughter? You promise to put them first . . . above anything or anyone else?"

"Always."

"Good. I know this whole thing hasn't been traditional. I also know it doesn't matter whether you have my blessing or not, but I appreciate you pretending that it does. I like you Devin, and I think you're good for each other. So, yeah, you have my blessing. But hear this. If you ever break that promise, they'll never find your body."

I can't help but smile. Callie reaches across for my hand and gives it a squeeze.

"I understand, sir."

"And cut the *sir* crap. I'm Greg."

"Got it."

He laughs. "Now that the bodily threats are out of the way, when's the big day?"

"That's something else we need to talk to you about," Callie says. "Can you be here next Saturday?"

"Oh . . . really?"

She frowns. "You don't want to be?"

"Sure I do. You two just seem the impatient type. I figured you were headed to Vegas."

"We thought about it," I admit with a laugh.

The car grows quiet again, and I know what he's thinking. He wouldn't have wanted to miss this for the world.

"This is better," Greg says softly.

Callie and I smile at each other.

"We know," she says.

Chapter 35

Callie

"Out of all the jewelry stores in Nashville, you picked this one?"

Devin sighs and leads me through the doors. "Megan suggested it."

"I'm sure she did."

I've been trying hard to get over my money issues, and I think I've been doing a pretty good job. But now, surrounded with towers of pretty blue boxes in one of the most expensive jewelry stores in the world, I'm suddenly wondering if my concerns weren't justified.

Note to self: Kill Megan.

A brunette sales associate greets us, calls Devin by name, and then disappears. When she returns, she's holding two of the pretty blue boxes. I nearly hyperventilate when he hands her his platinum card.

"Oh my God, how much is it?" I whisper.

Devin chuckles and wraps his arm around me. "No way."

"You won't tell me?"

"Nope."

"Why not?"

"Because I'm not."

We'll see about that.

She returns with the little bag and his receipt. We thank her and head for the parking lot. Devin knows he's in for a fight, but that doesn't keep the smile off his face as he helps me into the car. I snap my seatbelt with a huff as he climbs inside.

"Are we seriously going to argue about this?" Devin asks as we head home.

"I don't want to argue. I was just . . . caught off guard. They only sell one kind of ring in that store."

"What kind is that?"

"The expensive kind."

He laughs. "And this is bad?"

"Not *bad*. But I don't need an engagement ring from one of the most expensive stores in the world."

"I thought we were past this money thing."

"I thought we were, too."

"What's changed? You were okay with the house."

"That's different."

"How?"

"The house is for both of us. And our daughter."

"I see. So, it's okay for me to buy expensive things as long as it's for *us* and not just for you?"

"That's right."

"Then problem solved, because there are *three* rings in that bag. Your engagement ring and our wedding bands. It was a collection—all sold as a set. So, see? Something for you *and* me. Something for us. Happy?"

When he puts it that way . . .

"Yes, I'm happy."

I think.

Devin must hear the uncertainty in my voice, because as soon as we reach the house, he takes me by the hand and leads me upstairs. Thankfully, everyone's gone. It's the quietest the place has been in days.

We walk into the nursery.

"Stay here," he says.

He heads down the hallway, and I decide to try out my new rocking chair. While he's gone, I take a good, long look at the room. The guys did such a great job on the furniture. The mint-green walls are apparently good for blood pressure because I can feel myself calming down as I rock in my new favorite chair.

When Devin returns, he kneels in front of me.

"Do you see this?" he asks, holding up our latest sonogram picture.

I nod.

He then takes my hand and presses it against my stomach.

"Do you feel that?"

Our child kicks right on cue.

Daddy's girl.

"You've given me everything, Callie. No man deserves

this much happiness—least of all me—but I'm grateful for it."

He pulls the little blue box out of his pocket, and my eyes immediately fill with tears.

"When I started looking for this ring, my only intention was to find a ring that reminded me of you. It had to be beautiful. Flawless. Like you. I had to fall in love with it at first sight—just like I did with you. You were wearing some faded hoodie and jeans, and I knew in that moment I'd never seen anyone more beautiful."

I sniffle quietly. "You actually remember what I was wearing."

Devin gently brushes his fingers along my tear-stained cheeks. "I remember everything about that night. I found my soulmate that night. I fell in love that night, Songbird."

He slowly opens the tiny box and lifts the lid. I can't stop the soft gasp from bubbling from my lips.

"Don't you understand? You've given me so much, just by saying yes. This house? This ring? They're just *things*, Callie. Beautiful things, definitely, but still. It's just stuff and can't compare to everything you've given me. But I want to give them to you, anyway."

Devin takes my hand and slips the ring on my finger. Tears trickle down my face as I gaze at the gorgeous square diamond. Once again, I'd taken a gift given with love and focused on the money instead of the sentiment behind it. When would I ever learn?

"You bring me joy that is priceless. Will you marry me?"

I smile into his adoring eyes. "You know I will."

"And the ring? Do you like it?"

"I love it."

"The band's engraved," he says, taking the second ring out of its box. "I don't even know if you'll get the reference, but . . . it was important to me."

I peer at the platinum band, and my eyes fill with fresh tears when I read the tiny engraved words I'd sung to him that night in the piano bar. The night that changed my life forever.

To you, I'll give the world.

My tears are uncontrollable now, but so is my smile.

"I love you."

"I love you, Songbird."

Later that night, when we're snuggled in our bed and wrapped in each other's arms, he whispers close to my ear.

"You didn't say yes."

I brush my lips against his heated skin.

"Yes. A thousand times yes."

Chapter 36

Callie

"Morning sickness sucks." Lorie groans and nibbles on a cracker.

"I remember." I smile at my reflection in the mirror until Megan winds my hair around the curling iron a little too tightly. "Ow!"

"Hold still." She counts to ten before releasing the blonde tendril. I watch, fascinated, as it bounces into place. Devin had only one request during this whirlwind wedding experience and that was for me to wear my hair down. Megan, my matron-of-honor and Nazi hairdresser, was determined to make his dream come true.

"Are you nervous?" Meg asks.

"Nope."

I give my gigantic stomach an affectionate pat. Maybe I should be anxious. It is my wedding day, after all. But honestly, all I feel is happiness. The baby's happy, too, if her constant movement is any indication. We've had many discussions this morning regarding the intensity of her kicks, but she doesn't listen to me. The only time she's calm is when Devin's reading to her. I can't help but feel a little jealous. Father and daughter already have this sweet bond. Meanwhile, she's using my ribs to practice for her future career as a soccer player.

It just doesn't seem fair.

"I want a hot dog," Lorie mutters.

I stifle my laughter. All those hormones mixed with her natural bitchiness is sure to keep Owen busy for the next seven months or so.

"You just had breakfast," Megan remarks.

Lorie turns her murderous glare toward my hair stylist.

"Please don't kill each other on my wedding day. Someone give me my phone."

Megan sighs and fishes my cell out of her pocket. If anyone can sympathize with wild pregnancy cravings, it's me. I text the best man.

Your woman wants a hot dog.

Like a good daddy who values his life, he replies right back.

She sent me out for a hot dog at midnight last night. With onions and cheese!

I crinkle my nose in disgust.

"Lorie, dear. Would you like your hot dog with onions and cheese again?"

She makes a retching noise and quickly rushes to the bathroom.

"I take that as a no," Megan says. She unclips my hair and wraps another strand around the curling iron.

Minutes later, Lorie returns and sweetly requests a plain hot dog. I quickly text Owen and hand the phone back to Meg.

"Please tell me the barfing and cravings won't last the whole time."

"Mine didn't."

Lorie slumps down onto the bed. "Can I do this?"

Megan casts her a disapproving look. "Would you stop whining? This is Callie's day."

Lorie's eyes flash with anger. Since Megan has yet to experience the pleasure of being pregnant, there's no way she can comprehend that yelling at a hormonal mommy is probably the last thing you want to do.

"Please don't kill her, Lorie. Just remember she's clueless and I need her today."

Lorie's face relaxes. "Fine. But I make no promises about tomorrow.

"Hmph." Megan grins excitedly. "Finished! What do you think?"

Turning toward the mirror, I smile at the girl in the glass. She has long, wavy hair . . . just as the groom requested. And the make-up is minimal, just like I wanted.

"I love it. Thank you, Megan."

Just then, someone lightly knocks on my bedroom door.

"That better not be you, Devin McAllister!" Lorie yells.

Valerie walks inside. "Nope, just me. Has my eager son been trying to sneak a peek?"

"All afternoon," I tell her.

Valerie gives Lorie a hug. I love seeing the two of them together. Like me, Lorie's never been close to her mom. We're both lucky to have her.

Megan rushes toward the closet. "You're just in time, Mrs. McAllister. We're ready for the dress!"

The girls had really outdone themselves in helping me find the perfect dress. I didn't ask for specifics. I didn't want to know the designer, the type of material, or the price tag. My only requirements had been to find a gown I could actually walk *and* sit in and that it fit around my enormous stomach. I'm still blissfully clueless and I want to stay that way. All I know is that it's the most beautiful and comfortable dress I've ever worn.

And it fits.

The three of them help me into my dress and zip me up. When I turn toward the full-length mirror, Lorie suddenly bursts into tears.

"Stupid hormones!" She groans, reaching for the box of tissues.

Valerie dabs at her eyes, too. "Callie, you're beautiful. And I have something for you. I hope this isn't presumptuous of me, but William and I wanted to give you something today."

"Oh, Valerie, you didn't have to do that."

"We wanted to. You've brought so much joy to our family." Her eyes fill with more tears as I blink away my own. "Anyway . . ."

She offers me a long gift box.

"The day Shyann and Devin were born, William bought each of them something to wear on their wedding days. Devin's gift was a pair of cuff links. He's wearing them today. And this necklace was for Shyann."

I open the box to find a thin Y-drop necklace with tiny pearls and earrings to match. Lorie starts to cry so hard she finally excuses herself and heads downstairs.

"Are you sure? I mean . . . you want me to wear them?"

Valerie nods.

"Don't cry. You'll ruin your make-up," Megan says softly.

I try to get a handle on my emotions as Valerie walks behind me and slides the necklace around my neck. With trembling hands, I place the pearls in my ears before facing the mirror once again.

"Devin and Shyann shared a very special connection. A special love," Valerie whispers, her voice full of love and emotion. "Shyann would be so happy that Devin's wife is wearing her jewelry today."

"Thank you, Valerie."

I smile through my tears as she kisses me on the cheek.

There's a knock on the door, even though it's wide open. I look over to find my dad standing there, his eyes red-rimmed. *Did he hear all that?*

"Hi, Dad."

Valerie and Dad introduce themselves to each other

before she heads back downstairs. A tearful Lorie comes back, but only to tell Megan that the caterer has a question. The girls excuse themselves and leave me with my dad.

"Is she okay?" Dad asks.

"Lorie? Yeah, she's just pregnant."

He nods. "Must be something in the water."

"Must be."

I smile and offer him a seat on the bed. Megan will kill me if I wrinkle my dress, but my feet are killing me.

"You look great. I told you a tux wasn't necessary."

"Sure it was. How many times does a guy get to walk his little girl down the aisle?"

"Hopefully just the once."

"Better be just the once."

I grin.

"You look beautiful."

"Thanks."

"Nervous?"

"Not a bit."

"That's good. I feel like I'm supposed to say something profound, but I'm hardly the expert on happy endings."

"It's okay. You don't have to say anything. Just don't let me break my neck when I walk down the stairs."

It's a joke, sort of. I'm not really afraid of falling today. As the very pregnant bride, I'd opted for ballet flats instead of heels.

"I won't let you fall, Callie."

My eyes well with tears. "I know, Dad. You never have."

He nods. "Before we go down, I need to tell you about an

unexpected guest."

"What unexpected guest?"

"Your mom."

My breath catches in my throat. I'd debated whether to even invite her, but Devin convinced me I'd regret it forever if I didn't. I never expected her to show up.

"She walked right in like she owned the place...snapping at the caterer and yelling at the kid with the camera. You know, typical Kim."

Poor Oliver. He offered to take the wedding photos in exchange for a bottle of wine. We'd have to order him a case now.

"I was going to give her a piece of my mind, but Devin beat me to it. He told her she was welcome to stay but only if she kept her opinions and snotty comments to herself. If she couldn't do that, he'd have her tossed out, and the only glimpse of this wedding she'd get would be a postcard from your honeymoon. Then some big black guy came up and asked if there was a problem. She shut right up and promised to behave herself."

Sweet Malik. No longer my bodyguard, but a trusted friend. We'd have to buy him some wine, too.

"Devin's a good man, Callie. He'll take care of you."

"I know."

"Are you okay with Kim being here? Because I can't lie. It'd give me great pleasure to have her escorted out."

Am I okay with it? Not really. Whether she's here to confirm the square footage of the house or to actually enjoy her daughter's wedding day remains to be seen, but we invited her, so I'll deal.

"It's okay. She made the effort to be here. We should let her stay."

Someone softly knocks on the door.

"Hey, you two," Megan says. "Are you ready?"

Dad and I smile at each other.

"Ready, Cal?"

"I'm ready."

Lorie's right behind my matron-of-honor, holding my bouquet of white roses. She glances down at the flowers and smiles.

"And to think, this all started with a single white rose."

I feel my cheeks heat. Dad looks confused, but he doesn't ask questions.

Soft instrumental music resonates through the house, and I lace my arm through my dad's as the four of us make our way downstairs. Just like he promised, my father holds on tightly as we walk to the landing.

I face the living room, where our family and closest friends are seated, but I don't see any of them. Because Devin's standing at the altar, and my eyes can't focus on anything but him.

"Here we go," Dad says.

Here I go.

The bride and groom are eager—and my feet are swollen—so the ceremony's a short one. We recite the traditional vows. Devin's smile is a mixture of happiness and pride when the preacher tells him to kiss me.

As the wedding flows into the reception, Devin holds

me close to his side while, one-by-one, we thank our guests for coming. I force a smile when the last person in line—my mother—makes her way to us. She leans in to kiss Devin's cheek before offering me a nervous smile.

"You look beautiful, Callie."

"Thank you."

"And happy."

"I am."

Devin wraps his arm around me and kisses my temple. Mom's eyes soften when she sees the loving gesture.

"Could we talk? Not right now, of course."

"I won't let you upset her today," Devin warns.

Mom smiles. "So protective. I promise not to upset her."

Oliver interrupts us then, his camera in hand. He casts a sideways glance at my mother before smiling at me. "Your bulldog wedding planner is insisting on pictures before the first dance."

I grin. Megan wore so many hats today. I have no idea how I'll ever thank her.

"We'll talk later, Mom."

She nods and congratulates us before heading to the bar.

"I don't think I've ever seen my mom that nervous."

"She should be. I swear, Callie, if she upsets you . . ."

"I won't let her. Not today."

From across the room, Megan waves frantically. Devin and I laugh as he takes my hand and leads me to my crazy wedding planner.

"Your home is beautiful," Mom says as we make our way upstairs.

"Thank you."

The party is finally starting to die down, so I'd taken the opportunity to get the talk with my mother out of the way. It'd taken some negotiating, but I'd finally convinced Devin to dance with his mom while I gave mine a tour of the house.

She gasps with surprise when we pass the nursery.

"May I?"

I nod and follow her into the baby's room. Happy to have an excuse to get off my feet, I sit down in the rocking chair while she marvels at the furniture and decorations.

"We still need to put up the curtains, but it's pretty much ready."

"It's a lovely nursery. Have you chosen a name?"

"Elizabeth Shyann."

"That's pretty. Beth?"

"Yes."

She nods and sits down on the loveseat. "What a great idea."

"It was Devin's. We didn't see the need to buy two rockers, but we know there will be times we'll both want to sit in here with the baby."

"He's going to be a good husband, I think."

"Yes, he is."

"And you're going to be an amazing mother."

I bow my head and play with the soft pleats of my dress.

Mom sighs and leans back against the couch. "I owe you an apology. Actually, I owe you a lifetime of them. I've let the bitterness I feel about my choices in life tarnish my relationship with you. The decisions your father and I made were our decisions. I never meant to punish you for them, but I know I did. Getting married so young is the worst thing that's ever happened to me, but you . . . you are the *best*. Can you see the distinction?"

For a moment, I can. I'd had my own mini breakdown when I found out I was pregnant. I wouldn't call it the worst thing that's ever happened, but the idea definitely took some getting used to. Still, I will never regret it, because my unexpected pregnancy has brought me here. To this beautiful day, in this gorgeous house, where I just married the man I love.

"Seeing you and Devin together reminded me of how much I used to love your father. That might surprise you, but it's true. I just didn't love him enough to spend the rest of my life with him. We were just two kids, crazy in love. Your dad and I tried to make it work, but we're two very different people, and sometimes, those differences drive people apart. That's what happened to us."

"But Devin and I aren't you and Dad."

"I know."

Mom sighs softly and looks around the room. "This really is a lovely nursery. And I would love to be part of my granddaughter's life . . . if you'll let me."

I study her face, trying to make sense of everything she's saying.

"Mom, you have to understand that I won't let you be a negative influence in her life."

"I understand."

"She's not ruining my life. She's making it complete. She's not taking my dreams away. She's making them all come true."

I watch as she wipes a stray tear from her eye.

"She's going to be spoiled rotten with *stuff*. It's inevitable. But she will be taught that those are just *things* and there's more to life than just material possessions. I won't have you trying to convince her otherwise."

"Like I did with you."

"That's right. And you will love her because she's your granddaughter. Not because she's pretty or successful or smart. But because she's your granddaughter. That's all she has to be."

"I love you because you're my daughter," she says softly. "Not because you're pretty, successful, and smart. You're all those things, but I love you because you're mine. I will love my granddaughter just the same."

It's the first heartfelt compliment my mother has ever given me.

"I'm sorry, Callie. For everything."

For all I know, these are just words. My mother's made me cynical and untrusting of every syllable that comes out of her mouth. But, for my daughter's sake, I'm willing to give her the chance to make a believer out of me.

I can accept her apology, but I can't forgive her.

Not yet.

Maybe someday.

The house is finally empty, and I'm nestled in the lap of my husband while we sit in the nursery's love seat.

"Wow," he whispers when I finish telling him the story. "Do you think she'll disappoint you?"

I shrug. "I have zero expectations. If Mom keeps her promise, then I'll be pleasantly surprised. If she doesn't, I'm no worse off than I am now. It's all good."

"Still, it was quite the wedding gift." He lifts my hand and kisses my knuckles. "And that's quite a ring, Mrs. McAllister."

Without another word, Devin helps me to my feet and leads me to our bedroom. With it so close to my due date, we'd decided to forego the honeymoon for now, choosing instead to spend our wedding night and the rest of the week wrapped in the quiet solitude of our new house.

"You looked so beautiful today," Devin murmurs. Standing behind me, he runs his hands along my arms before slowly unzipping my dress. The flowing fabric slides down my body and pools at my feet. A sigh escapes my throat when he brushes my hair to one side and peppers my bare shoulders with soft kisses.

"I can't believe you're my wife."

"I can't believe you're my husband."

I feel him smile against my heated skin.

Reaching for his vest and shirt, I unbutton both and let them fall to the floor. As always, our never-ending need for each other consumes us, and he gently lays me down on the bed. Breathless, his lips leave mine and immediately latch onto my neck. I have to close my eyes, overwhelmed with the sensation of his hands as he touches every part of me.

Megan and Simon had told us that married sex is so much better. We'd laughed, neither of us believing it could be better than it was before.

We were wrong.

"Will you always drive me this crazy?" he pants against my skin.

I find his eyes in the darkness and whisper the truest words I've ever known.

"For as long as we both shall live."

DEVIN

They say the first year of marriage is the hardest, but if the first month is any indication, I can honestly say they're a bunch of morons.

Marriage is *unbelievable.*

I'm a married man.

Callie's my wife.

I'm going to be a dad.

I can be having the shittiest day in court and those three little sentences can instantly remind me that life is freaking amazing. Whether I'm dealing with a frustrated client, an ill-tempered judge, or an inflexible jury, none of it matters because I am a happy man.

After the week-long honeymoon at home, I went back to work while Callie started her leave of absence from the paper. With so much free time, she's become Betty Crocker, and each day, I come home to dinner *and* dessert. Sometimes, dessert is peanut butter cookies. Other times, it's my sexy, beautiful baby mama in lingerie.

Either way, it's heaven.

As Callie's due date approaches, she's become increasingly uncomfortable with just about everything. She's been having trouble sleeping because she can't get comfortable, and sitting doesn't help because of the pain that's started in her lower back. She's rarely content, and as the man who put her in this discomfort, it kills me that I can't do anything to make her feel better. Dr. Clifton tells us these are just the "joys" of the last trimester, but as terrible as Callie feels, I have a feeling Elizabeth Shyann may be an only child.

Tonight's definitely been a challenge. Her lower back has ached all day. Even my massages did nothing to relieve her of the pain. She finally falls asleep on the sofa just before midnight. I don't have the heart to wake her, so I wrap a blanket around her and kiss her forehead before heading into the study to work on a brief. The living room and my office are on the same level of the house, so I take comfort in the fact that I'm close by in case she needs me.

An hour passes, and I've barely made a dent in my brief when my eyes start to grow heavy. Stifling a yawn, I check my email one last time. I'm just getting ready to log out when I hear soft footsteps against the hardwood floor. I look up to find Callie in the doorway.

"Hi, baby."

"Baby." She nods slowly. "I think . . . yeah. Baby."

"Baby? As in, *baby*?"

"I think. I mean, I'm pretty sure—"

I spring out of my chair and rush to her side.

"Devin?"

"Callie?"

"I think my water just broke."

"Deep cleansing breaths, baby."

I struggle for air. How pathetic is it that my beautiful wife—who's lying in a hospital bed waiting to bring our baby into the world—is coaching *me* on how to breathe?

Is this what an anxiety attack feels like?

We've been here eight hours, and with each passing minute, my ability to think rationally fades just a little more. Callie, of course, is the epitome of calm.

Epidurals are God's gift to mothers. Why can't they make something for the fathers?

Just then, another contraction registers on the machine. My wife, however, doesn't make a sound. She just closes her eyes and squeezes my hand, breathing slowly and deeply until it passes.

"How are we doing?" Dr. Clifton walks in and checks the machine.

"I'm okay," Callie says as she crunches on ice. "I think Devin could use a drink, though."

The doctor does a quick examination before grinning up

at me. "We'll get you a drink afterwards. She's fully dilated. Are we ready to do this?"

Callie grips my hand tightly.

"Remember, Devin. You work up there. I work down here."

I nod lamely and brush a lock of hair away from Callie's face. At this point, I'm just happy to be given instructions that make sense in my muddled brain. From this point on, our lives will never be the same, and despite my nervousness, I'm actually really okay with that.

"Do you know how much I love you?" I whisper, pressing a kiss to her forehead.

With a quiet sigh, she nods.

"Okay, Callie," Dr. Clifton says. "You can push."

And with those words, our world changes forever.

"You can't leave me," I whisper softly into the brown eyes I love so much. Shyann smiles weakly, trying to be strong as I fall apart. The doctors say it will be soon, but I refuse to believe them. I lay my head against her pillow. It's all I can do not to climb into her hospital bed and hug her tightly to my chest.

"Listen to me," my sister says softly. "I want you to graduate. Go to college. Be happy and healthy."

"Not without you . . ." My voice shakes, because I have no idea how to exist without her. We've always been Devin and

Shy. Shy and Devin.

"You love me so much. I love you, too. But you have to let me go, Devin."

"I don't know how."

Her smile is serene. *"I'll send you someone new to love."*

"I don't want someone new to love."

Shyann's face is pale, but so angelic. *"I'll send you someone new to love, and she'll have your brown eyes."*

"Our brown eyes," I whisper.

"Our brown eyes."

That was the last conversation I ever had with my sister. It's been years since I even thought about it, but as I gaze down at my beautiful baby, Shyann's final words weave their way into my mind. I'd forgotten her promise to send me someone new to love, but as I rock my brown-eyed daughter in my arms, it's undeniably clear that my sister kept her word.

"Your eyes?" Callie asks hopefully.

I smile and place our baby on her mother's chest.

"My eyes."

My beautiful wife smiles and cuddles our daughter close. There's a flurry of activity behind us, but it's all so easy to ignore. The three of us exist in our little bubble of whispered words and tender kisses.

"Look at her, Songbird."

As if on cue, our five-minute-old child opens her eyes.

Callie laughs softly. "See? Such a Daddy's girl."

"And to believe there was a brief moment when I wished she wasn't mine."

"You didn't mean it. You were just scared."

"I'm *still* scared. But I'm not afraid to be her father."

"What are you afraid of?"

I slide my fingertip along our baby's soft cheek. "Failing her. Failing you."

"You won't, Devin. I know you won't. You love us too much."

The nurse checks on us one last time before everyone finally leaves us in peace. I know our family is waiting in the lobby, and I need to let them know all is well, but I just can't tear myself away.

"Thank you, Callie." I envelop my wife and baby in my arms.

Callie smiles at me and kisses my wet cheek. "What are you thanking me for?"

"For you." I lean in and kiss our baby's forehead. "And for her."

Chapter 38

Callie

"Thank you. I really did want to try."

It's true what they say. Modesty is long gone after the birth of a baby. The general mechanics seemed easy enough, but Beth had been stubborn, so I called Grandma for assistance.

"You're very welcome. Sometimes babies have trouble breastfeeding at first, but she's doing wonderfully." Valerie smiles adoringly at her grandchild in my arms. "I'm going to head on home."

"You can stay." I probably don't sound too convincing. I just can't tear my eyes away from my baby long enough to have a normal conversation with anyone.

"Take this time to bond with that beautiful girl. We'll come visit tomorrow."

She smiles and kisses both of us on the cheek before

walking over to where her son is fast asleep in the chair. Valerie adjusts his blanket and kisses his cheek, too, before whispering goodnight and closing the door behind her.

While Beth eats, I close my eyes and try to relax.

What an amazing day.

Our entire family had surrounded us all day. Dad had broken multiple speed limits to get to the hospital just in time for the baby to arrive. Later in the day, our friends arrived. None of them really stayed too long, but the constant stream of loved ones made it impossible for either of us to get much rest. Now, in the quiet stillness of the hospital room, I can finally do the one thing I've wanted to do all day.

I get to stare at my baby.

The nurses are still stunned, since apparently most newborns are born with blue eyes. Even Dr. Clifton warned us that Beth's eye color might change within the next few months. Time will tell if she inherits my blonde hair, but Devin and I both believe the brown eyes are here to stay.

I hum a few bars of Van Morrison's *Brown Eyed Girl* until I finally remember the words. While I sing, Beth keeps eating, and I breathe a sigh of relief that our baby has a good appetite. That day in the baby store, the mere thought of breastfeeding had made me nervous, but now, I can't imagine not doing it.

"I love to hear you sing," Devin whispers from his chair. "Perfect song, too."

I smile sheepishly as I switch the baby to the other side. "Sorry, I didn't mean to wake you."

"I'm glad you did. I wouldn't have wanted to miss that."

He folds the blanket before walking over to our bed. Leaning down, he kisses both of us. "Or this. I see she finally decided to cooperate."

"Finally. Well worth the initial frustration."

"Just like us," he says softly.

"Exactly like us."

Devin nuzzles her head. "She smells so good. And all she does is sleep, poop, and eat. This parenting stuff's easy."

I grin. "Yeah, it's all a breeze when she's twelve hours old. Just wait until she starts dating."

"Over my dead body."

"Right. What if my father had that philosophy? We never would've met."

"I bet your dad *did* have that philosophy. You just didn't listen."

"Beth won't listen, either."

Devin chuckles and stifles a yawn.

"You should sleep."

"And miss this? Not a chance."

When Beth finishes her feeding, Devin places her in the nearby crib.

"I'm glad she gets to stay in the room with us."

"Me, too." Devin leans down to kiss me softly. "You're the one who should be sleeping, baby. You have to be exhausted."

"I miss our bed."

He grins. "Me, too. But we'll be home before you know it. Then the real fun begins."

Devin pulls his chair as close as he can get to me. We lace our fingers together, and within minutes, he's sound asleep. Tears fill my eyes. To my left, my daughter is sleeping peacefully. To my right, my husband snores.

I'm surrounded by so much pure love and simple joy that it nearly takes my breath away.

"Devin?"

I reach for him, but his side of the bed's empty. The house is quiet, except for the soft sound of Devin's voice as it flows from the baby monitor.

He's reading *The Velveteen Rabbit*.

With a smile, I throw back the blanket and climb out of bed.

It's our second night at home. Like a lot of first-time parents, we've both had a hard time leaving the baby alone in the nursery. *What if she stopped breathing? What if she needed us and the baby monitor malfunctioned? What if. What if.*

The baby's only four days old and we're already walking zombies. Like clockwork, Beth wakes up every three hours for her nightly feedings. Otherwise, she sleeps great.

It's not the baby that's keeping us awake all night. It's our irrational fears that prevent us from getting a decent night's sleep. The uncertainties consume us, but neither of us are ready to surrender. We're determined to use the crib in the nursery . . . for as long as we can stand it.

I stop just outside the baby's bedroom and sneak a peek.

Sure enough, Devin's sitting in the rocker with our daughter snuggled close to his chest while he reads. He glances up from his book, and our eyes lock.

He smiles sheepishly. "Beth was lonesome."

I grin. He knows he's not fooling me, but I can't fault him. I want her in my arms every second of the day, too. Thanks to breastfeeding, the baby and I have so many chances to bond, but sometimes, Daddy feels left out.

"Stay with us," he says softly.

"Okay."

I lie down on the loveseat and listen while he continues to read.

"Once you are Real, you can't become unreal again. It lasts for always."

This past year has been a whirlwind of emotions. From that first night in the piano bar to the birth of our baby, we've had more ups and downs than some couples have in a lifetime. Despite that, we're unbelievably strong and more in love than ever.

We're *real*.

I glance toward the windowsill, where the baby presents from our family and friends are displayed. Right in the center is a huge bouquet of white roses—Shyann's favorite flower and a gift from Devin's parents. The birth of our child was, naturally, the most emotional moment at the hospital, but the delivery of the lovely white roses came a close second. Devin actually teared up when he saw the tangible reminder of his sister's never-ending love. After spending so much of his life in an endless shadow of sadness and isolation, my sweet husband doesn't have to be alone anymore.

And neither do I.

Devin closes the book and continues to rock our baby girl while she sleeps peacefully against his chest.

He's such a good dad. I knew he would be.

Our beginning was far from traditional, but our forever will be bliss. And that thought fills me with more comfort than I've ever known.

"I love you, Songbird," he whispers.

I smile, because it's true what they say.

Time heals.

Love heals.

And with that peaceful thought, I finally drift off to sleep.

ABOUT THE
Author

USA Today Bestselling Author Sydney Logan writes heartfelt stories that feature strong women and the men who love them. In addition to her novels, she has penned several short stories and is a contributor to Chicken Soup for the Soul. She is a Netflix junkie, music lover, and a Vol for Life. Sydney and her husband make their home in beautiful East Tennessee. To learn more about Sydney and her books, visit her online at sydneylogan.com.

CONNECT WITH
Sydney

Website: www.sydneylogan.com
Facebook: www.facebook.com/SydneyLoganAuthor
Twitter: twitter.com/SydneyALogan

Acknowledgments

Thank you to Denise Strand, a sweet reader from Northern Ireland, who planted the seed that has now become *this*—my sixth book. I hope you love this updated version.

As always, thank you to my editor, Kathie Spitz, for working so hard to make my books the best they can be. Thanks to Wendy Depperschmidt, JA Hensley, Terri Gislason, Patti Jaeger, and Rachel Lawrence for proofreading and providing valuable feedback.

T.M. Franklin designed my beautiful book cover. Thank you for being such a good friend.

Thank you to my review team, all the book bloggers, and Sydney's Sweethearts on Facebook for showing your support in *so* many ways. I can't tell you how much I appreciate you!

Special thanks to Nazarea Andrews and Inkslinger PR for introducing my books to new bloggers and readers!

Thank you to Fleetwood Mac for the musical inspiration.

I am blessed to have a husband who not only encourages my writing but who never fails to tell me he loves me every single day. I love you, too.

Finally, to my readers. Without you, these are just words on a page. Thank you for reading, reviewing, sharing, recommending, and encouraging. Your support is priceless.

Psalm 91:4